THE BUSINESS OF PLEASURE

JUSTINE ELYOT

First published by Xcite Books Ltd – 2010

This edition printed 2012

ISBN 9781907016424

Printed and bound in the UK

Cover design by
Zipline Creative

To Carl, Tricia, Sandra and Amy, who have been with me on this trip from the start. Warmest thanks to all who have offered advice, support and positivity on the way.

Lucky Number

AT THE FAR END of the hotel lobby was a mirrored wall, and Charlotte watched herself and her two companions as they checked in at Reception, seeing what the staff and guests must be seeing. She tried it through their eyes – two sharp-suited older men and a rumpled girl, flushed and sticky and grimy from the train and cab rides that had brought her here. What conclusions could be drawn?

Surely only the right one. The reflection of the senior man – she still did not know their names, though they knew hers – bent to sign something on the desk. The receptionist beamed brightly and glanced at her, curious. *She knew*. Charlotte sought some comfort in the junior man's eyes and found it; there was kindness as well as command and tension in those wells of blue.

'Enjoy your stay,' the receptionist said, and to Charlotte the words seemed to drip with arch knowingness. The senior man took the keycard from her.

'I'm sure we will,' he said.

In the mirror, Charlotte saw the senior man turn to her and, without any form of by-your-leave, place a hand on her bottom, nudging her forward towards the lifts. At the same time, the other man slung his arm low around her waist, and that was how the trio approached the mirror, their images growing larger and more distinct with every step; the girl with the sheer blouse and rucked skirt

1

flanked by the immaculate men.

She could see the faces of the passers-by, see the questions and assumptions behind the eyebrows and forehead creases.

And so, it seemed, could her companions.

'They all know what you're here for,' said the senior man, once the lift doors had swallowed them, spiriting them away from the safety of the open space. His hand was already under her skirt, taking possession of the knicker-free expanse beneath. 'Don't they, Bryant?'

'Oh yes.' Bryant – a name! – had his lips against her neck, then the tip of his tongue traced an upwards path to the hollow beneath her ear. 'Pretty obvious, I'd say. You're here to get fucked.'

'And not just by one man, you greedy little slut.' The senior man's hand shadowed her clitoris, his palm flat between her thighs. 'They know you're opening your legs for both of us, maybe one at a time, maybe both together.'

'Oh, yes, they know all about you, Charlotte.' Bryant undid the top button of her blouse and slipped a hand inside.

The lift bell chimed and the doors slid open.

'Please excuse us,' murmured the senior man to the startled but interested-looking pair of guests waiting on the landing, then Charlotte was escorted, semi-dressed, with a different man's hand on each bare bum cheek, up the corridor to the room.

'She will need cleaning up,' said the senior man dispassionately, throwing off his jacket and rolling up his sleeves. 'Bryant, why don't you bathe her? I'll get things set up in here.'

Bryant took Charlotte's hand and led her through to the marble ensuite, drawing her into him and kissing her gently but thoroughly once the door was closed and the taps running.

'I know we said you weren't to speak unless spoken to,' he said, deftly unbuttoning the rest of her limp and crumpled silk blouse and letting it float down to the tiles. 'But when you're in here with me, the rule is suspended. If there's anything you'd like to ask, just say the word.'

'What's his name?' whispered Charlotte, still not sure she should be framing the unbidden question. 'Do you know him?'

Bryant chuckled, spinning Charlotte around to unzip her skirt. 'Yes, I know him. His name is Collins. But you can call him Master. And don't forget it.'

'Oh, no, I don't intend to. I wouldn't want to cross him.' Charlotte grinned shyly at Bryant, bending down to peel her sticky, heat-drenched hold-ups down her legs. Ah, the relief of bare skin in an air-conditioned room … though the steam was starting to build up as the giant tub filled with fragrant bubbles.

'He isn't as frightening as he seems,' whispered Bryant. 'But don't let him know I told you that. You asked for a distant, cold man and he can play the role to a T.'

Charlotte let Bryant unclip her bra and leaned against him for a while, feeling his crisp white shirt on her back, letting him cup and caress her breasts while they waited for the bath to be ready. 'What did you ask for?' she asked.

'I'm sorry?'

'The Number. What did you ask for when you contacted them? When you filled in the form, did you do it together? Did you both ask for a submissive female to take to a hotel and fuck? Or did the number hook you up with each other as well as with me?'

3

'Ah … well … I'm not sure I can tell you.' Bryant was hesitant and his fingers pinched at her nipples a little more tightly than was comfortable. 'We aren't meant to talk about the Number.'

He let her go and turned off the taps, contemplating the tower of fluffy bubbles on the water's surface.

'If I let you into a secret, Charlotte, do you promise not to tell?'

Charlotte, standing naked on the bathmat, nodded.

'We are the number. Collins and I. We set it up. It's one of our businesses. But we have never actually used the service until today.'

'Really?'

'Really. Truth be told, we have been waiting a long time for a girl like you to come along.' Bryant smiled. 'And now you're here. Come on. You must be feeling a bit seedy after your long journey. Let's clean you up.'

Charlotte felt the accumulated dirt and dust loosen and lift in the water's warm embrace. She leaned back and sighed, letting the perfumed suds envelop her body, taking away the traces of the journey's exertions. Not that those exertions had been all bad, by any means. All the same, her skin needed priming for more, much more. She needed to be clean and fresh, a blank slate to be chalked full of the perverse demands of her two mysterious lovers.

Bryant's talented fingers pinned up her hair and massaged her neck and shoulders while she luxuriated in the bubbles, using the time to reflect on what had passed and preview what might be to come. Her reflection in the washstand mirror opposite portrayed dewy cheeks and shining eyes, a taut kind of excitement radiating out to the corners of the room.

'Not so dirty now?' murmured Bryant in her ear, his

hands sliding down the slippery slope of her collarbone to find her breasts, just below the water's surface.

'Perhaps not in body,' replied Charlotte, smirking at the double entendre.

'You'll need to bathe again before you leave,' he reminded her. 'Because, believe me, Charlotte, every inch of your gorgeous body is going to be used long and hard tonight. So don't use up all the hot water, will you?'

He stood up behind her, causing the water to splash and foam around her, and reached for a towel.

'Chop chop. We don't have all night, do we?'

Charlotte stepped into the warm embrace of the thick towel, feeling its gentle friction against her hard, wet nipples and dripping thighs. She allowed Bryant to wrap it around her and then begin to pat it and rub it vigorously against her skin.

'Arms up,' he commanded brusquely, drying her armpits, then moving down to the vulnerable teardrops of her breasts, dabbing their underside with the velvety pile, then instructing that she part her legs so he could attend to the dampness within.

When all the soapy wetness was absorbed and Charlotte's skin tingled with vitality and anticipation, Bryant escorted her, one hand on a shoulder, over to the mirror and had her watch while he took a complimentary bottle of baby oil from the cabinet and tipped some into his palm.

'Let's get you ready, shall we?' he suggested lightly. Charlotte immediately felt her loins flood and her stomach flutter. Ready. The words were subtle, almost innocent, and yet so utterly thrilling; their nuance melting her so that she was a distillation of pure submissive desire.

She saw herself tense and then her shoulders sagged

when he began to apply the oil to them. Her head dropped and she half-closed her eyes, placing her entire self in his hands, feeling them descend along and beside the curve of her spine, then back up to her arms, enveloping them, rubbing briskly downward until she was slippery-slick. The bottle was tipped again and then there was a firm but gentle circling of her stomach, a covering of her hips and a blissful, delicious application to her breasts, lengthier and more thorough than ever. Charlotte dared to open her eyes a little wider and groaned at the sight in the mirror opposite – the elegant, signet-ringed hands, fingers splayed across her sheeny mounds, bright red nipples peeking between them. Bryant was looking down, captivated by his work, like a craftsman caught up in the joy of creation.

'Oh, these are lovely,' he crooned, 'but I mustn't get carried away.'

The bottle was tipped again, and the treatment extended to Charlotte's legs and feet; she had to tilt forward and grasp the washbasin while Bryant knelt behind her, cupping her calves and gliding upwards, up for the grand finale, up for the bells and whistles and rounds of wild applause, was he there yet? Oh yes. Her inner thighs were thickly coated and now he was oiling her bum, buffing each cheek until it shone and even greasing the length of her crack, from tip to root, now at her perineum, making her sway and grip the basin all the harder.

'Oh God,' she whimpered involuntarily as the baby oil was splashed between her sex lips and daubed across her light triangle of fleece. Bryant's fingers lingered all too briefly at the pleasure portal before withdrawing. He pulled her back by her shoulders and directed her towards the mirror, silently indicating that she should take a moment of self-examination before events moved on.

Her body glistened back at her. 'I am ready,' it said. 'I am prepared.' And the signs were all there, from the stiff little nipples to the flush at her throat, none of which could be hidden by the plentiful coat of baby oil.

'I think you'll do,' smiled Bryant. 'Do you feel ready?'

'Yes, I think so,' she said, turning her neck to shoot a small smile back at him. 'I think you both know how to make an occasion memorable.'

Bryant chucked her beneath the chin, his knuckle lingering, caressing. 'Oh, you can count on that. But don't forget, once we are out of the bathroom, we go back to the rules you set us. You do exactly as you are told and you don't speak unless spoken to. That's unless you want to earn yourself a punishment, and something tells me you wouldn't be completely averse ...'

Charlotte giggled, then mentally composed herself. This was her chance, perhaps the last chance, to live out her favourite fantasy. She was not going to ruin it by trying to humanise her co-participants. From now on, Bryant was Sir again.

'Let's go,' whispered Bryant, and he took her by the elbow and led her to the door, while Charlotte imagined herself as an auctioned slave about to be presented to her purchaser.

In the bedroom, Collins – or Master, as she must remember to call him – was sitting cross-legged in an armchair, reading the *Daily Telegraph*.

'Ah,' he said, looking up, sliding his spectacles down his nose and staring hard at her. Charlotte was tempted to cover her pubic triangle with her hands, but something told her that would be inadvisable. 'She is clean, is she?'

'Completely,' replied Bryant.

'And you have prepared her to my specification?'

'Come and see for yourself.'

'Yes, I think I shall.' Collins put down the newspaper and sauntered over, eating Charlotte with his eyes from head to toe. She felt like curling into a ball, shielding herself from the bright steel of his gaze, yet the fierceness of it compelled her and she remained straight-backed, though her head hung and her fists clenched. 'Exactly as we discussed,' he opined, circling her slowly. 'Oiled and ready. Nipples hard.' His hand hovered around them, without ever quite touching. 'I can feel the heat between her legs from here.' His hand wafted in front of her snatch, almost touching, almost, so close, but ... He retracted it sharply, opting instead to mould his palm against the lower right side of her face and draw her eyes upward into his. 'Look at me, girl.'

Charlotte almost couldn't, but she was mindful of her vow of obedience, so she blinked a little then focused on the man who held her under his control.

'We need to be clear on a few things,' he said. 'Before we start. We know what you like, Charlotte, but we want to hear it from you. Tell us what you like.'

'Oh.' Charlotte was confounded, reluctant to comply with Collins's order. 'I wrote it all down ... sent it to you ...'

'Yes, I know that,' said Collins, the ostensible patience of his tone laced with menace. 'I am asking you to tell us. We want to hear the words, spoken out loud, by you.'

Charlotte bit her lip and tried to turn her head away, to plead with the seemingly more supportive Bryant, but Collins's grip was inescapable.

'Don't make us wait, girl. You have already earned a

punishment earlier on, remember. I would be only too happy to add to it.'

Charlotte had, in fact, forgotten that she had been promised chastisement for speaking out of turn on the train journey. Words began to stumble from her lips, slowly at first, then picking up pace.

'I want to be controlled ... mastered,' she whispered. 'I want to be told what to do, and given no option but compliance.' She stopped, trying to remember what else had been in her statement. 'I want to be examined, probed, fingered, tongued. I want to suck my masters' cocks for them, and I want to be taken in every orifice, even simultaneously if that can be arranged. I want to be treated like property, and if I do not perform to my masters' satisfaction, I want to be punished.'

'Word perfect,' noted Collins, smiling into Charlotte's fiery blush. 'So let's go over that again, shall we? You like to be handled? Perhaps like a slave being examined at auction?'

'Yes!' Charlotte started at the accuracy of his surmise.

'Oh dear, Charlotte. That's "Yes, Master". Another addition to the tally, I'm afraid. You like to suck cock, I presume?'

'Yes, Master.' Charlotte was annoyed at herself for making such a basic mistake.

'You long to be used in every possible position, I presume.'

'I do, Master.'

'And you dream of a good, hard buggering?'

Charlotte's voice was becoming a squeak. 'Yes, Master.' If only he would let go of her face and she could stare at the floor. But he had no intention of alleviating her discomfort.

'You realise you will be made to beg for your own orgasm. Does that arouse you?'

'Yes, Master, yes.' Would this interrogation ever end? Charlotte was already alive with desire, longing to be thrust on the bed and taken, hard and repeatedly, until all three of them were sated.

'Well, that's nice,' said Collins, unexpectedly flippant. Then his voice hardened again and his eyes were grey flint. 'All of that is to come, Charlotte. But first we have some issues to address, don't we? Speaking out of turn. Forgetting to use the appropriate form of reply. Some disobedience, some disrespect. How do you think this should be dealt with, girl?'

Collins's other hand had landed, quite unobtrusively, on her waist and was sliding slowly down to the swell of her hip. The lightness of his touch made her shiver and long to move towards him, into him, to force the pressure upward. He was tall and lean, his hand was large. How would that hand feel on her ...

'I should be punished,' she sighed, half-closing her eyes in premonitory ecstasy.

'Yes, you should,' agreed Collins in a low purr, tapping fingers against her oiled hip, baring his teeth in a feral grin before – no! – letting go of her and pushing her away. 'Bryant, do the honours, would you? I don't want oil all over these trousers.'

Bryant, standing behind her, caught her by the shoulders and propelled her towards the bed, pulling her down across his lap once he was seated on the silken covers. Hoping to please, Charlotte made sure her bottom was presented to its fullest disadvantage, raised high, taut and plump, ready to absorb whatever Bryant's hand could deal. Spanking was a favourite fetish, and she hoped her chastiser would not hold back – but that was before Collins seated himself at the corner of the bed, took a handful of her hair and yanked it so that she had no alternative but to look up at him.

'I want to see your face,' he explained. 'I want you to have no escape from your shame and humiliation, Charlotte. I want to watch every pained expression. I need to make sure that you are properly punished, you see. Do you understand?'

'Yes, Master,' she groaned in defeat. She had wanted a creative sadist, and Collins was certainly fitting that description. Perhaps a little too well.

'Good. Don't spare her, Bryant.' And with that, the first percussion of hand against rump rang out.

Bryant was an accomplished spanker, knowing exactly how to stop Charlotte reaching a comfort zone, varying his pace and the location of his strokes so that she had to wriggle and writhe and pant into Collins's face for the duration of the five-minute bottom-warming. The sting of Bryant's hand was one thing, but sharper by a good factor was the sting of having to have her reactions witnessed and relished by the dread Mr Collins. He kept up an embarrassing commentary along with the smack-smack-smack, sometimes even expecting her to reply to or acknowledge a comment.

'I believe the oil accentuates the pain,' he said. 'It certainly adds something to the sound quality … music to my ears. Does that hurt, Charlotte?'

'Yes, Master.'

'Good. You are going to be servicing us with nice hot cheeks; I always think that lends a certain edge to proceedings. I shall enjoy the sight of your crimson rear while I'm pounding away at it later. Oh, I almost felt that one myself. Bryant is a dab hand with a misbehaving bottom, isn't he? He has plenty of practice, of course.

11

You should see your face, Charlotte … quite the picture of woe.'

Collins's smile seemed so friendly and avuncular; it was hard to match the words with the face. Indeed, for Charlotte it was increasingly hard to process any thought beyond Ouch! any more. But in due course, Bryant's unstinting attentions to her behind ceased and she was left to recover over his lap.

'Is she wet? Or rather, how wet is she?' asked Collins nonchalantly.

Charlotte's shoulders shook at the sudden and welcome introduction of Bryant's fingers to the swollen, overheated area below her swollen, overheated bottom.

'Goodness, extraordinarily wet,' said Bryant, amused, massaging her clitoris and pushing one finger up inside her channel. 'I shall certainly take note. Our Charlotte is a girl who needs a good spanking.'

'I had a feeling she would be. Regularly and frequently, I'd say. Next time I'll bring a few items from my collection.'

Charlotte's head jerked upward, even as she tried to press herself down more firmly on Bryant's fingers. Next time?

Collins smiled down at her again and extended an elegant hand to ruffle her hair.

'Don't you think you need a close eye kept on you, Charlotte? By caring disciplinarians with your best interests at heart? I think such an arrangement might suit us all.'

His thumb pushed against her upper lips while Bryant mirrored the manoeuvre with her lower set. She parted them wetly, admitting both men, sucking on their knuckles with gratitude. Collins was right. The idea he proposed was giddying in its delicious perversity. She

12

would certainly give it her strong consideration … if only she … could … think …

'Her eyes are glazing over, Bryant; I think we need to bring her back to earth before she is made to come again. All the pleasure has been hers so far. I'm growing just a little impatient.'

'Yes.' Bryant's fingers made a reluctant departure from their playground. 'I, for one, am waiting for Charlotte to show her appreciation of my efforts. Come on, girl. Your vote of thanks, please.'

Charlotte saw Collins nod briefly, as if giving permission, and she lifted herself gingerly from Bryant's lap and knelt down between his knees. The upper part of his trousers was stained with oil from her stomach – perhaps the hotel laundry could save them.

'I'm sorry I spoiled your trousers, sir,' she said quietly. 'Would you like me to have them washed?'

Without warning, Bryant lifted her by the elbow, stood up, turned her away from him and smacked her sore bottom soundly.

'Speaking out of turn,' he explained curtly before pushing her back to her knees with a hand on the top of her head. He shed the offending garment, along with his boxers, before lying back on the bed, arms spread wide, cock pointing skyward. 'Now use that mouth the way it should be used, Charlotte.'

Collins stood up and folded his arms, watching her scramble on to the bed and crouch between the vee of Bryant's thighs. She reached out, placing reverent hands around her master's tool, tugging the foreskin down to reveal its shiny, eager head. Then she brought her head low, almost licking her lips, savouring the anticipation. Her tongue connected first, lapping at the tiny indentation with its drop of cream. Bryant hissed; she

13

flicked at his frenulum then began to enclose his shaft with her lips and mouth, gliding down, zigzagging with her tongue as she did so. He crammed her mouth with salty-tasting hardness, and still she battled to take more in until she had to stop, fearful of gagging.

'What a sight she makes,' commented Collins from behind her. 'Her bright red rear up in the air and her lips around your cock. I'm not sure how much of that sheen on her thighs is oil and how much is of her own making. She is a dirty little slut, isn't she? Is she sucking you properly?'

'Ahhh, yes.' The words seemed to leak out of Bryant like escaping gas. 'She can suck all right. Oh, Christ, yes, she can.'

Charlotte was gratified by Bryant's helplessness at her ... well, not hands. Mouth, she supposed. She liked to perform to the best of her ability, and she had honed her oral skills to what she hoped was near perfection. But a challenge to her cocksucking craft was about to be issued.

She heard the unbuckling of a belt and the rustle of fabric, then the mattress tilted downwards behind her. Collins was on the bed.

'Let's see how well she concentrates with another cock inside her,' he suggested. 'Spread those legs, girl, and keep that arse high. And don't you dare stop sucking either.'

Charlotte, almost mad with excitement at what was happening, kept up the enthusiastic pace of her gobbling, her head bobbing up and down obediently. She parted her knees as instructed, opening herself up, ready for impalement.

Fingers came first, digging industriously, finding her more than sufficiently lubricated, then the hands held on to her tender bum cheeks and one substantial cock ploughed up inside her, trapping her in position.

'Your mouth and your cunt, girl,' said Collins, slowly and deliberately, matching his thrusts, 'belong to us. We fill them and we own them. We will use them whenever and however we see fit.'

Collins succeeded in fucking her at a pace that seemed at once leisurely and energetic; he kept the rhythm measured, but every nerve ending Charlotte possessed tingled and jangled with each thrust. It was more difficult now to remember to suck; her hands, which had been playing with Bryant's balls, lapsed into inactivity while her brain's receptors struggled to cope with her new dual purpose.

'You are to ask permission for your orgasm, girl,' Collins continued, his voice a lower and lower growl now. 'Which is difficult, I know, with your mouth full. Never mind, eh?' He began to pick up speed, slapping against her warm bum with his pelvis, forcing Bryant's cock even deeper into her mouth, causing her to sway and tug the mouthbound member this way and that. Just as she was beginning to worry about choking, Bryant began to whisper a string of obscenities, then he yelled 'Fuck, yes!' and her mouth was swimming and swirling in liquidy emission.

Charlotte knew implicitly that she must swallow Bryant's gift and she gulped it down, her mouth still filled with the instrument of the issue, while Collins continued to work her from behind.

'Keep it in your mouth,' grunted Bryant, whose body was pliant and relaxed now, his hands playing tenderly with her hair. 'Just let me look at you like that. Mmm, you're taking a good pounding, aren't you? Don't forget, you have to ask permission to come.'

Bryant's final mocking words elicited a moan of lewd despair from Charlotte. She knew her crisis was impending, but how could she speak with her mouth occupied? Collins was finding every secret hidey-hole of sensation along the furrow he ploughed, wickedly and effortlessly, as if he had been studying some diagram of her inner workings beforehand.

Bryant, to her eternal gratitude, took pity on her plight. 'You can speak now,' he chuckled. 'I think you might be feeling the need. Do you think so, Collins?'

'She is hot, Bryant, hot and wet and tight. Just wait till you use her. You'll see.'

A sound, like the mewing of a kitten, came from Charlotte's mouth. Eventually, the men were able to discern that it was the word, 'Please,' being repeated at a helplessly high pitch.

'Please what, girl?' asked Collins, hanging on to his own orgasm by a whisker. 'Say it, now.'

'Please may I come?' she squeaked meekly.

Collins slid his cock backward until it almost parted company with the sorrowing quim that wanted it so badly. 'Well, let's see …' he said.

'PLEASE!' she shrieked.

'I'm a reasonable man …' He shot back up, swift and hard, to the hilt. 'You may.'

Charlotte twisted like a dervish, howled like a banshee, felt and sensed and rushed like every other mythological creature in the canon, leaving the tangible far behind, while Collins continued to slam and bang until he too was spent.

'Let her rest a little while.' Collins stood up and returned to the armchair and the newspaper, still wearing his shirt and tie, as if Charlotte were simply a document he had finished with.

She remained crouched on the bed for a while, feeling Collins's semen puddle and trickle around her sex, while Bryant kept her head cradled in his lap, stroking her hair.

'Good girl,' he soothed, 'Good girl. You did so well.'

Charlotte allowed her eyes to close and her mind to drift, swooping in and out of reality. She might have dozed off; coming to, the full surrealism of the situation struck her four-square. She lay on the plumpest of duvets, hearing the air conditioning's muted whirring, feeling the warmth of another body beside her. A slight catch in his throat suggested that Bryant was sleeping as well. The tiny snores were joined by the sudden inconvenient rumbling of her stomach and she remembered that she had not eaten in ... what? ... five, six hours?

There was a click and then the urgent voices of a rolling news channel broke the dreaminess. She sat up to see Collins watching the television, still in shirtsleeves and spectacles but bare-legged, sipping at a glass of iced water.

'Ah, she surfaces,' he said dryly.

Charlotte wondered if this was an invitation to speak, or merely an observation. She stalled, not sure she wanted any more wrath visited on her bum just yet.

'I'm considering calling room service,' he continued. 'We should eat. You will need to keep your strength up for our grand finale. Come over here and look at the menu.'

Charlotte, feeling muddle-headed and thirsty, did as she was told.

'Stop there,' ordered Collins as she drew level with his chair. 'I want you to kneel down on my lap, knees either side of me, facing away from me.'

Charlotte was unsure, finding words a little hard to

understand still, but Collins posed and manoeuvred her body until she was in the required position, her upper torso sloping down upon his legs so that her head almost rested on his ankles. Her legs were tucked either side of him so that his immediate view was of her still-swollen pussy and pink rump.

'Here,' he said, dropping the menu on to the floor so that it lay by his feet, open at the room service page. Charlotte's eyes travelled blearily around the script, trying to make a decision while Collins's thumbs prised her lower lips apart, inspecting them for damage.

'How are these doing then?' he wondered aloud. 'Still rather tacky ... not quite dried yet. Ah well, Bryant won't mind that. How is this?' He skewered two fingers up inside her, shaking her out of her dilemma over smoked salmon sandwiches or poached eggs on toast. 'A little sore?'

'Just a little, Master.'

'Just a little, eh? Well, that won't do. Can't have you walking out of here without a little bit of difficulty, can we?'

'No, Master.'

'No, indeed. Well, let's order food and then we can see to that. Bryant!'

Bryant awoke with a splutter and a few incoherent words.

'Wassup?'

'Sustenance is required. We can't leave the job half-done, can we?'

'Oh ... no, no, we can't. Matter of pride.'

'Quite. So what will you have to eat?'

Twenty minutes later, the receptionist appeared with the trolley – she liked to do these kind of discreet services personally. Bryant, seated at the table in a robe, thanked her for his steak. Collins, who had settled for a club sandwich and a dozen oysters, waved at her to place them on the occasional table beside his armchair. And as for Charlotte's smoked salmon omelette … well, that was placed on the floor, by Collins's feet, cut up into squares.

Charlotte's eyes were tight shut, her face buried in Collins's shins. She knew the receptionist would be casting an eye over her compliant back and displayed bottom, legs splayed wide and everything between on show.

'Are you enjoying your stay?' she heard, in a perky, complicit tone.

'Very much. Aren't we, Charlotte? Well?'

Charlotte mmmed, and earned a slap to her bottom for her ambivalence.

'Lift your head, Charlotte, and answer the lady.'

Charlotte craned her neck and regarded the receptionist from beneath sulky lashes. 'Yes, we are having a very good time,' she whispered.

'Please let me know if there's anything I can do to improve your Luxe Noir experience,' smiled the girl before turning smartly on her heel and leaving them to it.

Charlotte was reaching down for her last square of omelette, wondering how bad for the digestion eating in this position actually was, when she noticed Bryant push his plate aside and grin broadly at Collins. She tried to twist her neck back, to see what the reason for this signal of complicity might be, but the first clue she got was the shocking splash of cold gel between the cheeks of her backside.

'Oh!' She tried to rear up, pushing her palms on the floor, but Collins replaced her with a firm hand on her spine.

'You knew this was coming,' he accused. 'Don't make a show of fighting it. We know it's what you want. Don't we?'

Charlotte's hesitation earned her another pink palm-print on her posterior.

'Y-yes, Master,' she muttered reluctantly.

'I suppose you like to pretend you are being forced into it,' surmised Collins, working the lubricant in tight circles, greasing her rear entry with fanatical thoroughness. 'Makes it easier to deal with, perhaps. You aren't the dirty girl, eh? It's the nasty man who makes you do the dirty things? Is that right?'

'Per…haps,' admitted Charlotte, holding her breath as one finger slipped in to the knuckle, remembering just in time to add, 'Master.'

'But you've done this often enough, I'm sure. I think you must enjoy it. I think you should take responsibility for the fact that you enjoy having your arse filled with a big, hard cock, Charlotte. I think you should admit it. Go on.'

Two fingers were working their way up the passage now, demanding to be yielded to. Meanwhile, Collins plugged her pussy with a lazy thumb, giving her a foretaste of things to come.

'Oh,' moaned Charlotte, beginning to experience a ferocious rush of blood to the head. 'I admit it. I … I …' She broke off as Collins popped the two fingers out, relubricated them, and added a third to the tally. She knew she was dripping the evidence of her excitement all over his other hand, she knew this shamed her, but she knew also that it thrilled her beyond measure.

'Go on.' His left hand pushed and shoved at her pussy while his right continued its attentions to her widening arsehole. Bryant stood up, smiling encouragingly, and

20

made his way over.

'We need to hear it, Charlotte,' he said.

'I want you to fuck me,' she said tremulously. 'Fuck my arse. Fill it up. I love it. Master.'

'Good, that's very good,' approved Collins. 'Well, you're ready, I think.'

His hands, coated with lubricant and intimate juices, slid out of their hidey holes and braced beneath her ribcage, pulling her upright to her knees. At the underhang of her bottom cheeks, Charlotte could feel the damp tip of his baton, prodding the soft flesh insistently.

'Sit down,' he invited, placing his cock strategically mid-cheeks. 'Sit on my lap, Charlotte.'

Charlotte had only tried this entry method once before – it was more difficult and more painful than the traditional all-fours version, but she was intent on pleasing her masters and herself, and she put her hands on the arms of the chair and moved her legs to a crouching position, slipping her feet down between Collins's loins and the edges of the cushion.

'Play with her tits, Bryant,' commanded Collins, and the subordinate Dominant obeyed, stepping between Collins's feet and taking both breasts in hand.

Charlotte shut her eyes, surfing the wave of sensation that emanated from her nipples, and took the first brave move backwards, settling Collins's cockhead right at the aperture that led to her darkest pleasure. She had to wriggle a little, and a few times she began the decisive move only to lose confidence and tauten the muscles once more, but eventually she made a stabbing downward motion and the portal was breached. Almost immediately, her disobedient body tried to clench, but Bryant's attentions to her nipples led her to relax quite quickly, and she edged back and further back, drawing

Collins's engorged rod inside her innermost recess, grimacing with the discomfort and alienness of it but grateful that he had lubricated her sufficiently to minimise pain.

'All the way.' Collins's voice was hypnotically low. 'All the way in, Charlotte. How it stretches and fills you – do you feel it?'

'Ah, yes, I do, Master,' she gasped, finally unable to reverse any more, her buttocks resting at the top of Collins's thighs.

'Sit there and stretch your legs out, Charlotte.'

She unbent and put her full weight down to bear on Collins's pelvis, stuffed almost to bursting behind now. Bryant had leaned down to suck on her nipples, and she hooked her feet behind his knees, laying her head on Collins's shoulders and revelling in the lewdness of it all. Collins's hands were on her pussy now; he spread his own legs wide and prised her thighs apart to mimic him, so that they were stacked on top of each other like moulded chairs.

'Your arse is full and your pussy spread wide,' he lapped into her ear. 'You are utterly and completely open.' He lifted his lips. 'Bryant, don't you want to fuck her? Be my guest.'

Bryant grazed his teeth against a nipple then stood up, peering down at the chasm that offered itself to him. How temptingly, juicily red it was, and how much more tantalising the glimpse of thick male root disappearing into her behind made it.

He shed his robe, hooked his elbows beneath her knees and plunged in.

Charlotte, held in an almost impossibly gymnastic position, gave herself up to the pounding in front and the pulsing behind, marvelling at how the two cocks that occupied her seemed to work together to overwhelm her entire body. It was only a few minutes before she had to ask permission for another orgasm, for the presence of Collins at her rear seemed to hasten her passage to heaven like a jetpack of climactic power. She came twice more before Bryant emptied into her, leaving them both exhausted, chests heaving.

But Collins had his own end in sight, and he stood, still connected to her by his cock, turned around and pushed her down on all fours, kneeling with her tits squashed into the chair cushion. Now he was free to pump and thrust and he did so with abandon, using Charlotte's bottom to the fullest extent, reaching down to scrabble at her clit, for it was a matter of pride to him that she should be made to come one last time.

She did so in a hissing, sobbing homage to his mastery of her body, begging him for mercy she knew he would not show, and that was what it took to send his seed flying, washing and coating her, marking her most private place as his.

All three of them shared the bath this time, sleepily soaping each other, with kissing and stroking to boot.

'Would you do this again?' Bryant asked Charlotte, his fingers releasing the tension in her scalp with magical efficacy.

'Oh, I might need a week off work to recover, but yes, definitely.' She looked at Collins, who smiled, a real smile.

'The Number gave us all what we wanted?' he suggested.

'It did. The magic number.'

Collins took her hand and kissed the bubbles off it. 'My lucky number,' he said.

Window Dressing

IT POPS BACK INTO my head every so often, usually in that hazy, heavy time between waking and sleeping, and when it does, I gorge on the scene, lingering over every detail until it is perfectly fixed in my mind. Only then can my hand creep down between my legs and turn the image into a story.

It starts with a window, a large, rectangular frame with its base at street level, ten feet high and about six wide. Beyond the glass can be seen a dressing table with sprays and lotions ranged around, a nest of cushions, some abstract pictures on the walls. All of these items look red in the subdued light of the overhead lamp and you have to adjust your eyes to pick out the smaller features, like the patterns in the prints and the labels on the bottles. But most of the many passers-by have no interest in these finer points of the scene, because in the foreground, sucking every iota of attention out of your mind and into her, is a nearly-nude woman.

Realistically, she can only be about five foot five, but somehow the frame, together with her state of undress, makes her seem enormous, a louche giantess wandering around beneath the red bulb, brushing her hair for the fiftieth time, shaking and uncapping a bottle, looking supremely indifferent to her status as an exhibit in a kind of human zoo. She is, of course, a prostitute, so the zoo is more interactive than most. She lounges in her powder blue silky scanties, flesh spilling from the cups of her bra and the hem of her boyshorts, but it is not her body that fascinates me – it is her face. More particularly, the blankness of it.

Don't you care? I used to wonder. *Doesn't it bother you that everyone who sees you knows what you are and what you will spend your evening doing? That anyone could point a finger at you and say 'Look at her – she fucks strangers for money. By dawn, she will have had cocks in her mouth, her cunt, up her arse, between her tits, lots of cocks, lots of different ones, maybe as many as ten in the one night. She is a whore.'*

I spent a long time trying to figure out why the thought of this made me wet. It wasn't the prostitution angle – the haggard girls hanging around by the industrial estate, while not much more discreet, did nothing for my libido. It was, I realised, something to do with the glass. It was the concept of being exhibited, shown to the world, framed within your little rectangle of reference and held there, until such time as a man decided he wanted to fuck you.

In my imaginings, obviously it is me behind the glass in that Amsterdam street brothel, separated from the lunging hands and lustful tongues of the passing men only by that clear, thin pane, but fully exposed to their hungry eyes. There is a madam there, behind the scenes, who has told me that I must make sure I get a lot of customers tonight; she will be checking up on me to see that I am doing enough of the come hither – rubbing lotion into the crests of my tits, bending over to brush out my long hair so that my buttocks tighten, sitting back on the cushions with my legs tantalisingly spread, licking my lips, putting a hand on the waistband of my knickers as if I am going to slip it inside …

My underwear is flimsy, and I only remember I am wearing any when it flutters against my skin. Sometimes the bras are demi-cups, or peepholes with my nipples peeking through. I have to apply a special cream to keep them erect, because it's important that the customers think I am a horny little tramp who can't keep her knickers on even when cash is out of the equation. Sometimes I wear French knickers, the curve of my bum peeking cheekily out from under the lace, but more often a thong, displaying the two soft rounds that anyone can handle for a fistful of Euros. My legs might be bare, or they might be stockinged, highlighting my pale thighs and the triangle of promise at their end point. Perhaps, as in one version of the scene, the tiny scrap of material calling itself a pair of knickers will have a dollar sign embroidered on the front, or the words 'For Hire'.

The furniture is not always the same as the Amsterdam tart had in her boudoir. If I am in a certain mood, there will be feather ticklers and jewelled masks and all the trappings of luxury. Another mood might fill the room with tethers and ties, ornamental riding crops hanging from the wall. My underwear might be silk, or another day it might be rubber. The fantasy is infinitely mutable, susceptible to my every whim.

Especially when it comes to what happens next.

Perhaps (at vulnerable times) a rich foreign prince will fall in love with me and whisk me away. More likely, I will be worked hard, in every orifice, in every position, until I am racked with exhaustion, my muscles unravelling like overextended elastic. I might even be tied up, or spanked, or blindfolded, or gagged, if I'm feeling especially tense.

This is where my fantasy diverges most seriously

from the reality of my Window Girl – because, in my fantasy, all the fucking happens in that room, in the full view of the citizens and tourists of the city. They stop and take photographs, they clap and cheer, they leer and offer the thumbs-up. They form a queue at the window, and I can see straight away what lies in my immediate future. A group of boozed-up solicitors on a rugby tour, a sleazy businessman, an attractive sadist. I do not have permission to refuse any of them – nobody's money is any better or worse than anyone else's. If they've got the funds, they get the fuck. Simple.

Oh, I sometimes think – disjointedly, fingers or vibrator on clit – if only I could really do that. If only there was a pocket of space, away from my life and reality, where I could be the whore for hire, parading in public, giving a show for anyone passing. But of course, I know the hard facts. Prostitution isn't fun, isn't safe, isn't a good choice of hobby for a respected member of the community like me. Even if I went wild and rented one of those windows for a day, it would be just my luck to have some representatives from the charity I work for take a fact-finding mission to Amsterdam for the weekend, strolling through the red light district in search of lost souls to save. The idea of them reeling and double-taking at my semi-clad figure always makes me giggle. And besides, even in Amsterdam, I wouldn't be allowed to enact the second half of my fantasy – the public sex.

Or so I thought.

I had the application form up on screen in front of me, but I kept deleting the information. Then re-inserting. Then deleting. This couldn't be on the level, could it? A bespoke service, providing the fulfilment of carefully tailored sexual fantasies, was the stuff of erotic fiction. But it had been recommended to me, by a real person (or at least, a real person I 'know' from a chat forum), so I supposed it wasn't a scam. I wasn't sure whether to celebrate or regret that one glass of wine too many, late at night on the Rude Girls site, that inveigled me into revealing my perennial fantasy. Shortly thereafter 'BoyToy1982' direct-messaged me, asking if I knew about The Number. It was, she explained after I replied in the negative, an invitation-only service. Expensive, but worth every penny, as she could attest, having spent the previous weekend trussed up like a chicken in the basement of a Soho sex shop. If I was that hung up on my Amsterdam fantasy, I should contact them. I had chatted with BoyToy1982 many times over the last two years, about subjects as diverse as herbal remedies for period pains and the introduction of identity cards, and had no reason to believe that she was not a real person. The website she introduced me to was classy and understated – no orgasmic, rolling-eyed females writhing on cushions, no crimson and purple, just plain text on the home page, some fascinating testimonial stories and an application page.

I sighed and began the process anew. I was going to do this, if it was doable. I wanted – no, needed – to know how it really felt. I had this odd presentiment that, if I finally ticked this box, I would be able to relax enough to accept that date with Joe from the office.

NAME: Saffron Miles.

FANTASY NAME (if applicable): n/a

I continued diligently, furnishing them with mobile phone number, email address for any queries, availability (weekends) and sexual orientation (heterosexual). There was a long list of fantasy type boxes to tick. I clicked on 'exhibitionism', 'prostitution' and hovered over some of the BDSM categories before deciding that I'd better not add too many constituents to the mix on this first occasion. Then I spent an hour outlining the ingredients of the fantasy, editing and refining it before I was content to press 'send'.

I pressed it! I actually applied to The Number. Immediately I took my mobile phone out of my pocket and stared at it, as if expecting it to ring or bleep immediately. Of course, nothing happened and I logged off the computer for the night, not even daring to check my email for a confirmation.

Confirmation arrived the next morning, along with a pre-payment request. It wasn't cheap, as BoyToy had warned, but there was a reassuring professionalism to the communication, as well as an understanding of what I was asking for, so I took a deep, deep breath, answered the extra questions I had been asked, and gave them my credit card number.

The number could send instructions at any time, I was told, so it was essential that I let them know in advance any dates or times that were out of the question. *Any time*. The idea sent a little fluting thrill through me. *Expect the unexpected.*

The next few weeks were piquant and exciting – I could not leave my flat without looking around for a dark car or a mysterious figure on the other side of the road. Every time my phone rang, I jumped a mile in the air – *is this it?*

And then, at ten o'clock on a Saturday night in the spring, it came.

'*Put on your trashiest underwear. Get dressed. Meet at Railway Café in Docklands.*' Beneath the message was The Number. Yes. It was time.

Which underwear was the trashiest? I had plenty to choose from. Should I go for leopard-print? Scarlet and black, with peephole bra? Vinyl basque with stretch lace panels? My Amsterdam fantasy had influenced these purchases and I liked to wear them when I was daydreaming in front of the mirror, practising my sleaziest poses, licking a lollipop or deep-throating a banana.

I went with the scarlet and black – the black parts are wet-look fabric with lurid red lace frilling around the peepholes in the bra, and forming a dramatic arrow down the front of the knickers in rude emphasis of what lies at the point. It is trashy in the extreme and I felt suitably whorish, pulling the thong up and looking over my shoulder at the reflection of my exposed bottom in the mirror. I buttoned an easy shirt dress over the hookerwear and added strappy sandals before applying more make-up than I have ever slapped on in my entire life. A whole Juicy Tube on my pillar-box red lips, false lashes, thick eyeliner, blusher that stopped only slightly short of clownish. Then I grabbed my coat and bag and rushed outside to meet my taxi.

'Railway Café. Docklands, please,' I said, stopping to catch a breath when the cabdriver sneaked a knowing peek at me in the rear-view mirror. *He thinks I'm a prostitute!* That part of town is a haunt of the local working girls, and the Café is where they congregate for a cup of tea to keep out the cold on long nights. I was going to be in appropriate company then.

'Going anywhere nice?' he asked, and there was a trace of contempt in his voice I couldn't fail to pick up on. It emboldened me, perhaps it made me rash, but somehow it transported me into the dark heart of my fantasy.

'Just the usual,' I said, mock-evasively. 'Work.'

'Oh yeah? Working girl. Well, it's a good night for it. Weather wise, I mean.'

True, it was a mild night, low cloud hanging overhead, muffling the seasonal chill.

'Oh, I work indoors,' I told him.

'Indoors? Do you? Didn't know there was a massage parlour down there.'

'There isn't,' I said mysteriously.

'Oh. I'm sorry. Must have got the wrong idea,' he said, suddenly red-faced with confusion.

'Maybe. Or maybe you didn't.' The taxi pulled up at the station forecourt, at one edge of which I could see the café, drab light spilling from its frontage on to the tarmac. Squint as I might, I couldn't make out any faces among the shapeless forms inside. 'Tell you what,' I said, handing over the fare. 'If you're still on shift in the morning, why don't you pick me up and I'll be able to give you an answer to that.'

He turned around to face me, making an elaborate show of counting out the money I had given him. His bulbous eyes travelled from my pancaked face to my varnished toenails, taking me in with a sweaty, animalistic greed I had only seen before in my dream. 'Might just do that, love,' he leered. 'Ask for Dave.'

'Dave.' I smiled sweetly and stepped out of the cab. The little charade had been keeping my nervousness at bay, I realised as soon as my spike heels stabbed the pavement. I was here. It was real. Something I had asked for was about to be given to me – would I regret my request? Might The Number, depraved as it already was, be a front for something truly evil? No, no, no, I consoled myself with the measured words of BoyToy1982. She had her head screwed on. She would not lead me into danger.

With renewed purpose, I strolled up to the Café. As I came closer, I made out more details behind the condensation-steamed window. The shapes were of gorgeous, mythical goddesses – pneumatic and amazonian, with great pompadours of hair – wigs I supposed. Curious to see these creatures at close quarters, I stepped through the door less self-consciously than I might have done, and looked about me.

'All right, darling?' enquired one of the goddesses, and I smiled so beatifically that they must have mistaken me for some kind of idiot. Of course. They were men.

Not all of them – some women, relatively dowdy and hatchet-faced, lurked at the counter drinking tea – but the main grouping, laughing and bitching around a large formica table, were transsexuals, transvestites and drag artists. They conferred glamour on to the shabby café, filling the air with their extravagant perfumes, which mixed oddly with the grease from behind the counter. Drawn to their insouciance, I took a tentative step in their direction, but I was interrupted by the harsh tones of the waitress, a faded brass in carpet slippers and a 1960s beehive.

'Saffron?'

'Oh … yes.'

'They're waiting for you upstairs.'

She held a door open for me, her face impassive despite my attempt to smile at her. Behind me, one of the men, or maybe a newly-minted woman, sang *I'm just mad about Saffron* in a light tenor.

The stair carpet was fusty and smelly, but I made it to the landing before the timer snapped the light bulb off, and blundered through the only open door I could see. In a tiny sitting room, a tall man in a suit sat cross-legged on a torn leather sofa, briefcase at his side.

'Miss Miles?' he asked, in a distinctive, not particularly reassuring, baritone.

It took me a second or two to gather the wit to reply in the affirmative.

'I must apologise for the setting. The Café is rather noisier than usual. There is a drag club behind the station and I gather it's Ladies' Night tonight. Do take a seat.'

I perched on a low leather-covered stool, the type of thing that used to be called a pouffe before people stopped wanting to use that term. From my lowly seating point, the man looked forbiddingly long and looming, but he adjusted his spectacles and smiled, transforming his face at a stroke.

'Such an inventive and interesting fantasy you sent us,' he said warmly. 'I could not resist it. It took a while to find the perfect venue, but I hope you will not be disappointed. I have hired some people from the very best sources – some will participate, others will merely observe. All are clean and discreet, though naturally, sensible precautions will be observed. I wonder if you would be able, at this point, to give me an idea of the number of participants you might like?'

I blinked. He was asking me how many men I wanted to be fucked by. In the nicest possible way.

'Well ... I'm not sure ... if I say a number now, would I be able to add to it later ... if I still wanted to?'

'Yes, of course. Conversely, you are, of course, free to stop the action at any time. You understand, however, that I would not be able to offer a refund, should you find the reality less palatable than the fantasy. I am paying for hire of the space, as well as a number of people tonight.'

33

'Oh yes, of course, I'm sure you've gone to a lot of trouble,' I assured him, a little in awe of this old-fashioned and stern-looking man. 'It's ... a very interesting job you've got.'

He inclined his head. 'Interesting, yes. You haven't answered my question.'

'Oh! Shall I say ... three? To start off with?'

'Three is a very good number. I have ten at your disposal, depending on how the night proceeds. On one occasion, ten was not enough for the lady in question, and I had to ring out for more.'

I laughed, stunned. At the back of my mind had always been the nagging idea that I was a freak, alone in my disgusting desires. Evidently not.

'Well ... I think ten would be perfectly sufficient! More than enough!'

He smiled, rather charmingly. 'Good,' he said. 'Shall we?'

He rose to his feet, offering me an arm.

'Where are we going?' I wondered, heading side by side down the creaky stairs and out through the bustling café.

'Into your deepest desires, of course,' he replied airily.

My deepest desires, it seemed, lay over the railway bridge and past the piles of container crates stacked up in a yard beyond. Warehouses, of a low-rise corrugated metal build, lay beyond this yard and we walked through the gloom past dozens of depots and storage facilities until we turned a corner, in the heart of the deserted estate, and found ourselves face to face with ... 'Oh!' I exclaimed loudly.

It was a static caravan, of a type you might find in a holiday park, but the front wall had been removed and replaced completely with toughened glass. I could not see inside, for heavy burgundy velvet drapes had been closed over the window. At the rear of the building, smoking and muttering and rubbing their hands around a brazier, was a group of maybe two dozen men and a couple of women. The performers in tonight's special feature, I presumed.

My escort disengaged from me, produced a key and stepped up to the caravan door, ushering me inside ahead of him.

I stood, staring around into its red-lit corners, noticing how all the walls and kitchen units had been taken out to provide an enormous space devoted to nothing more than the arts of pleasure. Only the small shower and toilet remained behind a partition door. A heart-shaped mattress took up the centre of the room, surrounded by multitudes of cushions in sumptuous fabrics. Shelves of bottles and lotions and lubricants ran the length and breadth of the caravan, including, in one corner, a supply of sex toys. The prints on the walls were of tacky nudes and highly coloured kama-sutra illustrations. Everything was rose or violet, everything was both dim and lurid beneath the lamp's red glare. There could be no doubt whatsoever that this was a tart's boudoir. And I was the tart.

'May I leave you to it?' enquired the man politely. 'I think you should be able to engineer things from here. This rope here –,' he tugged at a length of intertwined golden strands, '– will open the curtains. When you're ready. Oh, and the wastepaper basket is by the door. The gentlemen will dispose of the necessaries when they leave. Do you need anything?'

I shook my head, dazed. "The necessaries." The tissues, the condoms. The reality. The man from The

Number bowed slightly and took his leave.

I almost followed him. Almost. Then I took a deep breath, took another look at my lascivious lair and removed my coat. The full-length mirror behind the bed showed a shapely woman with too much make-up on. 'Whore,' I mouthed to my reflection. 'Trollop.' Then I unbuttoned my shirt dress, revealing the cheap scarlet and black underwear, and there I was – in the zone. Ready. Raring to go.

I shimmied my hips, shrugging the shirt sleeves along my arms and dropping the unnecessary clothing to the floor. This was what I was tonight. A sex-mad hooker, gasping for a fuck as badly as some crave a cigarette or a hit of their favourite narcotic. I laughed out loud, sticking a hand down my knickers and posing, porn-star style. Then I turned and pulled on the curtain cord. Showtime.

As if summoned by a bell, a knot of men appeared at the window, pretending to glance casually in, then stopping to chat among themselves, all the while looking over their shoulders at me. I dropped to my knees in the window and put my hands either side of my breasts, squeezing them together, running my thumbs over the protuberant nipples, licking my lips. Oh, I was wet already; I could feel the moisture seeping down to the lacy crotch of my thong, and I parted my thighs a little, to give my audience a clue what might be happening down there. Now two of the men drifted out of their conversation and were clearly watching me, nudging their friends. I swivelled my hips, then wetted my fingertips with a saucy tongue and pushed my hand down inside the knickers. All the men were watching now, watching me plant my fingers between my slick lips and rub, and I was trying very hard not to individualise them, not to pick out faces or hairstyles, but to keep them in role as everymen connected by the sharp gleam of lust for me in their eyes.

I lurched to my feet again and twirled around, bending over and pretending to fiddle with my shoe strap. I could feel that thong applying pressure to the crack of my behind, slipping inside my cheeks and straining over my pussy.

A knock at the door. My first punter.

I pulled it aside, registering only maleness, of a younger kind – if I were looking at him with the eyes of Saffron the person rather than Saffron the commodity, I might find him fanciable. But he was here to fuck me for money, and there was no point getting interested in him.

'Hellooo,' I said, trying to sound like Marilyn Monroe.

'How much?' he asked brusquely. 'For a straight fuck, like.'

His refusal to beat around the bush, as it were, was aphrodisiacal in the extreme. Rubbing my thighs together to try and quell the itch at their apex, I said, 'How much do you have? I don't mind.'

'You want it that bad, do you, love?' he asked crudely, putting a big hand on my hip. 'Well, I think the going rate is a bit higher, but you look to be about a fiver's worth.'

My eyes rolled into the back of my head with extreme delight. Yes, make me cheap, make me the cheapest fuck in town.

'Deal,' I whispered brokenly, drawing him on to the stage.

'Right,' he said, pausing to give his mates the thumbs-up and a wink in response to their fulsome applause. 'What do I get for that, then?'

'The lot. Whatever you want.'

'Whatever I want? Knickers off, then, and sit on the bed with your legs spread.'

I couldn't get them off fast enough, almost tripping in my haste to show all I had. I fell back on the heart-shaped bed, splaying out my knees in the process, lying luxuriously and wickedly spread, watching my john remove his jacket and T-shirt.

'No, no, no,' he said reprovingly. 'Your public want to see your face as well as your snatch. Sit up and face them.'

I wriggled upright, taking care not to hide any of the personal areas he had ordered me to keep visible, and decided I might as well unhook my bra too. Thus naked, I faced the world, or rather the small portion of it represented by the squashed up noses and hot breathy mouths pressed against the window.

'While I'm getting ready,' the man said, unbuckling his belt, 'why don't you have a little play with yourself? Get in the mood? I want you nice and wet when I fuck you.'

Obediently, I licked the fingers of one hand and began to strum at my already-juicy clit, using my spare digits to pinch my nipples and pluck at the wobbling flesh of my breasts.

'Look at them while you're doing it.'

I could see them, hands on crotches, hard bulges threatening to dent the heavy-duty perspex of the window. They were cheering and punching fists in the air, lifting me up on a wave of delirious debasement; the rougher and readier their response to me, the faster I flicked at the swollen bud, bending my neck to lap at a nipple with my tongue.

'Very nice.' The john stood at the side of the bed, a

condom already applied to his solid, curving cock. 'Now get on your back and get those legs in the air. No, sideways on – I don't want that lot getting an eyeful of my arse. It's you they want to watch.'

I shuffled my bottom ninety degrees and lay flat, imagining the picture I made in that window, the rise and fall of my breasts, the way my arse curved and my thigh flexed. I gripped the undersides of my knees with each hand, holding myself strenuously open, watching the john as he took the base of his cock in his hand and dropped to his knees before me.

Ragged cries from outside filtered into my brain. 'Go on, my son!' 'Give her one for me!' 'Fuck her brains out, mate!'

'I know what your kind wants,' he said to me roughly, rubbing the tip of his cock against my lubricated entrance. 'No kissing. No affection. Just a good, hard shafting. Am I right?'

'You're right,' I fluttered.

He shoved himself in, with wonderful unceremony. I let out an 'ah!' of delirious contentment, in awe at his perfect reading of my fantasy and his unforgiving steeliness. Filled and fucked, and in public too. This was better than I had imagined it, by a factor of about a thousand. Fists banged on the glass, in dull rhythmic accompaniment to the john's merciless thrusts; I turned my head to watch my audience through blurred eyes and when I saw the atavistic lust of their expressions, I came, while my punter held me down and continued to fuck through my climax.

'She's loving it!' 'Get in there, my son!' 'Give it to her!'

He gave it to me, with interest, pounding me long and hard while the bedcover rumpled into the crack of my bum and my head began to hang over the edge of the outlined heart. I wondered if I would come again, and realised that – of course! – the john was screwing me with no regard for my pleasure, only his, so if I wanted another orgasm, I would have to fix myself one. I frigged myself again, much to the appreciation of the crowd, and brought myself off just as the punter spurted into the rubber teat stuffed far inside my cunt. The crowd went wild – they thought it was all over and, well, it was.

'Thanks, love,' he panted, puffing into my face for a few minutes prior to pulling out. 'You're a great fuck. Wish I could have shot my load inside you, but modern times being what they are …' He broke off and half-chuckled. His face was beet red and shiny with exertion, and it occurred to me for the first time that he was quite a handsome man in a rough, amateur boxer-ish kind of way, sandy-blond and freckled with a big broad mouth and gym-schooled body.

'It's me who should be thanking you,' I pointed out, lounging on the bed, limbs akimbo, past caring about the men outside. 'You've made this a brilliant experience. Or, at least, a brilliant start to it.'

He grinned, pulling on his pants and jeans then smoothing fingers through his hair in front of the mirror. 'Any time, love,' he said with a wink. 'I suppose you ought to freshen up for the next one. They're lining up out there.' He half-waved, a little awkwardly, and high-tailed it out of the caravan.

Yes. Freshen up. Try to find some reserves of energy. A real prostitute would not have used up so much on one fuck. I needed to remember to lie back and think of … well, just think of what's happening to me. But in a passive way, sparing my muscles.

Mindful of my waiting queue, I slipped into the tiny

bathroom and sponged myself down, applying scented lotion and perfume before putting my knickers back on – I really didn't think there was much point wrestling with the bra. Out in front of my crowd once more, I brushed my hair and touched up my make-up, taking it slowly and ostentatiously, sticking out my bum, letting my tits jiggle with every move, waiting for the whites of their eyes to show.

Once I had teased them enough, I flung open the caravan door once more and stood in its backlight, hands on hips, shivering at the blast of cold air that met me.

'Who's next, boys?'

An eager young man in a hoody and loose jeans stepped up.

'I want a blow job!' he demanded urgently. 'And my mate here wants to fuck you. Can you do both of us?'

I smiled. 'I don't see why not. It's specials night tonight. Two for the price of one. Come on in.'

Once more in profile, my naked body outlined in the window, I crouched on the bed, my eyes shut, all the better to see what my audience saw. I knew what was happening by the feel of it; the men looking in could see my mouth wrapped around a cock, sucking and licking with slutty relish, enjoying the owner's hands braced on top of my head to prevent any escape from my oral duties. If they shifted their eyes a little to the right, along my curving spine and around the smooth, well-presented endpoint of my bottom, they could also see the thick stalk of another cock, planted between those cheeks and angled low, so it was clear that my pussy was taking the brunt of its blunt thrusts. Now that I was here, where I had always wanted to be, I felt disconnected from the action, which I could only interpret from the false perspective of the audience. Yes, the hard shaft at my

41

rear felt good, sliding into the slippery slickness created by my previous customer (on which this man commented at length before deigning to dip his wick where wick had been dipped so lately); yes, I was fully engaged in sucking my head-end john into an ecstatic emission. But somehow I was not here. I was above it all, looking down; or in front of it all, looking in. And now, I finally understood the fantasy. What I was doing was exquisitely filthy, but I would not truly experience my desire until I got to watch myself in this condition, utterly debased and whorish, opening my orifices to all and sundry.

The epiphany coincided happily with another climax, first from me and then from the man in my cunt. On his withdrawal, the man I was sucking explained that he needed to finish off inside me, and I obligingly spread myself for my third cock of the night, not even demurring when he stuck an experimental finger in my anus before arriving at his blissful end.

Mindful of getting my money's worth, I took two more clients – riding on top with my bottom grinding enthusiastically for the pleasure of my windowgazers – before conceding that my pussy was too sore and well-fucked for further incursions. How do the professionals manage, I wondered? Is there a special balm?

Resolutely I drew the curtain on my clapping, wolf-whistling crowd and took my final shower of the night. The clock read 4.12 a.m. That taxi driver may well have still been on shift, but I didn't think I'd be able to offer him any specialised tip tonight. Even after a lengthy lathery soak in the scented steam, the area between my thighs throbbed and felt raw. It would be a day or so before I could walk without a little reminder of my night on the game.

Once I was dressed again, I wondered whether any of my fans were left outside the caravan. Presumably they would all have drifted off home to their Halls of Residence, or hostels, or open prisons. How were these men recruited exactly? So many questions …

Before I could ponder further, there was a knock at the door.

'I'm done,' I shouted cautiously, hoping there was not still a large and unruly queue at the step.

'It's me – your … facilitator.' The man from the café's voice was unmistakable and distinctive. I let him in, smiling shyly, wondering how much of my performance he actually saw.

'Well, Miss Miles,' he said, sitting on the rumpled bed before checking it for stray condoms and tissues. 'Can I add another satisfied customer to my ledger?'

'Yes, I'd say so. It was so perfectly prepared and executed … funnily, though, I realised halfway through that I really wanted to be *watching* myself. Lovely as all the sex was. That sounds ungrateful, I suppose.'

'Not in the least. We have found that, from time to time, as a fantasy plays out, the buyer finds that there are extra dimensions they would like to explore. Often these are followed up in a further session.'

'I see. I'd better start saving up for next year then.'

He stood, chuckling, and reached up to a corner of the ceiling. Oh! I had not noticed that! He plucked a tiny camera from its bracket and handed it to me.

'Not necessarily,' he said. 'It's all here. Though, of course, we'd be delighted to see you again.'

'Wow. A souvenir.' I turned the tiny metallic eye over and over in my palm.

'You need to connect it to a computer,' my host explained. 'What you do with it after that is up to you. If

43

you wish to release it for public consumption on the internet, please let us know – we'd like our proper credit. We might even pay you for some advertising.'

'Oh! I don't think I'll be letting anyone else see this!' I exclaimed with conviction. Though I did kind of like the idea … 'Thank you. I will definitely recommend you. It's been …' I could not finish the sentence, shrugging and blushing instead.

The man inclined his head, accepting my inarticulate tribute, before standing to escort me back to the taxi rank.

When I think back to it now, it seems like an elaborate dream – but now, instead of fantasising, I have the film to watch, over and over, finding a new aspect of mortifying pleasure every time.

And I'm saving up for next year all the same.

Lucky Break

CHARLOTTE HAD FOUND A new way to deal with the drone and drear of the weekly office meeting. Instead of doodling on her desk blotter and ticking off the number of times her manager used the phrases 'ball park figure', 'ducks in a row' or 'corporate vision', she drifted off into her mind, imagining the ineffectual chinless man to be Collins or Bryant instead, preparing to call her in for a very personal performance review.

Office life with those two in charge would be quite a different proposition. The appearance of the trolley-lady would no longer be the highlight of the working day. They would make her wear bizarre and skimpy outfits. They would call her in for staff exercises, which would be of the pelvic-floor-strengthening type. And the penalties for poor performance … ah, well, they would involve bending over the desk, for sure.

'Did you get that, Charlotte? Is it minuted?' She jerked back to reality, her inner self responding with a sulky *What if it isn't?*, even as her outer one understood that Jim Bennett – not *Mr* Bennett, not even James, nothing to command respect, just plain man-of-the-people Jim B – would only have responded with a knitted brow and a puzzled shake of the head, and perhaps a little gathering of perspiration on his upper lip. Mr Collins, on the other hand, would have ordered her into his office – perhaps even lifted her roughly by the upper arm and dragged her – perhaps he wouldn't even do it in the office – perhaps he would make a public example of her … oh, how quickly could she get to the bathroom?

'Yeah,' she said to Jim, daring a shrug.

'Good, jolly good,' he said nervously, eyeing her as if she were an unidentified beast who might bite. 'That's all, folks.' He said it in imitation of Bugs Bunny at the end of a Looney Tunes programme. Charlotte felt her will to live draining away. Then she jumped as the phone rang – just once, signifying an internal call.

She picked up the receiver and dutifully trotted out the Litany of the Department: 'Hello, this is Charlotte Steele, Human Resources, how may I help you?'

'Oh, hello.' The regal received pronunciation immediately identified the caller as Merle from reception. 'This is Reception. I have a visitor at the desk for you.'

Before Charlotte could enquire further the dial tone kicked back in. She was not expecting anyone. Perhaps a union representative unhappy about something or other? Perhaps somebody handing in an application form in person? Whatever it was, it was bound to be dull.

Except it wasn't. When Charlotte arrived in reception after five flights of stairs and a maze of corridors, her visitor was standing at the far end of the lobby they shared with the Crown Court, reading a poster about some fundraising event or other. He had broad shoulders and a blue suit and perfectly cut hair. He was … surely it was …

'Charlotte.' He turned and smiled and she almost screamed aloud.

After an age during which her jaw seemed wired in an

unattractive gawping mode, she managed to utter the words, 'Mr Bryant.'

'Thank you for coming down,' he said smoothly, advancing towards the desk where Merle sat arranging papers and pretending not to watch. 'I wonder if I could steal you for the rest of the afternoon ... Miss Steele?'

'Oh.' She put a hand to her mouth, suddenly filled with wild and wicked merriment. 'I can't flex off till four ... it's only quarter past three now ...' She wished she had worn anything but this dreary grey skirt suit with black polo-neck and ballet flats. She looked ten years older than twenty-four. She wondered if Bryant remembered her as he had last seen her – rumpled and exhausted, sticky and sweaty, dazed and confused and thoroughly used.

'I'm sure I could arrange something. What's your boss's extension?' His hand hovered over Merle's telephone, to her blatant annoyance.

'Four-three-three-seven. Oh, you can't!'

But he had punched it in and stood with the receiver against his ear, smiling benignly at both members of his female audience.

'Ah, hello, yes, I need a fairly urgent conference with Miss Steele from your office – I'm from Bryant and Collins and she has been in dealings with us regarding some personnel issues ...'

Charlotte snorted. Personnel? Personal, more like. Intimate, indeed.

'... Oh no, I'm afraid it can't be conducted over the phone. "Face time," as you say, is essential. I would be most awfully obliged to you ... well, that's thoroughly decent of you. Thank you very much. I'll tell her she can go home after our meeting, shall I? Splendid.'

He replaced the receiver with the air of a man who

had the world at his fingertips.

'There,' he said, nodding at Charlotte and extending a hand. 'All squared.'

'But didn't Jim say …?'

'I find, Miss Steele,' he said, taking her by the wrist and exerting just the smallest pressure to jump-start her in his preferred direction, 'that an authoritative manner goes a long way with a public servant.'

'I think you're right,' she replied fervently, casting a brief backward glance to Merle, whose half-moon glasses rested severely on the bridge of her nose as she followed their figures to the doorway and out to the steps of Colliton Town Hall.

'So you got my email?' she asked nervously, allowing him to lead the way down and past the library, towards the town centre.

'Yes, we did.' He squeezed her wrist, which he was still handling, then laced his fingers with hers and smiled down. 'We were so pleased to hear from you.'

'Were you? Even though I said … you know. I can't afford to do it again.'

'That's what I'm here to see you about. I have a proposition for you. Business.' His eyes twinkled. 'With perhaps a bit of pleasure thrown in.'

Charlotte's chest tightened and she gulped down air, almost jumping when they stopped abruptly at the car park entrance and Bryant pointed a key fob at a sleek silver-blue Bentley.

'Why don't you come for a drive with me and I'll explain it all to you?'

Get in a car with a strange man? But he wasn't a stranger … exactly … All the same, she knew very little about him, except that he had a taste for filthy kinky sex. As did she. He was no dodgier than she was, then, she supposed. He had told Jim Bennett the name of his business – they could check if she didn't show up at work the next day.

Bryant seemed to read her face; his eyes crinkled kindly and he stooped down a little, to level with her.

'I'm not going to hurt you, Charlotte. Not without your consent. You have your mobile? Good. You can text a friend if you like – let her know where you are. Tell her I'll have you back for supper.'

Charlotte smiled and slid past the door Bryant was holding open for her.

The upholstery was divinely comfortable, smelling of luxury, and when Bryant started up the engine, the car barely registered the movement, gliding into an easy purr and pulling out on to the road as if propelled on a cushion of air.

'Where are we going?' asked Charlotte as Bryant switched off the Vivaldi CD he had been listening to earlier, presumably.

'Some lovely spots around here, Charlotte. Good places for walks. I envy you. It's so very far from that dirty, crazy city I have to operate in.'

'Oh, I like the city. I would love to live there.'

Bryant turned his head, his expression satisfied. 'Good. I was hoping you might say that.'

'Why?'

'Collins and I ... we have been discussing you. After your little performance the other week on the train and at the hotel ... well, let's say we were impressed. And not just with the action. With the way you conveyed your fantasy to us. With your enthusiasm and articulacy. With your quick grasp of what our operation entails. And we liked you as a person as well. So we thought ... maybe you might like to work for us.'

Charlotte gripped the edges of the leather seat, trying to calm the wave that had rocked through her.

'What? Work for you? For The Number?'

'Well, yes. Given that our client base is overwhelmingly female, it seems wrong somehow that we don't have a woman on board. We thought you'd fit the bill. Female fantasy consultant. What do you think? Could you see yourself in that role?'

Charlotte could not speak for a moment, staring ahead blindly at the narrowing roads and disappearing street lamps as they reached the outskirts of the small market town. The word 'role' made her think of the part she had played in the hotel – but that had not been so much a role as a hidden part of herself, let out to play for once.

'It would mean living in the City.'

'Well, yes. Collins has a little flat he would be happy to rent you.'

'Really?'

'Very close to the office. You would be involved in research and development. Some marketing. And … a little road testing, I would imagine.'

'Road testing?'

'Seeing if some of our clients' fantasy expectations can be met. Logistics … risk assessments …'

'With you? And Collins?'

'You could always expect our full support. And we'd take care of you. We'd see that you were never endangered or compromised.'

Charlotte watched Bryant drive. He was assured and steady, handling the steering wheel confidently, his feet playing the pedals without undue hurry. They were driving past fields now, and heading towards some of the forest that had been left behind when the new bypass had hacked through it. She felt safe with him, even driving through these overhanging branches in the gloom.

She did not even lose her head when he turned the car down a narrow single-lane track, having to put on his headlights. A lay-by appeared from the murk and he brought the car to a skilful stop before turning to Charlotte and asking, 'Well? Are you interested?'

He had taken off his jacket before getting in the car, and Charlotte concentrated intently on the creases at the elbow of his starched white shirt, thinking.

'Yes,' she said at last. 'I think I am. As long as I have enough to live on …'

'You will. More than enough. Limitless earnings potential, if the site really takes off.'

'Then yes.' She laughed, feeling weightless and free. No more mind-numbing meetings. No more hateful college course. No more reading *Psychology in the Workplace* on the train. 'I'll work for you.'

Bryant clapped in delight. 'Wonderful! Excuse me, I must just email Collins.'

He tapped away on his netbook while Charlotte took the opportunity to text her flatmate. As soon as the communications were sent on their way, Bryant turned back to Charlotte, seeming immediately intent on some dark purpose.

'You won't be dressing like that in our office,' he opened forebodingly.

'Oh … really?' Charlotte fluttered, scrunching up her toes inside the soft leather ballet flats.

'Really. Knee-length skirts? Flat shoes? And … are those … tights?'

He reached out a hand and patted Charlotte's opaque black knee.

'Yes. But if I'd known …'

'No excuse, Charlotte. You should always be

prepared. You never know when a masterful man is going to come and make demands of you. You of all people should be bearing that in mind. Shouldn't you?'

'Yes. Sir.' Charlotte's body tensed in excited anticipation. Her thighs jammed together, the opaque tights feeling thick and damp. He was right – they would have to go.

'Never mind. A reminder might be in order, though, before we proceed with contractual matters. Get those tights off, please.'

Charlotte knew better than to quibble. She lifted her skirt delicately at the hem and wriggled out of the offending garment, placing it in Bryant's waiting hand once her legs were bare.

'Hmm, you'll have to put those shoes back on, I suppose. For now,' he sniffed, stretching the lengths of heavy-duty nylon and wrapping them around his fingers experimentally. 'Actually, I could find a use for these,' he noted. 'Right, take off your jacket and get out of the car. We're going for a nice walk in the countryside.'

Charlotte obeyed the instruction, stepping out on to crackling twigs and uneven tracks in the dried mud. It was not cold, but nonetheless the air breathed goose-bumps on to her bare legs and her nipples tightened beneath the serviceable polo neck and cotton bra. Bryant came around behind her and nudged her forward with a hand at the small of her back, taking her off the track and into the wood-scented depths of the forest.

'Collins and I like heels. So you'll be wearing them. Maybe knee-high boots on occasion … patent leather perhaps. And stockings – always stockings. No trousers, of course, and keep the skirts no longer than mid-thigh. We don't want you to look like a tart, necessarily … but we do want you to look sexy and available. A few shirt buttons undone, lots of lip gloss, the suggestion of wantonness. I'm sure you know what I mean, Charlotte. Do you ever dress like that for a lover?'

Charlotte thought back to her personnel course, to the sub-module on appropriate dress codes. How surreal it all was.

'For a lover, maybe. For work though …'

'Work is play. For you, Charlotte, from now on. Work is what you make of it. Are you wearing knickers?'

'Of course!'

'Take them off.'

Charlotte stopped, peering through the ferny half-light to make sure no rogue dog-walkers or birdwatchers were in attendance. Then she reached under her skirt and squatted to pull down the plain white knickers she wore for the office.

'I'll have those if you don't mind,' said Bryant peremptorily, and they joined her tights in a bulging trouser pocket. At least, she thought it was a trouser pocket …

They walked on, and Charlotte's attention was focused less on the dry scrunch of leaves underfoot and more on the breezes that ventilated the interior of her staid grey skirt, whispering around her crotch while her bottom rubbed against the cool nylon lining. The overhanging trees meant that the warmth of the early autumn sun could not penetrate here, and Charlotte shivered, as much from cold as anticipation.

'A bit chilly, my dear?' enquired Bryant mildly. 'We should do something about that. Warm you up. Your little lesson about the tights could serve a dual purpose. What do you think?'

He put an arm around her shoulder, drawing her close

to him – an affectionate gesture even as he discussed the matter of punishment.

'I think … I'm wondering what is going to happen. Here in this wood.'

Charlotte looked about her for signs of civilisation, but all she could hear was the rustling and sighing of leaves in the light wind.

'What do you think?' repeated Bryant, looking down with a tilted eyebrow.

'A punishment of some kind.'

'Don't you think you deserve it?'

'Yes.' She smirked self-consciously. Bryant was too anxious of her consent, too solicitous of her feelings, to play the truly cruel master. Collins would have played this scene differently, she thought, dragging her unceremoniously to a tree and delivering a summary whipping. Perhaps, she mused, she would prefer that … all the same, Bryant was here, and it was no disappointment when she considered the pleasures that might lie ahead.

'Yes. You do. Well, then, Charlotte, I think you should find me a nice, strong switch, don't you? Plenty to choose from here. Of course, autumn isn't the birching season – they are drier and more brittle than their springtime counterparts – all the same, a serviceable enough instrument can usually be made. Well, hurry up, then. What are you waiting for?'

He patted the seat of her skirt, encouraging her forward, to explore the lower-hanging branches of the surrounding trees and assess their branches for flexibility and potential sting. Her hands were trembling as she snapped off long, thin wands of birch and willow, thinking of how they would soon be employed in striping her quivering pale rear.

When she had selected five of the rods, she proffered them hesitantly to Bryant. Rather than accepting them, he produced a Swiss Army knife from an inner pocket and flicked out a blade.

'Do you know how to trim these?' he asked urbanely. 'Have you ever done it before?'

'No,' Charlotte whispered. 'I never have ...'

'Never felt the kiss of the switch, eh? Oh, you're in for a treat then, aren't you? Come on, take the knife. Any rough spots or old buds need to be sliced off. We need the rod to be as smooth and sleek as possible, or it can be nastier than even we would like.' He smiled. He had such a *kind* smile. It was so *strange*.

'Really?' Charlotte asked, nervous as she began to hack at the knobbly parts of the switch with Bryant's blade.

'Oh yes. I like to make a mark, but I don't like to draw blood. Nice stripes, but skin unbroken – that's the sight I like to see. Would you mind if I took a photograph when I'm finished?'

'Oh ... I suppose not.' She looked up at him briefly, vividly. 'I seem to trust you for some reason. I hope I'm not misguided.'

'Thank you, Charlotte. I'll do all I can to be worthy of your trust.'

He took the switch, denuded of bumps and loose flecks of wood, and swung it through the air, adding a blood-chilling topnote to the endless leafy whispers.

'Ah yes. Good work. This will do very well. Now, can I assume that you will keep still while I'm thrashing you, or should I tie you to the tree?'

Charlotte was not sure if the question was rhetorical or not.

'I've never done it before,' she prompted, 'so ...

55

um … I don't know if I'd be able to keep still.'

'You think you should be tied? Yes, that's probably sensible.' Bryant removed the balled-up pair of tights from his trouser pocket. 'Your tights might not have been such a bad idea after all. Though of course I'm still going to punish you for wearing them. That goes without saying. Well, then.' He ripped the offending hosiery in half with the aid of his knife, then took Charlotte gently by the elbow and led her over to a tree whose trunk offered the perfect width and circumference for a whipping post. After turning her to face the tree, Bryant looped one stretchy tight leg around her waist, securing it with a firm double knot, before manoeuvring her arms to embrace the trunk and tying them together at the wrists, her palms pressed together as if in prayer.

'You're in my power now,' he murmured softly into her ear from behind. 'How does that make you feel?'

'Scared, a bit,' admitted Charlotte. 'But in an exciting way. I feel helpless … but in the way I fantasise … not in a bad sense.'

'Perfect little submissive,' he crooned, nipping at her earlobe before grasping her around the waist and roughly pulling up her polo-neck top until it was stretched above her breasts, exposing most of her back and her bra to the chill-tipped woodland air. His hands moved to the cotton bra cups, easing them down over her nipples until they were bunched low beneath the underhang where breast met ribcage. Charlotte's nipples now brushed the ridged wood, painfully sensitive, so that she thought sparks from them might ignite the dry bark. She lay her cheek flat against the whorls, pressing her tits to the trunk, embracing the chafe and the soreness, waiting for the next move, which would not be of her making.

'I'm sure we won't be needing this.' She felt the hook

and eye fly apart, the zip slice down, the slippery lining of her skirt slide slowly over her hips, then thighs, then tickle the backs of her knees before landing in a heap around her ankles. She was naked from the waist down, and there was no way she could do anything about it. The white moons of her bottom would be seen by any off-the-beaten-path rambler with dogs or binoculars and, once Bryant had encouraged her to spread her legs a little by slipping a hand between her thighs and tapping at her spreading pussy lips, so would her unprotected sex. There was no way around it. She, Charlotte Steele, was a horny little slut who needed a good switching from a man who was not afraid to lay it on hard.

But how hard would he lay it on? Charlotte bit her lip, tensing everything in anticipation of Bryant's opening strike. She flinched and squealed at the sudden touch of the rod, but it was not a hard stroke – not a stroke at all, and she cursed herself for expending vital energy on a little introductory tap. He continued to brush it over her bottom, down her thighs to her knees, then up again, prodding between the sensitive lower lips, jiggling the wand a little, getting it up nice and high until the tip was sodden with her immoderate leakages.

'You look perfect,' Bryant told her. 'My damsel in distress, lashed to the tree, writhing and naked. If only I were the hero instead of the villain, eh? If only I was here to save you ... instead of ...'

The switch sliced the air and a row of firecrackers lit and danced on Charlotte's behind. She moaned and wrenched at the tights around her wrists.

'Ahhh,' Bryant exhaled with satisfaction. 'How did that feel, Charlotte?'

'Like fire,' said Charlotte, when she could speak. 'It burns.'

'Mmm, a lasting burn. I don't know how many to give you, sweetness. How many do you think you could take?'

'I … don't really know. It hurts a lot. Maybe … six.'

Charlotte found that she was growing impatient with the negotiation. She wanted him to pronounce the sentence and be done with it, rather than canvas her opinion.

'Six it shall be. But if you can't take any more, tell me. Say my name. Say Bryant.'

'Yes, yes,' muttered Charlotte, and Bryant chuckled.

'Impatient for more? Oh, you are such a find, dear Charlotte.' And the second stroke was delivered before the sentence was finished, causing her to jerk and hurl herself closer to the tree bark, rubbing her bare stomach against the brittleness, finding distracting comfort in the lesser pain.

'It makes such a pretty mark,' mused Bryant. Why did he have to be so damn verbose? It was nice to be appreciated; all the same, Charlotte found herself thinking again of how Collins would have done this. Differently, more severely, the mood would have been darker, he might have been silent or he might have issued low-toned orders. Bryant was like some kind of gentleman dilettante in comparison. 'Two lovely lines of red. Let's add another.'

So he did, and Charlotte was remembering now to breathe through the stroke, even though she still reared and howled. Should she say his name? Should she make him stop? This was three – halfway through, halfway there. To stop before the end would be shameful – he would be disappointed in her. She would be disappointed in herself. No. She would grit her teeth and get to the end and have the memory and the sweet after-pain that made it all worthwhile. And now she was annoyed afresh that she was even having this debate with herself. Collins would have brooked no refusal. He would not have made her have to do this irksome *thinking*.

Halfway through an open-air switching, Charlotte was starting to make some startling realisations about the nature of her submissive tendencies. Funny how things were so different in theory than in the field, so to speak. If asked before, she'd have said that the Bryant model would have suited her far better, and yet ...

'Owwwww!' The fourth stroke caught her unawares, mid-self-analysis, and she resolved to stop thinking and limit herself to feeling from now on. The stripes he had already laid were beginning to throb. A switch was well-named. It switched her on, made her feel nothing but the fiery rawness of the welts, crossing her arse like a collection of sore red ropes, tied to her, inescapable.

She had collected herself for the fifth and sixth, almost enjoying them in the knowledge that they were the final strokes, after which lay ... who knew? Hopefully a pleasurable way of maximising the sensual stimulation the whipping had precipitated was on the cards. Would she have a say in the next step, or would Bryant guide the proceedings?

'No more tights then?' he said brusquely after the sixth stroke.

'No more tights,' Charlotte repeated, her voice a little shaky, bits of bark sticking to her cheeks and forehead now, not to mention her breasts, which were hurting more than she had realised from their rough acquaintance with the tree. She flexed her hands and wriggled her bottom, trying hard to calm the angry stripes painted across it, but to no avail.

'One more to make sure then,' said Bryant to her

surprised consternation, taking advantage of her relative relaxation to give her a stinger of momentous proportions, catching her just at the lowest line of her buttocks, where any attempt to sit down thereafter would remind her of it.

'Oh fuck!' she cried, completely blindsided by her assumption that the whipping was over.

'Oh, Charlotte!' purred Bryant, throwing aside the switch and running his hands across his handiwork. 'Such language. If I were a cruel man, I would probably have to add more strokes for that. I'm not though.'

'No, right,' Charlotte laughed ironically. 'Not cruel at all. It's not cruel to tie girls to trees and whip them.'

'Not when it's what they want,' pointed out Bryant laconically. 'Is it? Do you think?'

Charlotte clenched her teeth, not wanting to admit that he had a point. She began to think she might have underestimated the extent of his capacity for sadism – it seemed to her that he was crueller in persistently pointing out her consent to this than Collins might have been in pretending to act against her will. The flood of shame quickened to a wild lust, a need to be forced and overwhelmed and taken.

'And now,' said Bryant into her ear, his palms flat and large against her glowing bottom, 'I suppose you'd like to be fucked, would you?'

Charlotte whimpered, pushing her arse back against him, sighing when he parted her cheeks with his thumbs and began to massage the area.

'You'd like to be fucked here ...' One hand moved between her legs, gliding into her wetness. 'Against a tree ... my stomach slapping against your hot red arse ... until you come ... and I come ... and then I might leave you here, Charlotte. What if I left you here, tied here, with my spunk running down your legs and your poor, striped bum on display. How would that make you feel?'

'Ohhhh,' Charlotte could barely string a thought together, let alone a sentence. 'I don't know … humiliated. Ohh, God, yes, so humiliated and used and ashamed.'

'You like that, don't you? At least, the idea of it. But I wouldn't leave you, Charlotte. I have too many uses for you.'

Zips, buttons, fumbling and then a swift, hard, much-needed cock was slid snugly into Charlotte's tight snare.

'There,' whispered Bryant. 'Sore bum, full of cock, for the world to see, Charlotte. Take a moment to think how you must look.'

Charlotte took that moment. She took that moment to look down at her hips, where Bryant's fingers could be seen holding on. She took that moment to listen for distant voices or car noises, hearing nothing but the eternal leaves and the slight clinking of Bryant's belt, swaying against their sides, the cool leather sometimes stroking her skin. For the duration of that moment only, she realised how her arm and shoulder muscles ached from the tension of the whipping, and she wondered how distracting the intense sting of her switch marks would be when Bryant began to thrust against them.

But then all that was forgotten when Bryant began to withdraw, slowly, then sheath himself once more, without thought or care for her poor bum or her sore nipples, rubbed against the bark again. This was no slow, sensual coupling but a hard ride, Bryant grunting with each forceful stroke, the tree creaking as if their fucking might snap it. His pelvis slapped against her bottom cheeks, and she clung tight to her support, her feet sometimes raised from the ground as Bryant's cock plunged deeper and faster. Bryant pushed urgent fingers against Charlotte's clit, needing to get it over with, needing to fill her while she moaned in defeated ecstasy, and she let her orgasm scorch out from her cunt and along the searing lines of the switching, overtaking her exhausted body with thrilling, painful pleasure. Bryant snarled and pinned her so tight to the tree that she had to fight for breath, spilling inside her while he sank teeth into her shoulder.

He slumped against her, his arms encircling her and the bark, breathing heavily. Charlotte felt that she was melting into him, her body smudged and dirty, her pussy slick with their combined fluids, the sweat of sex seeping into her welts and making her bottom feel as if it had caught fire. It was so uncomfortable, so sticky and icky and mucky, and yet she could stay like that indefinitely, she thought.

She had a moment of panic when Bryant pulled out of her, having to hug the tree all the more desperately to keep upright.

'Mmm,' she heard him say, then there was a click and a flash of light, and she knew he had photographed her, all shiny and sweaty and streaked, her thighs clammy with his semen. She wondered if the picture would go up on the website, and the idea excited her, a tiny pulse of lustful shame awakening her tired sex.

Then Bryant's hands were on her shoulders and he was pulling down the polo neck to kiss the soft flesh there, stroking the fabric where his teeth had snagged it, whispering into her ear.

'Good girl ... well done ... you are spectacular. You will take the job, won't you?'

'Oh yeah.' Charlotte let her head loll back against Bryant's smooth cheek, losing herself in the momentary intimacy.

'Marvellous.' He began to untie her, releasing her wrists first, then holding on to her waist when she was able to step back from the tree. She found that she needed the support; her legs were watery and her body stiff as a broom handle. Bryant continued to hold her while she stretched and flexed and shook out pins and needles until she was able to stand again, still naked from the waist down with the bra cups underneath her breasts and the black top, rumpled and soaked now, above them.

Charlotte looked about for her skirt but Bryant chuckled and shook his head.

'No, Charlotte,' he said, then he put the tights about her neck and knotted them into a form of collar and leash. 'You stay like that – it suits you so well. Come on. I'll take you back to the car.'

Yanking on the nylon, he began to pull Charlotte forward across the leaf-carpet of the woodland, like a man taking his dog for ramble. She could not remember how far away the car was, and she hoped upon hope that Bryant had marked the route they had taken. Despite the raw heat of her backside, it really was getting cold now. Her nipples were like pebbles of ice and the spunk on her thighs had chilled almost to dryness by the time the long march of shame was over and the car came into welcome view.

Without releasing her neck, Bryant opened the car door and ushered her in.

'My clothes,' she said haltingly.

'You don't need those yet,' he told her. 'Sit down and get your seat belt on.'

Charlotte sat gingerly down, the leather seat feeling at first wondrously cool and soothing against her angry switch marks. She pulled the seat belt across her exposed ribs and stomach, clicking it smartly so that the bottom part of it lay atop her nude upper thighs and the diagonal part cut between her breasts, parting them in a way that drew emphasis towards the goose-bumpy mounds.

Bryant leaned over and loosened the tights around her neck, leaving them swinging like a noose, but then he attached the other end to her wrists, wrapping it round and round until they were secured in her lap.

'I want your legs spread wide,' he told her. 'Keep them apart. That's it.'

Charlotte opened her thighs until her knee backs hinged over each front corner of the leather seat. Her tethered hands were forced to rest on her mons, fingers framing her gaping labia, close enough to reach in and touch her clit.

'Very nice,' approved Bryant, who climbed in beside her and started up the engine. 'You must be hungry. It must be time to eat, I think.'

'Where? How?' Charlotte craned her neck towards him in wonder and consternation, but he simply smiled and pulled out of the lay-by on to the dark forest track.

Charlotte was grateful for the quiet, unlit country roads, although she continually dreaded the possibility of a coachload of tourists pulling out in front of them. But it didn't happen, and eventually they reached a village where Bryant parked up in a secluded corner and prepared to get out of the car.

'What are you doing?' flapped Charlotte.

'Stay there,' he said with a reassuring wink. 'I won't be long.'

He wasn't long, but for Charlotte his absence may as well have been a geological age. Although the parking spot was at the far end of the village, and overlooked only by a sombre church tower, concealing her from the cottages beyond, she imagined the sudden arrival of a gaggle of old ladies, or bellringers, or choral singers. How on earth would they react, she wondered, unsure of whether to giggle or be aghast at the idea.

Thankfully, she didn't have to find out, for Bryant soon returned with takeaway cartons of Chinese food.

'Let's find a private place to eat these,' he suggested, hitting the road once more until they came to another lay-by, shrouded by overhanging trees, far off the beaten track. Bryant switched on the light and the radio, feeding Charlotte chicken chow mein while the evening news chuntered on in the background.

'You really are hungry, aren't you?' he said, impressed at her appetite. 'This is what I call eating out. Don't you?'

'Nnrgh,' said Charlotte, mouth full of noodles, feeling very small and helpless and well-tended-to.

'Have you had enough? Are you sure?' Bryant stroked her forehead and wiped the remainder of the sauce away with a pristine handkerchief. 'Shall we just sit here and relax for a little while. The others will be here soon.'

'The others?' Charlotte tried to sit up straight, but her bottom was sticking to the leather now and it hurt.

'I thought you were a local girl,' tutted Bryant.

'I ... am.' She tried to hide her mystification.

'Then you should know that this is a very popular spot after dark, Charlotte.'

'It is?'

'Yes.' Bryant laughed, genuinely surprised. 'It's quite well documented.'

'I ... look, I don't do this kind of thing ... at home. It's just been fantasies up to now. I've had boyfriends, but it's all been pretty … normal. Except in my head.'

'Conventional on the outside, shameless on the inside,' said Bryant. 'Oh look. Visitors.'

A car pulled up at the far end of the lay-by and four young men, strapping farmer types, shambled out on to the gravel.

'Up to you, Charlotte,' whispered Bryant – the words she never wanted to hear. 'I can start the engine now and take you home. Or you can give them a little show. Which one?'

Big moon faces were looming behind the toughened glass, squinting and peering. Charlotte looked down at her bisected breasts, at her still-parted thighs, at her tied hands. She looked abandoned and hot, especially viewing herself through their eyes. A lust object. Her pussy clenched and she shut her eyes for a few moments before opening them again, her decision made.

The evening passed in a blur of headlamps and greedy eyes, strumming fingers and her own neck tossing from side to side as she made herself come for the entertainment of the local yokels, once by her own hand, twice by Bryant's.

She would never forget her final view as Bryant turned the key in the ignition, causing the spectators to scatter. Their faces, red and parched with lust as their fat fists tugged on their pricks, and at the end of the row, the red, lustful face of Jim Bennett, his froggy eyes bulging from his head.

No need to write that letter of resignation then, she thought, as Bryant's Bentley carried her effortlessly away from it all, towards a future that held infinite lascivious promise.

Down and Dirty

IT'S ALMOST EMBARRASSING TO admit that this is my favourite fantasy. It is so commonplace, after all, and something plenty of women do every day and every night. If only I wasn't such a freak, I'd have done it myself long ago. But I can't bring myself to do it – I can't get past the thought that he might be contaminated. Any amount of fungus might be blooming beneath his perfect skin. His broad chest could be full of deadly spores. I might put my lips up to his be kissed, only to find the sweetish stench of decay wafting from his mouth. Ulcers, sores, nail infections – all might hide inside a fashionable suit.

I sound mad, I know. I'm quite aware that my scruples aren't normal. Not everyone wears surgical gloves to leave the house; not everyone flinches if a person comes within half a foot of them; not everyone has a weekly spend of £150 on household detergents. And other people have sex. They touch each other. They give each other pleasure. I have not had an orgasm other than by my deeply-disinfected vibrator in five years – not since Gerry left, citing irreconcilable differences. He said I should be cryogenically frozen because nobody would be able to tell the difference. He said I could cosy up to a bottle of bleach if that's what I wanted.

It wasn't what I wanted though. I don't want to be

this way. I want to feel a touch again, without fifty images of rotting flesh flashing before my eyes. That is why I dialled the Number. I suppose they are used to people asking for all kinds of perverted, disgusting stuff, but all I wanted was to pick up an attractive man in a bar and take him to bed. So simple, so dull in a way. But it would – perhaps – change my life.

I received an email a week later, inviting me to London to choose a suitable candidate and to witness the many, many tests I had stipulated in my initial contact. The address I arrived at was in Harley Street, at the back of a large private practice. I was shown to a rather nicely furnished waiting room, where I was introduced to a gentleman in a suit. At least, I say I was introduced – he did not give me his name. He simply said, 'Mrs Davies – I'm delighted to meet you. I'm from the Number.' Then he held out a hand, which I waved away as usual.

'You must excuse me,' I said. 'This is all … a bit like a dream.'

'I'm sure it must be,' he said, with a friendly chuckle. He had kind eyes, which was a relief. 'Your request was a very interesting one. We have had nothing like it before.'

'No, well, I know I'm a freak,' I said with a high-pitched laugh that did nothing to convince him that there was anything funny about it.

'Not a freak, Mrs Davies,' he said gallantly. 'We all have aspects that diverge from the norm. I assure you, I am probably substantially less normal than you are.'

'Oh, do call me Naomi.'

He indicated one of the chintz armchairs, but I did not want to sit down. This was a medical establishment after all. Who knows how many germ-ridden posteriors had brushed those floral cushions?

'Our candidates should be here very shortly,' the Number man said to break the awkward silence. 'We have three – you choose your favourite, obviously. Then we may proceed with the tests.'

'Ah.' At that moment, the door opened again, and the receptionist showed in three men, all mouth-wateringly handsome and very, very clean-looking. I turned to the Number man, suppressing an almost irresistible urge to giggle.

'Gentlemen,' he said, 'may I introduce Naomi to you. She is going to choose one of you to perform the scenario she has outlined to us.'

Perform! I actually laughed out loud. This had to be the crowning bizarre moment in a life full of them. They smiled warmly back at me, sizing me up, not that I minded. I'm a good-looking woman, still a long way off middle age, a trim size ten with long legs and unblemished skin. I wondered if they would look so pleasant and forthcoming if I was one of those slobby tracksuited types I see passing my window every day with their dirty-faced children. I supposed they were being paid for this ... so they probably would.

'Well, Naomi, the choice is yours. I'll leave you to your decision.'

The Number man shrank back in his armchair, picking up a copy of *Horse and Hound* and flicking through it.

'What are your names then?' I asked bravely, trying to maintain a calm demeanour in the face of raging nerves and excitement. Was I really going to end up in bed with one of these dreamboats? Perhaps I should have asked for two ... would that cost me extra though? This service was not coming cheap as it was.

'I'm Liam,' said the broadest one, a clean-cut,

farmboy type in properly-pressed jeans and a plaid shirt. 'I'm studying vet science.'

'Oh, a vet. How lovely.' I shuddered inwardly. Diseased animals – even worse than diseased humans. I flicked my eyes along the row to the next chap, a tall slight blond with a long nose.

'My name's Kai. I work as a chauffeur – paying my way through college.'

'A chauffeur! That's rather … unusual these days.'

'It's a limousine hire company. I drive hen parties around town.'

'Oh, gosh, rather you than me.' All those heifers in themed outfits vomiting champagne all over the upholstery. Ugh.

My final candidate was an elegantly-suited black man with glasses.

'I'm Justus,' he said. 'I recently qualified as a lawyer.'

Oh, now this sounded hopeful.

'What kind of law do you specialise in?' I asked, dreading that he might say criminal or family.

'Intellectual property,' he told me. Perfect! His only contact would be with clever people with enough money to pay him to fight their cases. He seemed by far the safest bet, and the most confident of the three to boot. He might well know his way around a woman's body, whereas the wet-behind-the-ears youth of the other two did not inspire such hopes.

'Intellectual property.' I repeated the phrase, rolling it around my tongue, eyeing his snow-white starchy collar and the way his gold signet ring gleamed in contrast to his matt skin.

'Are you a lawyer yourself?' he asked politely, perhaps a little confused by the way I was relishing his career choice.

'Me?' I laughed. 'Oh no, not a lawyer. Though I have used them before. Not your type though – the divorce type.'

'I'm sorry,' he said with a formal nod.

'Don't be. If I was still with him … Justus, I'd like to pick you. If you're absolutely sure … I mean, if you don't fancy me, please walk away, but …'

'I'm delighted,' he said. 'I don't want to walk away! Just a moment.' He fished in his pocket and brought out something I recognised only too well. Surgical gloves. After slipping them on, he held out a hand to me. I was captivated – it was such a strong and emotional feeling, it was almost like love. To think that a man could be so considerate … it was new to me.

The Number man had discreetly dismissed the other two, and now the three of us were alone, to get to the bare bones of the matter – the necessity for tests.

I watched through glass as Justus underwent a battery of examinations and swabs and needle pricks. I was impressed that he was willing to do all this for … OK, for money. Not for me. All the same, I thought, many men might have just shrugged halfway through the taxing afternoon and flitted off to find a normal girl and a bar job. Justus gave up every part of him, from epidermis to saliva to blood, just so that I could have this one shot at an ordinary life, with uncomplaining stoicism. This was a man, I thought. A real man.

'We will have the results in a week,' the lab technician told us.

'A week,' nodded Number man. 'Very well. Naomi, we will be in touch. Be prepared.'

I laughed, a little miserably. I was always prepared.

I had a text the next week to say that all the results

were clear, and I should wait for further instructions. Wait. Waiting is a thing I do well, walled up in my disinfected gleam-white haven. I see ordinary life through the screen of my television and I yearn for it, for the careless kisses and rough embraces I watch in the soap operas. I was watching one such soap opera – an omnibus edition – on the fateful Sunday afternoon. My telephone bleeped and I knew it was them. I never get text messages from anyone else.

I took it off the table and fumbled with the buttons, taking far too much time to call the message on to the screen in my anxiety.

'Hotel Luxe Noir, seven o'clock,' it stated. 'Introduce yourself at Reception.'

And that was it. No more than that. I had four hours to get ready and get into London. The journey would take an hour, so I should allow two, I supposed, even on a quiet Sunday.

I spent two hours in front of my mirror, scrubbing my skin and taking my cosmetics out of their tightly-sealed containers to apply them. I had no idea what to wear – I supposed I ought to look sexy – so I put on the slinky black dress I had not worn since Gerry's office Christmas party of 2002. That was my last night out, I think. It still looked brand new, and luckily I had chosen a classic cut and design, so it had not dated. Perfume. I should wear perfume, though I had a deep suspicion of scents, which I always suspected of being designed to mask the smell of rot. I was committed to appearing as normal as possible, though, so I took a deep breath and spritzed on a citrus thing from Jo Malone that my mother had given me for my birthday.

Before my mascara had dried, the taxi was at the door and I had no option but to grab my handbag and my cushion, shin on my surgical gloves and set off on my adventure.

All the way to London, I sat on my cushion and twisted my latex-covered hands in my lap. Every five minutes I had the urge to take out my phone and make a cancellation by text. All that money though – all the things I had sold on eBay to pay the fee. No. I was going to be brave.

I was much too early, arriving at the hotel with forty-five minutes to spare, so I took myself for a wander through the nearby park. Late-afternoon strollers, skaters, families hauling picnic baskets, lovers – normal people – passed me by and I felt the air on my skin, late-summer warmth and the scent of the flowers, which was a little too ripe and too rich, for they were past their bloom now. They were dying.

I felt giddy and had to leave the gardens, to catch my breath on the pavement, looking at the chalk art on the slabs. The hotel across the road looked reassuringly glitzy and pristine. I would go in now. I had only ten minutes before seven.

'Ah, you need to go to the Oyster Bar,' the receptionist told me with a smile. 'They are waiting for you there.'

The Oyster Bar had a small cordon in front of the door and a notice 'Closed for cleaning – will re-open at 8 p.m.' I crossed the barrier and opened the door, looking in and frowning. The place didn't look closed. There were people – about a dozen of them – lounging at the bar or in the booths. I caught sight of Number man, who smiled and raised his hand, beckoning me over to his booth.

I put my cushion on the cobalt-blue leather and sat down, my chest too jagged to force words from.

'Don't panic, Naomi,' he said gently. 'All these people are hired by me. They are all clean. And the bar was comprehensively blitzed before you arrived. It is as germ-free as your own home. We wanted to give you the illusion of a busy bar, so that you could have the experience of being picked up. The way you explained to us. We thought a bar empty of all but you and Justus would not give the right ambience. Do you understand? Is that all right?'

I let out a long breath, letting my chest rise and fall for a moment.

'I see. Oh. That's good.'

'I've got you a drink,' he said, pushing over a sealed bottle. 'It's a cocktail – it's been in this bottle since it was mixed. And there's a straw.' He handed over a prepackaged straw in its paper sleeve.

'You are very thoughtful,' I told him, taking off my gloves and unwrapping the straw. I trusted him. I trusted that the room and the surfaces were clean. My hands came out to play, feeling the polished table top and the smooth cool glass of the bottle.

'I'm going now,' he told me. 'Enjoy your evening.'

I wanted to reach out after him, to ask him not to leave me, but he didn't give me a backward glance. Alone in the bar, feeling prickly and self-conscious, I concentrated hard on my cocktail. What was it? A Harvey Wallbanger, I thought, orangey but with a deeper note at the back. When I next looked up, it was to see Justus, leaning one sexily negligent elbow on the bar, eyeing me up with unmistakable interest. I pricked the bubbles of nervous laughter rising in my chest and gave him my coolest, levellest look back before flicking my eyes tactically sideways, the way I used to. I used to do this! I used to do it well! Perhaps, I mused excitedly, it really was like riding a bicycle, and everything would be smooth and frictionless, all the way to the afterglow.

I stole a quick glance back. Oh, he looked good. He looked better than good, all suited and booted, with gold-framed spectacles seeming to magnify the look of naked want in his dark, dark eyes. The flash of his teeth showed that I had been caught in the act of ogling and I riveted my eyes to the cocktail, wondering if the heat in my cheeks was giving me away. Seconds later, a rich, amused voice in my ear, closer than I would normally like, asked me if I was waiting for someone.

I resisted the strong temptation to duck away and put a hand over my ear. Justus was clean. He was tested. And his breath smelled minty-fresh.

'No ... I ... um ... I'm staying here alone. Just having a drink before dinner.'

'Do you mind if I join you?'

'Oh ...' I had no idea how to play this. My riding a bike analogy had failed. Should I appear reluctant, and make him work for the grand finale? Should I be easy? After all, I didn't have to fret about him respecting me in the morning.

He made the decision for me, sliding on to the banquette beside me, putting his mineral water down on the table. He was close enough to smell and I took a lungful of the waves that radiated from him. None of them were reminiscent of decay and whatever cologne he was wearing was very light and fresh. Soap and mint and something piney – so reassuringly inorganic that I let him ease closer, close enough for his cuff to brush my bare wrist. That suit was brand new; it only lacked the tags. It had that brand new suit scent.

'You didn't wait for my answer,' I accused, without rancour.

'Didn't I? I thought I had your answer,' he said. 'Besides, it offends my morals to let a woman sit alone in a bar.'

'Your *morals*?'

'I have my own code, built up over the quarter century I've been alive. One of the most important precepts is to offer a lady company if she looks lonely.'

'That's very … good of you. What a big heart you must have.'

'Yes, it's very big. My heart, that is.' He grinned wickedly. 'What's that eye shadow you're wearing? It has a metallic look.'

Before I could move, he had put a finger and thumb beneath my chin, tilting it up for his inspection. I nearly screamed, nearly fainted, nearly … I remembered to breathe. This was what skin felt like on skin. There were people – lots of them – who would do anything for this, who were addicted to it. I thought his finger and thumb-pads must be burned into me, an indelible smudge mark on my face. His eyes were such discs of liquid chocolate that I could barely make out his pupils, but eventually I saw that they were wide and large, drawing me into them as if they had been enchanted to suck me into their blackness.

'Beautiful,' he whispered. 'I want you.'

'Bit sudden,' I managed to choke out, 'isn't it?'

'Life is short,' he said, and a shiver ran straight up my spine and into the nape of my neck. 'I don't want to miss a second I could spend with you. Come with me.'

'I don't know …'

'How can I convince you? Maybe like this.'

His breath, menthol and lemon, and then his lips, full and sweet, on mine, testing me for resistance at first and then … I did not want to resist, I could not resist, resistance was futile. He did exactly what I wanted him to, which was to take the option of resistance away from me so that my shrivelled, desiccated obsessions flaked away and what was left was the sensual woman I used to be.

He was gentle but assertive, easing me in, never rushing me, but never giving me the chance to withdraw. When his tongue began to flicker around my lips, I whimpered a little, into his mouth, but allowed him access. The thought flew through my mind that I needed a fanfare – this was a momentous thing. Instead, light R&B music continued to play in the background, accompanying my fizzing, floating sensations, until Justus released me and said, 'Does that help?'

'It was very convincing,' I replied dreamily. 'Very. Convincing.' Nowhere in my mind – well, OK, somewhere, but at the very *back* of it – was the fear that a million bacteria were making their murderous way down my gullet. Instead, my main fear was that he would not do that again.

He dispelled the fear. Then he dispelled it a second time, just to be sure, this time forging into me with his tongue in the first few seconds. His hands were capable, strong at the back of my head and his aftershave was so wondrously subtle he could almost not be wearing any. Nothing to mask, everything pure and without veneer. Perfection.

Once he was finished with the fear-dispelling, he kept in close to me and, with a nuzzle, said, 'Shall we take this to my room?'

'Your room?' My mouth felt full of cotton wool, thick and muzzy.

'Uh huh. Or we could carry on just here, but I think the barman might have a word or two to say about that.'

'I'm … not that kind of woman.' It was a token effort which I knew he would ride over roughshod.

'Baby, I'm not that kind of man either. But you have this effect on me – I can't help myself!'

I loved the cheesiness, the predictability of it – these oft-rehearsed lines were never spoken to me before. I was normal! I was a normal woman, getting propositioned by a normal man in a normal hotel bar! It was so thrilling I wanted to scream.

Maybe some normal women would have batted him away with a string of scornful words, maybe some would have suggested another drink first. But not this normal woman. This normal woman had a normal itch that needed scratching fast.

'Oh, well, if you can't help yourself … poor man,' I teased, running a hand over his cheek, which felt like velvet pile, almost too soft to be male.

'I need you in my bed,' he murmured, a subterranean rumble that made my senses vibrate. 'I'm ready for you. I'll turn your body inside out. You'll beg me to stop and beg me for more at the same time.'

'Ohhh,' I half-tittered, nervous now. 'Gosh. All right then.'

He stood and pulled me roughly after him, causing me to almost turn my ankle in my high-heeled shoe. I looked up at the fascinated barman and gave him a weakly apologetic grimace, though of course he must have known exactly what was going on. The amused faces of the customers struck enthralled guilt to my very core. It was so wrong, so swift, so immoral and so amazing I thought I might be flying.

I flew past the gleaming metallic fittings of the bar and into the lift (Justus pressed the buttons) and along the corridor, where he lifted me up so I really was almost airborne and into the room where it would all happen.

'Just you and me now, baby,' he crooned, kicking the door shut behind him and bearing down on me for another soulfully intense kiss. When I opened my eyes, set back down on the carpet, I noticed that the bed was sealed in polythene wrap, as were the easy chairs. The furniture shone so much it sparkled and everything smelled of divine nothingness.

The bed crackled as I put a hand on the clear covering.

'This is all so hygienic,' I exclaimed, impressed.

Justus, to his gentlemanly credit, pretended not to hear me. 'We are going to rumple this beautiful bed,' he told me. 'Together, we are going to make it look as if Tracy Emin and all her artist friends have had a party on it.'

I laughed, enchanted. That Tracy Emin unmade bed thing had always made me feel sick, but, right now, it seemed to have lost a lot of its emetic power.

Justus held me by my elbows, gazing with serious intent into my rapt face.

'You don't think I'm serious?' he said, dangerous as a panther on the cusp of a pounce. 'I am very serious. Let me show you how much.'

He released an elbow and let a hand trace the outline of my neck and shoulders, doubling back over my collarbone, then reaching around behind me to the top button of my dress. He scarcely fumbled at all; it was undone in a split second, and he eased the straps down over my upper arms then bent to kiss my neck and shoulder with a lightness I would not have thought him capable of. I bent back my head, eyelids fluttering, the golden light of the room blurring. His hand steadied me at the small of my back before I crumpled and I swooned into him, making the most of his skin against mine, his lips against my throat, his close-cut hair prickling my cheek and chin. Now his nose was edging down towards the valley of my cleavage, its slopes exposed by the sudden downward shrug of the fabric. His mouth lighted on the crests of my breasts ... untouched for so long ... I began to shiver.

'Let's lose this, shall we?' he whispered, chasing the straps down my arms until they were free and the dress began to collapse, the fluid silk rippling slowly over my ribs, my hips and whispering against my legs until I was standing – leaning – in my underwear.

Justus's hands went to my waist – to be honest, I was really needing the support now – and he took a step back, looking me over from head to toe. I wanted to shrink from his gaze, but I could not step away, could not look away. Eventually, he shook his head and my heart plummeted. I was too fat! Too short! Too old!

'Tsk tsk, Naomi,' he said. 'You have been keeping this hidden for how long? Five years, did you say? That is an unforgivable crime against the men of this world. How do you plead?'

I bit my lip, grinning coyly. 'You aren't a criminal lawyer!' I reproved. 'Nor a judge.'

'I certainly am a judge. I'm a judge of a fine woman, and you, my dear, fall into that category. So I'll ask you again, how do you plead?'

I said the word. 'Guilty.' For a moment, the emotions, the realisations it led to overpowered me. I held up my wrists. 'What is the sentence?'

'A stiff penalty for you, Naomi.' He grinned, but there was compassion in his eyes. 'I sentence you to an evening you cannot regulate or control. An evening of not being able to dictate what happens next. I bet that's difficult for you.'

'I haven't done anything like it … in years.'

'Shall we do it? Shall we … take you down?'

'Take me down.'

'I'm going to undo you.'

'Undo me.'

He unclipped my bra, freeing my breasts, which were too small, would not do …

'Lovely.' He bent to kiss each nipple, anointing them with the tip of his tongue, holding them in capable hands. His buzz-cut hair cried out to me to touch it, to feel the smooth curve of his scalp and the velvety fuzz that protected it. All these new textures and feelings were rioting together, striking me off-balance until I was tossing in a sea of unfamiliarity. People love the sea, but it is dangerous; I was not sure whether to melt or vomit. I gritted my teeth, took myself in hand, went with the melt.

He tipped me off my feet and lifted me into his arms, twirling me round so that the ceiling chandelier spun and fragmented into blurs of colour, then he threw me gently on the bed, which felt cold and tacky.

'Oh, let's get this plastic off!' I exclaimed. 'It feels awful!' Laughing giddily, I got to my feet and helped him rip the sheet off to expose the luxurious silkiness beneath. 'This is so much better.' I lay back against the covers, rippling my naked spine against them, wanting to print my outline on the silver-grey silk.

Justus was appreciative of my disinhibition; he threw off his suit jacket, slipped out of his shoes and hurled himself over me, crouching with his knees outside my hips, his tie swinging over my face, his teeth flashing predatory intent from a great height. He was so big and so beautiful, I just wanted to strip him down and feast on him while I could. I clutched at his belt and he clamped a hand down over mine.

'In a hurry?' he enquired.

'Yes, I'm in a hurry. I've been in the desert and you're the biggest, coolest drink of water I could ever have dreamed.'

'That's nice, Naomi. But we've got all night.'

'Don't make me wait.'

'The journey is the best part. Don't you think? Reaching the destination can be overrated. Let's have a good, long journey. First class. Great service. Great views.'

'Take off your clothes!' I yelped, tormented by the way his finger was travelling down my stomach to the elasticated border of the only garment I now sported. I wanted him to rip them off, to wrench my thighs apart and dive, clothes flying from him, into my canyon. Finally I understood the ridiculousness of my long abstinence; finally I knew what I had been missing. To make up for all those years, I would have to drain this poor man dry, to have him take up residence between my legs for the indefinite future, to have his cock lodged within me morning, noon and night. Oh, that would be fine. In the cab home, in the supermarket, cooking the dinner, with Justus joined to me at the groin. I could live like that. If only I could get him to take off his suit and fuck me in the first place.

'Let's take it nice and easy.' He took a mouthful of tit again, tonguing it and making low, vibrating sounds of ecstasy like a gourmet masticating a rare truffle. I plucked at his shirt buttons, and, even though he tried to bat me away, I managed to get a couple undone. My hand slid inside the gap, meeting warm solidity, perfect definition, curves and lines where they should be. His knees pressed into my hips, warning me that I had taken more than he had permitted. One hand fished me out of his shirt and moved my exploring fingers to the rocky bulge beneath his belt.

'Wow!' I sighed. 'Please ...'

He finished his meal of my breasts and shook his head, tutting tormentingly.

'All in good time, Naomi. I'm still hungry.' He made a lunge for my knickers then dropped them on to the carpet. His lips were upon me, his tongue spreading me wider, feasting and salivating while I squealed my shocked approval.

Even in the Gerry days, this was not something I had done a lot of. Somehow, it seemed too intimate, too revealing. I could not fake my response, or tone it down – the tongue worked its magic and I was enchanted.

'Oh, Justus, no, stop!' I pleaded.

He lifted his head, eyes wide.

'Really?'

'No,' I confessed. 'Not really. Carry on.'

'Yes, ma'am.'

And his tongue tripped along every little crease, covered every bump and mound with its bounty, never letting up until I gave it up, bucking into his generous face with no idea how to stop myself, and no care about how I looked, or anything but the blissful climax he had brought me to.

'You have to promise me, Naomi,' said Justus mock-sternly, kneeling up from his oral workout, 'that you will get that done to you a lot more often. I could feel that wave coming over you right from the moment I went down. You needed that.'

'Oh. Oh,' was all I could say. 'Oh God.'

'No, I'm a mere mortal,' he said. 'I know it's hard to

believe. I suppose I should let you get a breath back before I move on to the next part of my plan for you. Or … no, OK, we'll do it this way. Turn over on to your front.'

I obeyed, having no will whatsoever to do otherwise, and lay with my cheek against my arm, listening to the sounds of him undressing at last. I was not sure I would have the energy to do anything other than lie like a rag doll while he took his pleasure – but as it happened, that was not what he had in mind. Instead, he lay on his side beside me and gave me the gentlest of massages – not even a massage at all, really, more a sort of firmer, less irritating stroke. My shoulders, neck and back burned with the sweetness of his touch; I imagined his circular motions drawn on to me, like a map of his attentions, and my eyelids began to droop, my head to weigh ever heavier.

'OK,' he said, and he smacked my bottom so unexpectedly that my whole body leapt as if electrocuted. 'I know I said it was good to wait … but I think I've waited long enough. Judging by the state of this …'

He placed my hand around his cock. It was joyously fat and hard; my untensed body began to tauten again at the thought of its intentions.

'Turn over. Look at me,' he growled. I scrambled on to my back and drank in his powerful body and imperious face. I felt intimidated, but not by his physical stature – more from a kind of quasi-virginal nervousness. I knew what sex felt like, but I had forgotten, and it was like losing my cherry all over again. He reached for the condom pack out of his jacket pocket and began to snap the rubber on, never breaking eye contact with me. 'Tell me you want this, Naomi.'

'I ... I'm a little afraid ... but I want it.'

'What are you afraid of?'

'I'm afraid I'll like it. And then I'll have to ...'

'You'll have to?'

'Have to stop ... living the way I do.'

'Have to start living again, you mean. Good. Because you should. You do want it, Naomi, and you should want it. And you should get it. As often as you want.'

'Plenty of people live without ...'

'Don't go back to that. Open your legs. Open yourself up to me.'

His gruff injunctions were kindly meant, I realised. They were for my own good – he just needed to put enough force behind them to ensure I took them seriously. Again, I loved him for it, in a way. And I opened my legs.

It did not feel the way I remembered. It felt much, much better. I was filled, for one thing, both length and width-wise. And Justus knew how to get the right angle, how to go in hard and how to ease off and how to speed up and how to vary the intensity and how to nudge against my clit and how to find my g-spot. What a lot of things this man knew. Intellectual property law wasn't the half of it.

He knew how to take me from the front, from behind, from below and from on top. Also, from the side, over the side of the bed, in a chair, in the Jacuzzi, on the floor. He knew how to make me sigh, how to make me moan, how to make me crazy, how to make me come. There was nothing intellectual in it, but I would have liked him for my property.

By the time the hour the contract ceased had come, so had I, five times. I lay limply in the bath, half submerged in bubbles, raw, sore, chafed, satisfied, cured.

Well, perhaps not cured. Perhaps not as simply as that. But I still see Justus when I'm up in town, passing the Inns of Court, as I find myself doing quite often these days. I don't wear a mask and I don't wear gloves – or at least, not the latex kind. But I do wear a smile, and all the money I used to spend on Pledge now goes on underwear. Every day, in every way, I am getting better and better.

Lucky Charm

THE OFFICE SUITED CHARLOTTE well; it was not large but it was luxuriously appointed, with thick pile carpets and a smell of expensive leather from the chairs and the antique desk blotters.

With her opening day almost at an end, and nobody else in the office for the first time since she had sidled shyly in that morning, she went over to the window and looked down at the higgledy-piggledy Soho street life. The neon lights were just fizzing into lewd life in the sex shops of Brewer Street and the waiters in the Italian joint opposite were putting out menus, pristine napkins over their forearms. It was too far away to tell whether or not they were good-looking, but their bodies, in the dark red shirts and black waistcoats and trousers, were tempting enough.

Charlotte licked her lips. She was fantasising about any and every man she saw, these days, it seemed. Working in such a sexually charged atmosphere had turned her into a raging nymphomaniac – still, it was hardly surprising. She drifted off into pleasant reminiscences of her day while the streetlights popped on, one by one, in a golden haze before her eyes.

Walking up the final flight of stairs, she had smoothed her skirt down over her thighs, feeling the telltale bump of the stocking snaps beneath the silk-lined wool. Bryant's phrase had stayed with her – 'the suggestion of wantonness' – and she hoped she had captured the effect. The skirt was a dark red tartan with golden thread in the pattern; the stockings were seamed but nude; the shoes were black high-heeled slingbacks; the shirt was white silk, two buttons undone at the top. Was it a mistake to wear knickers? If so, she would have to accept the consequences – for she was wearing her favourite red and black lingerie set from the expensive knicker shop down the street. The black and red meant that the bra was plainly visible through the gossamer-thin blouse – perhaps a bit more than a suggestion of wantonness there. But somehow she doubted her employers would mind. Leeway might not be given in the other direction, though, and she hadn't bought a pair of tights since that fateful day in the forest.

Naturally, she was nervous – as anyone on their first day in a new job might be – but she was also excited. The lace stocking-tops rubbing together beneath the tight skirt might have been having an effect as well. Stopping to compose herself at the door, she realised that her nipples were pressing against the lacy confines of her bra. She took out her mirror compact, checked that her make-up was just that crucial bit overdone and tarty, and knocked on the door.

'Enter.' Both voices, dark and light, in shiver-inducing harmony.

She grasped the handle with both hands and turned it, standing in the doorway for a moment to assess how best to reach their twin desks, set at diagonal angles to each other, without tripping on the carpet fibres. The morning sunlight streamed in through the window, catching the imposing pair, who had stood to receive their new handmaiden, in its radiant beams.

'Good morning, Charlotte.' Collins was the first to speak. 'Are you going to stand in the doorway all day?'

She took a hesitant step forward, but he shook his head and frowned, tutting slightly, making a downward motion with one hand.

'Hands and knees, Charlotte,' he instructed.

'Oh!' She covered her mouth with her hand, feeling dizzy and giggly. They really were going to continue with this dynamic, even in the office. How ... interesting. Wondering if it would be possible to sustain total submission over the course of a working day, Charlotte dropped to her knees, thankful for the embracing plush of the carpet. She moved forward, unable to look her bosses in the eye, moving between chair legs and pot plants until she reached the desk interface, at the apex of which her new colleagues stood, side by side, smiling down at her if she had but known, though she imagined them to be stony-faced.

'Up,' said Bryant gently, and she perched up on her knees, back straight and shoulders back, breathing a little unevenly. She felt Bryant's hand cup her chin and lift her head up so that she was looking up his long torso to the overhang of his head, right into his clear blue eyes.

'Make-up is good,' he said, but to Collins, not to her. 'Nice shade of lipstick. What's it called, Charlotte?'

'Harlot.'

They chuckled in unison. 'How perfectly appropriate,' approved Collins. 'Charlotte the harlot. It's the very shade that always looks so good around a cock. Don't you think?'

'I certainly do,' replied Bryant. 'Good girl. You may stand, for the rest of the inspection.'

Charlotte rose to her feet, feeling shambling and awkward, her head hanging down over the flapping open collar of her blouse.

'And such a stylish bra too,' noted Collins with a vocal smirk.

'I love a girl who doesn't match her underwear with her clothes. Dark bras under white shirts …'

'Visible panty lines are supposed to be such a fashion crime,' mused Collins. 'I never understood that. I once followed a girl the length of Oxford Street because she was wearing such an obvious pair of high-cut knickers under a very tight miniskirt. It defined her arse rather wonderfully.'

'Oh, I wish I'd seen that.'

'Perhaps we could get Charlotte to do it.'

'Good idea.'

'One more button, Charlotte. You look wanton, but today I think I'm in the mood for slutty. No, I'll do it for you.'

Collins reached out to undo a third pearl button, leaving her cleavage exposed right down to the front-fastening clip of her bra.

'Do you get many visitors to the office?' asked Charlotte nervously.

Bryant put a finger to his lips while Collins shook his head, giving his colleague a tragi-comic look.

'Oh dear, speaking out of turn,' he said. 'Charlotte, you did not give us time to outline the rules, my dear. But now you have forced our hand, let me make it clear to you that, when you wish to speak, you must first ask permission. "Please, sir, may I speak?" is the preferred form. Do you understand?'

'Yes, sir,' whispered Charlotte.

'Good. To answer your question, no, we do not receive visitors here very often. But those that we do will be perfectly aware of your position here, make no mistake. So there will be no need for rapid covering-up. Barring a police raid.'

She managed not to splutter, but gave him a very wide-eyed look instead.

'What we do is not illegal,' Collins explained. 'We are not a brothel. But we do procure sexual services, although it would be very easily defended if any complaint was made. Bryant and I are lawyers. We know the law. But just be prepared – plenty of people do not. It is why we keep the service limited by word of mouth recommendation.'

'Anybody who comes here will be a friend. We don't bring clients to the office – we think it best that as few people as possible are aware of its location. So if we ask you to work naked, you may do so with the assurance that no shock or dismay will be caused by your nudity. At least, not to the visitors.' Bryant paused to smile fiendishly at Collins, then at Charlotte, who was biting her lip. 'That skirt is rather long. Perhaps you could lift it a little. I see it comes with a handy pin.'

Bryant reached out for the silver pin that adorned the corner of Charlotte's kilt, unfastening it, while Charlotte rumpled the fabric diligently up her thighs, waiting for somebody to say 'when'. Nobody did.

'I like kilts, but I prefer the shorter, pleated version,' commented Collins, watching the inexorable rise of the hem above the lacy ends of Charlotte's stockings. 'They always make me want to reach for my cane.'

Charlotte looked around her, as if she expected to find a cane somewhere within reach, but there was none that she could see.

'I'll introduce you to it sometime,' Collins said, the words a tender promise rather than a threat. 'Keep going then.'

The skirt had concertina'd almost to the crotch of Charlotte's red and black knickers. Any higher and it would no longer qualify as a skirt, surely. No suggestion of wantonness any more – nothing less than a blatant broadcast. With megaphones.

Charlotte took a breath and hiked it ever upward. Even though the office was well heated, her thighs felt cold and her knickers struck her as ridiculously flimsy now that they were all that protected her modesty from the iron stares of her bosses.

'You wore knickers.' Bryant's observation was on the obvious side, but hinted at another reading – that perhaps knickers were surplus to working requirements.

'We have rules about knickers,' said Collins. 'You will find them on the rules we have prepared for you. They are rather complicated, so I won't go into them just yet. The rules, that is. Not the knickers.'

Bryant laughed. Charlotte pressed her lips together, hoping that the wet spot developing beneath her was not spreading too visibly. The skirt was around her waist now, an inelegant bunch that showed off the high-cut briefs in all their silky boudoir glory. Bryant pierced the spare tyre of material with the safety pin, holding it precariously in position at one edge.

'Hmm, it will have to do,' said Collins. 'We'll buy you some suitable office wear. Perhaps after work, if you aren't busy. Or sometime during the week. Would you like that?'

'You'll … buy me clothes?'

'Yes. I think, in the circumstances, a clothing allowance is only fair. We can't reasonably expect you to have a wardrobe as diversely whorish as we have in mind for you.'

'Mmm, yes,' fantasised Bryant. 'Uniforms. Latex.

Very short skirts. Very high boots. Scraps of slave-girl toga.'

'Corsets,' added Collins. 'Special corsets, with special additions.'

'I know a woman who makes those. Shall we book an appointment?'

'I think we should. Or rather, Charlotte should. Remind her to call Miss Frost later.'

'Well, I think you'll do,' said Bryant breezily. 'We'll keep you like that for today. Come and look at your workstation. All the documents you need can be found there.'

Thus had Charlotte been introduced to the place where she would pass her nine-to-fives in the least nine-to-fiveish manner imaginable for as long as the three of them should find each other's working company agreeable.

She had spent the day at her new desk in the corner of the office, her bottom in its silken casing perched on an ergonomic swivel chair with a kind of nubbed rubber cushioning which felt altogether too sexy to be businesslike. It kept her mind focused on her lower regions, which she supposed was the intention, but it did rather distract from the spreadsheets, as did the constant sight of her bare thighs above the stocking tops every time her eyes made a downward sweep.

Collins and Bryant came and went, never both present at the same time, popping in for a few minutes here and there to make sure that she hadn't had a software crash or a particularly bizarre email request, but most of the time she was alone, reading requests, tweaking the website, checking over the accounts and noting down ideas for planned fantasy scenarios.

At lunchtime, Bryant had brought her a paper bag of

edibles from Prêt-a-Manger and asked her, quite politely and without any trace of demand, if she would mind sucking his cock when she had finished. She did not mind in the least, and rounded off a good lunch of crayfish and rocket sandwich, packaged grapes and a fruit-of-the-forest smoothie with a generous mouthful of spunk.

All in all, it had been an interesting day. She thought she had the measure of the job now and, as the Italian waiters beetled around below, she drifted off into possibilities for fulfilling her clients' dreams – venues, fixtures and fittings, transport, suitable men for the jobs.

She came to with a jump when the office door clicked open, spinning around to see Collins, his tall, angular frame striking her anew with its imposing presence. Had it been Bryant, she might have caught her breath, relaxed her shoulders, smiled an 'oh, it's you!' but it wasn't. She remained, spine stiff, face frozen in an expression of mute supplication, awaiting his terrifying pleasure.

'Charlotte,' he said, his voice so velvet low she had to strain her ears to snag its words. 'How was your day?'

'It was very good, thank you, sir,' she said deferentially, feeling as if she ought to curtsey. 'Is it over? I'm not exactly sure when it's over.'

Collins moved further into the room, switching on a tall lamp in the corner.

'You will be told when you are no longer needed. Every day will be different. Some days will take you out of the office. Sometimes you will be needed in the evenings, sometimes in the middle of the night. But that was explained in the Rules, I think.'

'Yes – I just wondered if there were normal office hours – when nothing extra was planned. But I know to wait for your permission to leave now. Thank you, sir.'

There was a loaded silence.

'Do I have it, sir? Your permission to leave?'

'Have I given it?'

'No, sir.' Blood rushed to every extremity of Charlotte's body, lighting it up with mortification, anxiety and excitement.

'I have come here to review your day's work, Charlotte. This is going to be a weekly feature of your employment here – a performance review. I think in general it will be held first thing on Monday morning, but I wanted to familiarise you with the procedure, so tonight's version is simply a taster.'

He opened a store cupboard and drew out a high stool, of the kind Charlotte had not seen since school science lessons, made of varnished wood with an oval seat and a strut halfway up the legs to act as a footrest. This he placed in front of his high desk before moving behind it to take up his seat.

'Sit down, Charlotte.' He nodded at the stool. 'And put your skirt back up. Nobody gave you leave to unpin it.'

Cheeks ablaze, Charlotte rolled the kilt back up to waist level and re-fastened it before perching herself, as demurely as she knew how with her knickers and bra on show, on the stool.

'Don't cross your legs. Open them. And you needn't fold your arms either. Keep your hands holding on to the edge of your seat please.'

Under Collins's close scrutiny, Charlotte rearranged herself as instructed, her thighs wide and legs dangling from the edges of the seat, highly conscious of what an inelegant and lewd sight she must make.

'Your nipples are hard,' said Collins with a flash of wicked teeth. 'I can see them through your bra. Are you feeling a little bit hot and bothered, Miss?'

Charlotte knew she could not lie, not to Collins. 'Yes, sir,' she muttered.

'I didn't hear you.'

She looked up and repeated herself, a little belligerently. 'Yes, sir.'

'You like to be told what to do, don't you, Charlotte? You like to be treated like a bad girl who needs constant supervision. Am I right?'

'You're right, sir,' she whispered, the words so uncomfortable to speak, more uncomfortable than her ungainly position on that damned stool.

He relaxed his sternly locked brow. 'Just as I hoped,' he said pleasantly. 'I am going to give you permission to speak, Charlotte, so that you can give me your impressions of your first day at work. Anything you wish to tell me, you can tell me now.'

Charlotte sat up straight, gathering her thoughts, hoping to please Collins with her ideas and insights. 'I think the job will suit me very well, sir. I am getting to grips with the website and all the different procedures you have to go through. All the vetting! Wow! I had no idea you were so very meticulous. But it's good that you are, of course. I've had loads of ideas about how to put some of the clients' requests into practice too. I know the perfect venue for that banquet one. And I've found a really good florist that can undercut the one you use. And I thought about advertising in the Student Unions for men to add to our roster – though obviously not everyone wants a *young* man … so we'd have to stick to the men's magazines for the older candidates … all the same …'

Collins held up a hand, smiling indulgently. 'This is good, Charlotte,' he said, 'but not what we are here to discuss. We can bring up all these ideas when we meet as a team with Bryant. I just wondered … if you liked it here. That was all.'

Charlotte looked down at the slopes of her breasts rising above lacy bra cups and between gauzy flaps of shirt. She looked at the skirt bulked around her waist and the spread milky thighs, striped with ruched black suspenders. The portion of stool seat visible to her was slightly slick with damp; a damp that must have proceeded directly from the heat generating between her legs.

'Yes, sir. I like it very much.'

'Better than local government, eh?'

'Much better, sir.'

'Good.' Collins, who had been eyeing her sidelong, hungrily, but with enough restraint to realise that his meal would be tastier if he took it slowly, snapped back into severe business mode.

'Bryant says he is satisfied with your performance today, but we have a few small matters to address.' Collins flicked open a leather notebook, reading from it. 'Speaking out of turn on three occasions. Wearing an overly long skirt. Using the washroom without asking.'

Charlotte gasped. 'But nobody was here! Who could I ask? And how do you even know?'

'Because, dear Charlotte, you have just told me.'

'But … I … oh my God! How was I supposed to …?'

Collins drummed elegant fingers on the desk. 'Phone? Email? Text message?'

'What if neither of you is available?'

'You wait.'

'What if I *can't* wait?'

'You work on strengthening your pelvic floor, dear Charlotte. Which will be a useful thing for you to do anyway, because believe me, you are going to get thoroughly used in every orifice while you are working here. But you knew that, didn't you?'

Charlotte was mutely open-mouthed for a while, electrified by the intense, almost savage, delivery of Collins's statement of his intent for her.

'And there was an awful lot of disrespectful *tone* in those last few exchanges,' said Collins contemplatively. 'Dear, dear, dear.'

Charlotte felt outwitted, realising too late that Collins had been winding her up with the deliberate intent of provoking her into a rule break. She determined to grit her teeth and accept whatever it was he had in mind for her. After all, it was unlikely to be anything she didn't want, in the final honest analysis.

'I'm sorry, sir,' she said meekly.

'Not sorry enough. Not yet,' he said softly. 'Push those knickers aside and play with yourself.'

The abrupt command surprised Charlotte, who had been expecting something along more traditional disciplinary lines.

'Go on,' he prompted. 'Put them to one side. Show me how wet you are.'

Charlotte unveiled her glistening pussy lips, wondering if Collins would approve of their newly-shaven look. She had done it especially for him, thinking he would approve. He made no comment on it, though. He simply nodded and leaned forward a little, squinting through the lenses of his glasses.

'I thought so. You're soaking wet. That stool will need a good wipe down by the time I've finished with you. Well, what are you waiting for? Finger yourself.'

Charlotte was by nature an assiduous person, and when she set out to do a job, she made sure it was done to the best of her ability. She inserted three doughty fingers between those weeping lips and began to strum, looking up at a corner of the ceiling initially until Collins ordered her to face him, to watch herself being watched.

This was so difficult, she thought. It was almost impossible not to break the eye contact, unless she pretended she was doing something altogether different. Rather than frigging herself in the office for the entertainment of her strict boss, she was … making a sandwich. Cheese? Chicken? Butter, not that horrid low-fat spread stuff. Her fingers skittered manically, mechanically across her clit, a butterknife spreading their goodness.

'You are thinking of something else,' Collins realised indignantly. 'Stop daydreaming. Is it because you are afraid you might come?'

'Yes, sir,' shuddered Charlotte, forcing herself to obey. 'No, sir,' she amended, aware that this was not the complete truth. 'It's embarrassing, sir.'

'Good.'

Charlotte curled one finger up into her tightly-furled bud, finding it slick and slippery with her juices. Was Collins going to fuck her? Was he going to let her come? Was he going to punish her? Oh, the thought of it made her body convulse as she pictured herself bent over the stool, maybe tied to the wooden legs, taking stroke after stroke of Mr Collins's belt.

'Your face is very red. Are you going to come?' Collins could have been asking her if she had settled the stationer's account.

'I … think so …, sir.' Her fingers were blurs of activity, scrabbling, squishing, pressing, pushing.

'You'd better stop then.' Charlotte, almost tearful with reluctance, took her supercharged fingers from the channel and lifted woeful eyes to her tormentor. 'Hmm, orgasms must be earned, dear Charlotte,' he admonished her. 'Stand up now and come over here.'

Now so wet that she made a tiny sucking sound with each step, she approached the desk, her knickers still dragged diagonally across her mons, baring the largest part of her nether regions.

'Hold out that hand.' Collins took it and held it to his beaky nose, taking a good long lungful of her female scent. 'You're incorrigible,' he said. 'I shall have to whip the lewdness out of you, shan't I?' He mock sighed and Charlotte tried not to break into a grin. 'Very well. Bend over the desk then.'

Exhilarated and yet afraid, Charlotte tilted herself over to press her warm breasts and stomach into the cold mirror-shine of the desk. Collins took her hands and pulled them up to his side of the desk, so that she could cling on to the edge. She heard him open a desk drawer, but she did not dare look up, keeping her cheek flattened to the surface while he stood and moved around to the other side where her red and black frilly bottom adorned the polished oak. One hand descended on the cascading frills, ruffling them lightly.

'These are nice,' he said, his voice sardonic. 'Favourites, are they?'

'Yes, sir.'

'All the same, they're coming down.' He bared her bottom, letting the scanty panties fall until they snagged against her suspender snaps and were held captive at mid-thigh.

Charlotte could feel two hands now, squeezing the mounds of her buttocks then brushing them, following the curve down to the cleft of her sex.

'I'm wondering how much these can take,' Collins

explained, his voice, as ever, unaccountably dark and melancholy. 'Do you know? Do you know your limit, Charlotte?'

'No,' she said. 'I've never really … gone that far.'

'These Performance Reviews are partly designed to find it. We balance your achievements against your transgressions and your shapely little rear here pays for any deficit. You will inevitably make mistakes. We all do. Most of us do not have to reap quite the same consequences as you will, though, Charlotte. Because you are special, and you need this.'

Charlotte felt warm. Special. She was special to him.

She felt warmer still on the first measured crack of his hand against the bare flesh of her arse, shocking her out of contemplation, shocking her into the moment.

'Just an introduction then,' he said. 'Just a taste,' and his hand continued to rise and fall, with sharp impact, while Charlotte kept her fingers tense at the ledge, working hard at keeping her squirms minimal.

'You won't forget the rules now, will you, Charlotte?' The smacks were hard, but in a considered kind of way, as if he was making sure he didn't peak too soon. They left their imprints across the widest part of her bottom and downwards, pinkening her thighs to the stocking tops. Charlotte knew that this was nothing, that this was mild, that this was a mere feather-duster tickling compared to what lay in his reserves, but it was still getting a little uncomfortable and before too long she thought she might have to utter a low cry or a squeak. She tried to clench her buttocks, but he responded by putting extra weight behind the next few strokes, and she conceded defeat, offering him her full soft globes to do with as he wished.

Once they were warm and the colour of strawberry

pulp, Collins changed his tactic, picking something up from the desk – whatever the thing was he had taken from the drawer, she supposed.

'As a reminder to keep the hemlines high,' he said, gripping the roll of skirt material for a moment as a tactile cue, 'I shall give you twenty strokes of my best leather strap. This one is supple, Charlotte, and has proved rather popular with my submissives through the years. I suspect you will find much to appreciate in its combination of strength and sting.'

Charlotte was just processing the words '*my submissives through the years*' and surprising herself with a pang of jealousy when the strap swung and caught her across a bar of skin already well-prepared by Collins's hand.

Her pelvis jolted against the desk and she yelped, feeling the burn more intensely than she had ever imagined she would in all her years of fantasising about it. She managed to take the first half dozen without breaking position or yelling the place down, but as the strapping continued her broken vocalisations turned into cries of outrage – 'that hurt' or 'ouch, ouch, ouch' – but never did it occur to her to ask him to stop, or beg for mercy. By the twelfth, she was biting her lip hard and letting go of the desk periodically to try and shield her bottom. Each attempt to do this was met with a firm replacement of her hand in its permitted station and a warning that she would get more for disobedient conduct during a punishment. *He wants me to cry*, she realised by the fifteenth. *He wants me to plead through my tears.* And, despite the tightness and soreness of her rear, her final thought was, *I won't.*

He added one more to the total of twenty, catching her off guard so that she howled in surprised pain, but then he put the strap aside, laid a hand on the fervid heat of her bottom and said, 'You take it well. Repeat after me: "Thank you, sir, for correcting me."'

Charlotte, spluttering and gasping a little in the wake of the onslaught, said, 'Thank you, sir, for correcting me.'

'Well, Charlotte,' he said, his hand still enjoying her posterior heat wave, stroking the scarlet flesh in a way that somehow offered no relief, 'I don't think we're anywhere near your limit yet. But I will find it. Trust me.'

Charlotte shivered, wondering, not for the first time, what went through the mind of a man like Collins. Why did he want to hurt her? Why did he want to master her? But then, she might as well ask why she wanted him to hurt her – she was no closer to finding that answer.

'Open those legs wider,' he commanded with a sharp smack to her humbled flesh. 'I'm on the horns of a dilemma here … it all looks so tempting.' She heard him open and close a drawer.

'Damn,' he said. 'No lubricant. Well, that solves my problem, I suppose.'

The sound of his swift footsteps mingled with the jingling of his belt buckle and the soft shush of fabric, then there was flesh on her flesh, his hands on her hips, his knees bending hers at the back and his cock, large and thick, slipping speedily into her cunt. She cried out and kept her fingers tightly wound around the edge of the desk, for he began forcefully and only carried on more so, his thrusts making her knees knock against the wood and her bottom take a secondary pounding from his lower abdomen. She was being used, pure and simple; she was a tight hole and a hot cushion for him to pound into and against, a slippery wet cavern to fill with his seed. She could have any face, any form; she was just a convenience. The thought made her come, a first time, but Collins was not finished. He held back, keeping the rhythm measured but brutal, making sure that he wrung a further, sob-inducing climax from Charlotte before releasing inside her.

She felt so tired, so used, so defeated – he had, after all, made her cry – and yet so happy. So complete. So exactly where she wanted to be in the universe.

'Get dressed,' was Collins's curt command. 'We're meeting Bryant for dinner. Then we're taking you shopping.'

'At this time? Won't the shops be shut?'

Charlotte made an attempt at emergency repair of her outfit, which was now crumpled and sweaty beyond redemption. She looked like a girl who'd just been well fucked after a hard spanking. But Collins wasn't going to let her escape the truth of that, and she was going to have to parade it in front of all the patrons of the hotel where they would dine.

'Not the kind of shops I have in mind.'

Charlotte was pretty sure that their little trio had raised a few eyebrows in the hotel restaurant, especially the way each man would pause to squeeze her hand or stroke her cheek. Her feet were locked at the ankle, her left in Collins's right, her right in Bryant's left, and, at one point, Bryant's fingers found their way under the snowy tablecloth to investigate the wet, sticky interior of her knickers.

'I see you didn't just review her performance,' he said ruefully to Collins, withdrawing his hand and wiping his fingers on the pristine linen napkin. 'You road-tested her as well.'

'Wouldn't you have done?' asked Collins, holding up

104

a hand for the bill.

'Well, yes. Of course I would.'

They shopped in the backstreets and alleyways of Soho. They bought clothes of barely-there silk and shiny vinyl, buckled leather and stretchy lace. Accessories of metal and maribou, silicone and whalebone, were scooped up in armfuls. Charlotte modelled and demonstrated all of them, in cramped back rooms behind coloured door strips, for her bosses' pleasure. All of the purchases came in so handy for the office, in their many and various ways. But that's an entirely new story.

Girl on Film

OBVIOUSLY THERE IS SOMETHING wrong with me.

Women are meant to like wafty costume romances with bedroom curtains blowing symbolically in the wind. They are meant to like chocolate box fairy stories of the Richard Curtis variety. They are meant to want something left to the imagination.

That's what Aunty Mavis always said. 'Oh, I like to have something left to the imagination.' But she didn't have one, so I've always thought she meant 'Ugh, that filthy sex, get it away from me.'

Well, there's nothing wrong with my imagination. But I want to *see*. I want to see the lips licking and the thighs spreading, the stiff cock and the glistening sleeve and the way they come together. I want to see the look on her face while she's humped fore and aft with her mouth wrapped around a third hopeful erection. I want to see the mechanics and the bare bones of it. I even want to see the ridiculous overacting, hear the heavy huffing and ersatz begging and share the plastic ecstasy of it all.

But there's more to it than even that. Shameful enough as my porn-viewing habit is, I want to go further. I want to be the girl in the picture.

You see, I like to watch a skinflick, but I always have this unease of conscience. Is the girl cracked up to the eyeballs? Was she abducted from an outpost of the former USSR? Is she trying to escape a myriad of childhood demons by becoming a faceless fuckdoll? I don't know. But I feel I should know. I feel I should disapprove of myself for potentially green-lighting exploitation and international sex slavery. How will I know for sure that nobody is being exploited in a film? It seems there is only one sure-fire answer. Take the lead role. Make sure the only holes being filled are mine.

Easier said than done, though, especially when you are a well-respected district nurse.

Or so I thought, at least, and yet today I sit here in a back-alley branch of Starbucks, talking with an elegantly wasted man in eyeliner about fucking on film.

'So, to get down to the nitty gritty,' he says, fidgeting with a pencil, 'what do you want in this picture?'

The pencil could be his twin; so long and thin he is, with a burgundy stripe blazer that only reinforces the effect. Is he hard lead or soft graphite, I wonder. 2B or not 2B? But I really have to stop avoiding the question, because it is THE question, the answer to which will take me far inside my deep-down fantasies – only now I've been asked it, I really don't know what to say. Isn't life always like that? Aren't we always stuck for words in Starbucks with a famous indie porn director?

'Well?' His eyes, red-rimmed as if he has been up all night, widen. 'Carmella? What's in the script? Anal? Sixty nine? Dildos? Strap-on? Bondage?'

'Stop! Stop!' I beg in a fierce whisper, my hot chocolate going down the wrong way. 'Sheesh! This is Starbucks, not bloody … Spearmint Rhino.'

'If you want me to direct this film, you need to tell me what you want in it,' he says, toning the impatience down. 'I have the experience … but this is about what you want, isn't it? That's what the people at the bureau told me when they commissioned me.'

'How much are they paying you for this?' I ask.

'What's that got to do with it? Anyway, it's you that's paying, isn't it? So you need to start telling me what you want.' He takes a sip of his Americano and grins suddenly, his slightly sulky face ghoulish with glee. 'Quite a set-up they've got there, isn't it? Kind of like *Jim'll Fix It* for sex fiends.'

I laugh, despite a slight prickle at being called a sex fiend. Perhaps he has a point, after all. And surely, as an up-and-coming director of filthy films, he can't exactly distance himself from the description.

'It doesn't come cheap,' I tell him. 'You're right. I really need to get over my scruples and give you a list. It's just that this is so … weird.'

I look around. The cognitive dissonance between our conversation and our surroundings frightens me. At the neighbouring table, two smart women with enormous handbags compare manicures.

'Just tell me what sexy stuff you want in it and we'll work a storyline around that, yeah?'

He is unbending a little now. When we met, he had seemed so uncomfortable, almost angry at finding himself in this position. I had thought about quitting then and there but … he was pretty in a slightly exotic way, with the cheekbones and the mildly slanting eyes and he didn't use too much of that chaotic wax in his hair like most of the young media boys did, though I guessed he was about thirty, so maybe past all that. So, yes. Pretty. So I stayed.

I take a deep breath. I am going to outline my fantasies to a very attractive, but completely uninterested-in-me-as-a-person-slash-sexual-partner man. Why couldn't we have done this by email?

'Well, I think I'd like … you know, some straight sex. Umm, not fussy about positions.'

'One man or two?' he interrupts. 'Two is popular.'

'We aren't selling this, are we?' I blurt, alarmed.

'Oh, no. True. I forgot. OK. So one man then?'

'I think … yes. One man. Unless I think of a reason for having two. And maybe … a girl?'

'A girl!'

'But I'd have to know she was, you know, not being exploited.'

He laughs. 'How about my girlfriend? She isn't being exploited, I promise.'

'Really? Your girlfriend?'

'Yeah. She's more the typical porn star look than you, though. You might not want that.'

'She doesn't look like a real girl, you mean? More like a blow-up doll?'

'She's 100% real,' he huffs, a little offended. 'I don't do those plastic porn shows. I mean, she's a bit more … let's say … amply provided for. In the T&A department.'

'Oh. Right.' I consider this for a moment. 'Can we hold the girl thing. I'm not sure I want to be the second prize in my own private sex tape. I want all the attention on me.'

'OK, so we've established that much. I know plenty of skinny girls, by the way …'

'Forget about the girl.'

'Right. You're the boss,' he says, with an edge of feline pique.

'Let's get this list down,' I murmur, glancing sidelong at the modish women and their Mulberry bags, hoping they haven't heard any of this. 'OK. Straight sex, any position. Something involving a vibrator. Umm, oral. Both kinds.' I'm trying my hardest not to use any rude words; it's quite a challenge. 'And, you know, I think I'm not averse to a bit of, um, back door ...'

'Really? Anal? Excellent. One of my favourites.' He smiles, reminding me of the devil. The Mulberry women look utterly scandalised and move away to a more distant table, whispering to each other. When they look back, I hold their eyes. Then I turn to Dimitri and raise my voice above its terrified quaver.

'Yeah. Anal. I'm up for that.'

Our next meeting takes place in the more congenial atmosphere of an ill-lit bar in Soho, near his office. I wonder why we don't actually use his office, but he shrugs and says it's too annoying and too busy and he would never be off the phone before finding a suitably inaccessible booth in which to continue our dealings.

'So we can do it in this order,' he says, taking out his notes from before. 'Oh, do you want kissing? It's not compulsory.'

'Er, yeah, I think kissing would be fine.'

'So kissing, then he undresses you, masturbates you ... with a vibrator? Yeah. Then sixty nine, then straight fucking, then you give him a blowjob to get him hard again, then anal.' He dashes down his notes and gives me a querying look, as if he has just asked me to confirm the accuracy of some accounts. 'Of course, there'll be breaks between most of it,' he says, noting that I can do nothing but blink. 'We'll try and get it all done in a day though.'

'What about the setting and all that?' I ask.

'It can't be too elaborate. Budgets are always tight, though I have a little more to play with than usual. What do you want? I'll tell you if it's feasible.'

'I don't want cheesy cliché. No plumbers. No horrible wallpaper.'

'Yeah, but I can't do country estates either.'

'That's fine. I'm not into costume drama. The man can look and dress like a person you'd see in the street. Though good-looking would be nice ...'

'Good-looking, eh?' He smirks and makes a note. 'We need to do a casting. Next week?'

'OK. This time next week. We cast my ... opposite.'

'Your opposite.' The smirk deepens. If his cheekbones got any higher they'd be flying. His fingers are long and knobbly, always busy, always fidgeting with that damned pencil.

'Doesn't it bother you?' I ask, out of left field, not sure why I care. 'Your girlfriend.'

'What, that she's a porn actress?' He looks up at me, his eyes hooded, trying to assess whether to take offence or not. 'No more than it bothers her that I make the films. It's how we met. We can't exactly ...'

'Is it serious between you?'

'Not ... deadly serious.'

'She fucks other men for the camera. Do you ever ...?'

'Fuck other women? Yeah. I started out in this business as a performer. In college. Paid the rent.'

'You're not the usual type. You aren't beefcake. Or blondy Nordic-looking.'

'Right. I don't have a moustache either. Have you seen any non-mainstream, post-80s porn, Carmella?'

'Not so much,' I confess.

'It's not like that any more. I got the gig because I've got a big cock. And I'm sexy. Or so I was told.'

He is. He is sexy. Not obvious-sexy, but sinuous,

graceful, elegant, sardonic, jaded. It's the way he moves, and the tired eyes, and the look of a lightning rod he has. A lightning rod or a whip handle – better images than a pencil, after all.

'Why are you doing this?' he asks, betraying an interest in my motives that has been entirely absent up to now.

'Because … I'm bored with watching it. I want to do it. My way.'

'Your way will be my way,' he reminds me. 'I'm the director. Are you kinky?'

'Well … isn't this a bit … kinky?' I am floundering. I wish he would lose this sudden forceful interest in me. I'm not sure I can handle it.

'You know. Any shameful little secrets? Do you fancy it in leather? Do you want to walk a man like a dog? Do you like a good whipping? I can do all that. Cater for it, I mean.'

'I might want to walk before I can run,' I say with a nervous laugh.

'Ah, fair enough.' He sits back, dispirited, the pencil twirling madly between his long, slim, sexy … oh, stop it! … fingers. 'I've been wanting to get into the kinky market,' he confesses. 'Jazz won't go for it.'

'Jazz. Your girlfriend?'

'Yeah. Jazzy Jewel. That's her pornstar name. She won't let me tie her up.' He sighs. 'You think, when you date a porn actress, that she'll at least be broadminded.'

I laugh. I can't help it. He looks so forlorn.

'Maybe … we should just see where the wind takes us,' I tell him.

The casting session takes place in an odd little corrugated shed that might once have been a hall

112

attached to one of the less popular churches.

Dimitri meets me outside the tube station, slouched so perfectly against the wall with a cigarette and a sharp suit that he could have come straight from the cover of a Jam album. God, he is fine. I wish I could stop thinking it. He is the director of my porn film. He is the means to my end. He is ... a commodity. Just like those exploited porn people I worry myself over. I must objectify him, or I won't be able to do this.

Inside the hall, five men sit on iron-framed chairs, chatting awkwardly with cups of tea. Two of them are topless, towels slung over their shoulders, as if they have come fresh from the shower.

'OK!' says Dimitri, taking charge of the scene with ease and a click of the fingers. 'I have some lines of script for you to read through, and Carmella here is going to act out a scene with each of you.'

I stare at Dimitri. 'What scene?' I ask sharply. He emailed his first draft to me earlier in the week, and it is pure filth. I keep my clothes on for roughly two minutes. Luckily, those two minutes are the ones we will be going through.

I pretend to be standing cleaning a window in a skimpy, revealing outfit, while each of the five men acts the role of passer-by, stopping, staring, then responding to the blatant invitation of my (imaginary) breasts and stocking tops with a predatory stare and a knock at my door.

'Special delivery. Did somebody order a good, hard fuck?' is the line the men must attempt. Only three of them seem able to read. Of those three, one is far, far too pumped-up for my taste. One has hideously bad breath. The other ... I don't know. I just don't ... I just can't see myself with him. He is quite handsome, well-built, tall, I

113

like his clothes, I like his tan, I just … don't find him very sexy.

'I'm sorry.' I turn to Dimitri. 'I didn't realise I was this fussy, but …'

'What? None of them?'

'Sexy is an elusive quality,' I tell him. 'I don't find that many men have it.'

'So … what? Put out another call? Give up? Do you want your money back?'

'No. But … I was wondering …'

I really can't say this. I shouldn't even think it. It's madness. Sheer folly.

'Go on.' He leans against the radiator, tapping his teeth with the pencil, his eyes narrowed at me.

'You've heard of actor-directors, right?'

I almost have to look away for fear of how he will react. He removes the pencil just half an inch from his mouth and stares, a big mooncalf stare. Then the sides of his eyes crinkle and he shouts out a laugh.

'Seriously?'

'I kind of picture you … every time I look at the script,' I admit shiftily. 'But if you don't want to … don't worry. Do another casting. I'm sure that's best, actually, yeah, just make a few phone calls and …'

He puts a hand on my shoulder, steady and firm. 'It's OK,' he says gently, his eyes amused below raised brows. 'I'll do it.'

'You're … sure?'

'Uh huh. I've got a friend who can stand in behind the camera. I know how things look on film too, so it's likely to need a bit less in the way of editing. So shall we meet at my, uh, studio, same time next week?'

'Yeah. Same time next week. Your studio.'

*   *   *

I drive to the studio, which is an unremarkable bungalow set back from the main road, surrounded on all sides by a ten-foot hedge.

'This is your studio?'

'Yeah. Well. It's my parents' house, actually. But they've moved to Spain so ...'

'Do they know it's been immortalised on film?'

'Not as such,' he confesses.

Inside, in the spacious living room, there are cameras and big microphones with those spongey jackets on and a tea tray with biscuits and ... that's about it. A bored-looking young woman and a man are waiting for us, sipping tea on the cream leather sofa.

'Hi, guys, let me introduce our star for the day, Carmella. Carmella, this is our cameraman, Dale, and our runner, India.'

I smile at the thought of this production having a runner. Though, alas, there appears to be no Best Boy Grip.

'So, India, get us a cup of tea and we'll run through the first scene, yeah?'

India glowers, obviously unhappy at her place in the pecking order. I wonder if she is an aspiring porn actress – she is certainly attractive and somewhat pneumatic. Something occurs to me, something rather dismaying, and I ask, straight out.

'So do you have to have a ... fluffer? For this?'

Dimitri laughs and puts a hand on my thigh. 'I think not,' he purrs. Oh, the relief. I am sure I don't want to watch India getting him ready for me. I think that might be the most depressing thing I could possibly imagine at this moment. 'My screen name was Woody Woodward. I think that tells you all you need to know.'

The tea is drunk. I feel drunk. I'm not sure I want to

go through with it now I'm here.

'So, Carmella,' says Dimitri, once Dale has started fidgeting with the camera and India has retired to the kitchen to wash the cups. 'Is that what you're going to wear for the first scene?'

I have taken off my coat to reveal a very skimpy, see-through blouse and teeny stretchy miniskirt. I have worn black lacy hold-ups rather than stockings because the thought of a million retakes while Dimitri struggles with suspender snaps did not appeal, and on my feet are skyscrapers, black and patent leather in style.

'Well … yeah. Don't you think it's tarty enough?'

'On the contrary. It's exactly tarty enough. Can't wait to see what's underneath. Though I kind of can.' He grins and, sensing my nervousness, reaches over to stroke my cheek. 'Don't think about what you're doing, Carmella. Just … live it. Enjoy it. I'm planning to. I promise I'll make you forget what planet you're on, let alone anything else.'

That's what I needed to hear. My pussy clenches, sending a squirmy sexy feeling through me. I am going to get fucked senseless, on camera, by an evil mastermind of porn. This is what I want! I'm going to go for it.

He puts his thumb to my lips and I kiss it, almost absent-mindedly, drinking in his expression of … well, I can only describe it as a sort of lustful kindness.

'Come on. Scene one. I'm outside – you're "cleaning the windows". Let's go!'

Dale and Dimitri head out of the front door and mooch on the driveway, waiting for me to get into position in the large front window. In the doorway, India glares at me. She obviously thinks I'm too old, too flat-chested, not leggy enough. But I'll show her.

I pick up my bottle of Windolene and my cloth and spread myself luxuriously behind the glass, stretching up so the mini rides up past the lace, revealing plenty of thigh, pressing my sheer blouse to the cold, smooth glass so my nipples harden against it. Outside, Dale films Dimitri mock-strolling past then stopping and double-taking at the lewd display that confronts him. For a moment he folds his arms and watches, eyebrows aloft, so that I am encouraged to scale ever ruder heights of display, shoving the cloth into my cleavage and running a hand along my thigh, one high-heeled foot perched on the window sill so my leg is bent and the hem of the lycra miniskirt stretched so wide my knickers are visible. I love this. I put a hand on my breast, lick my lips, beam out the message through half-closed eyes to my audience. Come hither, come hither, come hither.

He winks at me and walks up the garden path – not in a hurry, but quite slowly and purposefully, then rings the bell.

I run to the door, pouting in a sultry manner at my visitor, ignoring Dale and his camera over his shoulder.

'Special delivery,' says Dimitri. 'Did somebody order a good, hard fuck?'

'Yes,' I say, as huskily as I can without losing sound quality. I perceive that India is behind me, out of shot, with the microphone. 'Do I have to sign for it?'

'No, but you might have to beg,' snarls Dimitri, stepping over the threshold and pushing me up against the wall, tongue down throat, rock-hard pelvis crushing my lower abdominals, hands wrenching my arms up above my head and holding them there, pinned at the wrist.

'Nice,' says Dale. 'Can I get a shot of your tongue … yeah. Good. Are you going to do that thing with the shirt?'

Dimitri keeps my wrists held with one hand and uses the other to rip my blouse in half, fondling my breasts with thorough finesse, poking the fingers down into the lacy cups so my nipples are visible to the audience.

Dale talks through the whole thing, so I can only assume we will have to overdub the sound later. 'That's it, mate. Can we see her nipple? Think it's time to move over to the couch?'

Dimitri's wandering hands have wandered down to my thigh now, lifting the skirt inch by inch for the camera, revealing slutty red string briefs.

'Did you know I was coming?' he asks breathlessly, plunging a finger inside the cheap nylon. 'Were you expecting this?'

'I do this every day,' I tell him, my mind hard-pressed to remember my lines, with his finger on my clit, painting itself in my juices, and his other hand squeezing a tit. 'I'm always on the lookout.'

Dimitri rips the rest of the blouse off me and wrenches my skirt down, all the way down, before pulling me by the wrist into the centre of the living room, then standing behind me, supporting me, so that we are both facing the camera. His hands cup my unclipped breasts, thumbs tormenting my nipples with their slightly rough whorls of skin. He nips and nuzzles at my neck, making my head droop to one side. I push my bottom into his hard cock. Woody Woodward. Yes. Very apt.

The bra comes off and I am standing, topless, in front of a camera, a man and a sneering girl, being comprehensively felt up by Dimitri.

'If you want it, slut, you'll have to get your knickers off,' he says, moving a hand down there and hooking it in place between my thighs. 'I can feel how wet you are. God, you're wet.' He slips a finger under the slippery silkiness, feels my slickness, takes it out and makes me lick it off. 'Do you want it?'

'Yes,' I sigh. 'I want it.'

'You know what to do, then.'

I arch my back and peel the knickers down while Dimitri holds me by the hips. As the twin globes of my buttocks present themselves to him, he slides one finger down the crack from the top, stopping at my secret little hole and prodding at it. 'You're getting it up the arse later too,' he says matter-of-factly. 'That's what happens to dirty girls who show off in windows.'

Oh, the rush, the shame, the thrill. I can't help the tiny moan of delight that comes out, though it's fine to make any noise I like. In fact, Dimitri had said, the noisier the better.

'Turn her around,' says Dale as I step out of the knickers. 'Let us see her arse properly.'

Dimitri spins me to face him and his hands reach around to spread my hind cheeks to the camera's unblinking eye. 'You've had a few cocks up here before, I'm sure,' he asserts, pushing at my anus once again. 'You'll know what to expect, eh?'

'Mmm.' I cannot remember any of the script now. Dimitri is going to have to improvise. He commandeers me around to the leather couch, pushing me down so my naked bottom puckers with gooseflesh on contact with the sheeny cold surface.

'Lie back and spread those legs. That's it. Feet up on the couch, wide as you can.' He stands aside to let Dale capture the glistening split. 'And play with your tits. Go on. I'm going to get something.'

Dimitri saunters out of shot for a moment, while I

119

settle into role, flicking my nipples and keeping the longest possible distance between my ankles. At Dale's request, I begin to touch my pussy, enthralled and amazed at how gushing wet I am down there.

'That's it, love,' Dale encourages, his rough-edged voice inserting itself perfectly into my erotic haze. 'I want to see that clit, big and fat as you can get it. Oh yes.'

Dimitri returns, wielding a large black vibrator.

'Whenever I pass your house,' he says, 'I always make sure I'm carrying this.'

He throws it on to the couch and drops to his knees between mine, gazing intently at the rippled, glazed flesh that so blatantly trumpets my need to be fucked. He pinches the lips between his fingers and urges them even wider apart, making sure that Dale has a good angle to capture the slow, precise fingering that follows.

The sound, that sweet, slithery sucking noise, is so loud I am sure the microphone must be picking it up. His fingers plunge and knead and strum, taking me almost to the edge, but never over it.

Very quietly he mutters, 'You're going to come and they're going to watch you. They're going to see what I do to you.' I begin to lose control and he takes his hand away, picks up the vibrator.

Speaking to the microphone again, he says, 'I don't think fingers are enough for a greedy girl like you. I think you need something thicker and longer. And more powerful.' He switches it on and begins to move it languidly over my pussy lips and clit, alternating the power settings when it looks as if I am starting to enjoy myself too much. Dale is now almost touching me with the camera, hanging over the arm of the couch, his lens focused right at the point where the rounded head of the vibe and my pulsing clit meet.

'Make her come, Dimitri,' he says, businesslike, and Dimitri homes in on my swollen bud, switching the vibrator to its highest setting, and pushes three fingers hard up inside me.

His face, so pale with lust that his eyes look almost violet, lowers over me.

'Come now, and come hard,' he grinds and there is his hot breath, a bit pepperminty, and the underlying smell of him, all dressed up and debonair while I lie here, naked and at his mercy.

So I do, I come hard, kicking my feet so Dale has to retreat a few inches, moving the camera to my contorted face, then down to my bum which is rising and falling on the couch, in time with the spasms that Dimitri has forced.

'Sexy, sexy, sexy!' approves Dale. 'Dimitri, you need to do something with that hard-on before it busts out of your trousers. Get on top of her and make her suck you.'

He crawls over me, moving me to a lying down position with my head slightly elevated, resting on the arm of the sofa. He unbuckles the belt and unzips the fly, and then clamps my shoulders between his knees, introducing his big stiff cock to my mouth and pushing it in. I suck like a professional, watching Dale and India from the corner of my eye and taking silent direction from the cast of their expressions.

'Hang on!' Dale interjects anxiously. 'This isn't in the script, is it? I thought …'

'Fuck the script,' says Dimitri energetically. 'Ever heard of improvisation?'

'Yeah but …'

'Stick to the camera stuff. I'm the director.' He shoves his cock an inch further into my mouth. 'Aren't I,

Carmella?'

'Nnrgh.' He obliges me by withdrawing from my now aching jaw and scooting down to lie flat on top of me, all long and bony but surprisingly comfortable, sealing our conspiracy against Dale and India with a kiss.

'What do *you* want?' he whispers into my ear. 'What do you want right now?'

His hand is playing between my thighs. I love the feel of his suit against my bare skin, the shirt buttons pressing into my chest.

'I want you to strip down and fuck me,' I tell him. He feels so good, those hands, those long fingers, that neat, glossy hair – could anything feel better? There is only one way to find out.

'I'll be glad to,' he proclaims, jumping up and doing a sexy striptease, even though the camera is focused on me, on my shifting down and spreading wide, on my expression of studied dumb lust.

'More slut!' Dimitri urges. 'You don't look dirty enough. Look like you'll die if you don't get some soon.'

I push two of my fingers into my cunt and squeeze a tit, bucking and slithering all over the leather, channelling my inner nymphomaniac.

'Please, I can't wait any longer!' I declaim, and actually, there is some feeling behind the words. I really want this luscious cock of Dimitri's; I really want to see his face when he comes. I think it will be one to remember.

'Good thing you don't have to then!'

Dimitri, now naked, slender but sinewy, slides knees-first on to the couch and lifts my legs up so that my ankles rest on his shoulders. 'Good angle for the camera,' he mouths silently, and indeed it must be, for now Dale is very close to us, so close that his lens is almost a third element in our coming together, homed in on Dimitri's cock as it hovers ever closer to my jewel-red pussy. I try to take no notice and concentrate on Dimitri's face, which is intent and triumphant. He has a thin gold chain around his neck with a small charm – a coin of some kind – attached and it begins to swing over my breasts, brushing them, sending a tiny chill of cold through me, then it comes to rest just beneath my chin, and Dimitri is in, inside me, holding me by the hips. There are some obvious contrivances to be made to ensure that the camera gets what it needs – it has to peer through an arch of mixed flesh to capture the cock in action, and I must admit that at times my calves feel achey and I want to flatten my back, but I zone out of all that and keep my eyes on Dimitri, who is working so hard, slamming and thrusting and rubbing over the sweetest spot and bringing one hand to my clit to keep the pressure up, up, up.

We go at it hard and fast and his face becomes a tangled blur, his pendant zigzagging all over my neck and face, his upper arms corded and taut with the effort. He is the sexiest thing I have ever seen. My legs stay slung over his shoulders so that my upper thighs almost creak with the strain, my knees up near my ears, but Dale is happy. 'I can see it all,' he enthuses. 'Fuck, that is one good bit of action, man! Wait till you get to do the editing!'

'Like it hard, eh?' Dimitri grunts. My back is stuck to the couch so his ferocious fucking is inescapable. 'Like it hard and in public, being watched. How does she look, India?'

'Like a dirty fucking whore,' says India, and that's

when I come, whimpering into Dimitri's laughing face, into India's disgusted titter, into Dale's long-drawn-out 'Yeeeeaaaaahhhhh.'

Dimitri carries on, though, drawing yet another climax from me before he is ready for the 'money shot'. He shoots all over my tits and belly, and his face is no disappointment, crumpled and vulnerable, beautifully shocked for those few fragile seconds.

Then he is Dimitri again, sweating and puffing, but the lanky love god I have come to know, just a little.

'Sweet,' he says, brushing a plastered hair from my forehead. 'Nice one. Did you get that, Dale?'

Dale is busy filming my jizz-gleaming breasts and the flush that spreads from my collarbone to my hairline.

'OK, cut,' he says. And that's when I remember. It's not even over yet.

'What do you think of the show so far?' whispers Dimitri, leaning over to my ear and offering me some more popcorn.

'Rubbish,' I mug, but then I smile at him. 'No. I love it. It's so much better than I ever expected.'

We are in the same living room we made the film in, sitting on that same cream leather couch, with all the blinds drawn down, all the lights off, and the film running on a huge, wall-mounted TV screen. Dale and India are either side of us, making comments at key intervals.

'Your cock looks better than ever, D,' says Dale dispassionately. 'You keep it in good nick.'

'Do other porn actors let themselves go, then?' I ask, amused. 'Let their cocks get fat and hairy and dress them in dowdy boxers?'

Dimitri snuffles with mirth, chewing contentedly on his popcorn.

'Something like that,' he says.

'Nah, I mean it still gets hard really quickly and stays hard for ages,' says a mildly affronted Dale. 'It's a gift, man.'

'Some of us are born with it,' says Dimitri, 'some achieve it, and some have it thrust upon them. Like you.' He nudges me and we giggle like pathetic schoolchildren.

'Look, it's getting to the good part,' says India sulkily. 'Stop mucking about and let's watch the anal scene. That's my favourite.'

'Mine too,' I agree. Dimitri puts an arm around me and I lay my head on his shoulder.

It is so odd to see what we did this way. I can't keep my eyes off my face, which does not seem like *my* face. It seems alien, as if there is nothing of me behind the avid eyes. Is this what I look like to Dimitri, to others? Five feet six, one hundred and thirty-five pounds of sex. My voice is all wrong too. Do I really moan in that ridiculous drama-school way? Do I really sound that posh?

It is lovely, though, to see Dimitri's hands on me, and to see the way his body combines and flows with mine. The dance is intricate, compelling, almost beautiful to watch in a way – a bizarre performance art.

I watch myself bent over the arm of the couch, legs in a V, camera shooting me in profile while Dimitri, with cock rigid once more, fucks me standing up behind. During this scene, India was given a camcorder to use, and scenes of Dimitri pumping away are intercut with images of my screwed up, puffing face, or his hands, fingers splayed over my tits, squeezing them as he thrusts.

'Do you ever get enough?' he grinds out, spearing me

125

up against the leather, holding me firm for a moment, waiting for my answer before he will start again.

'Never,' I vow, and I'm impressed with how genuinely deranged with lust I sound as I say the word. This is one hell of a sexy film. 'I need it all the time.'

'That can be arranged,' says Dimitri, resuming his rhythm. Off camera, India hands him a bottle of lube. My body stiffens – at the time, I could hear him unscrewing the cap, and I knew what was coming. 'But you'll get a very sore pussy, won't you? Perhaps we should give it a break. Try something else.'

I begin to whimper like a kicked puppy; his finger is so swift and smooth, the lubricant cold as it is spread between my cheeks with no-nonsense professionalism.

'This is what you need,' he says, softly, just loud enough for the microphone to pick up. I can see what he is doing, see my split cheeks, see his finger working the little twisted opening, making it shiny sheeny with lubricant. It looks so obscene, but I cannot look away. I think I will be rewinding this scene, quite often.

The camera pans out a little, making it clear that the root of Dimitri's cock is still buried inside me; he is swivelling his hips in small rotations, just enough to ensure I still feel it there in full effect. Another close-up – Dimitri's finger, breaking the seal, sneaking up inside to the knuckle. My face, damp and gasping, eyes tight shut.

'I hope there's room for me up here. What do you think?'

'I don't know,' I whisper.

'Better find out then.' Dimitri's finger is two fingers now, and they are squelching lubriciously back and forth, widening the tiny aperture to suit his purpose. 'My guess is … yes.'

The hard, gleaming cock pulls slowly out of its sheath and places itself at the tiny hole vacated by Dimitri's fingers. It is slow, excruciatingly but very arousingly slow, watching the blunt round head push, push, push until it begins to stretch the arsehole enough to take it in.

On the couch, transfixed, I don't hear Dimitri's words at first.

'You like this bit, don't you?' he says, his fingers finding the dimple in my sweater caused by a hardened nipple. 'I can tell.'

Without looking away from the screen, I nod. 'Wow,' is all I can say.

'Dirty girl,' he teases, but I don't stop him pulling up my jumper and playing with the nipple, chafing it with the lace of my bra cup. 'You aren't the only one.' He pulls one of my hands over to his crotch, the fabric of which is straining with the force of his erection.

On screen, Dimitri's cock – the very cock I can feel right now – is edging onward. His cock, my face – looking astounded, my mouth and eyes wide open – then his cock again, further up now, getting to the point where I start to squirm and try to thrash.

'Your face,' chuckles off-screen Dimitri. I am starting to look very alarmed – I remember this bit being painfully tight. 'That hurt you, didn't it?'

'You're so big!' I excuse myself. 'I don't think I've had one that big before.'

He grunts with satisfaction, then pulls me on to his lap, making my skirt ride up in the process so he can get one big hand inside my knickers with ease. My bottom is on the zip of his trousers, the cheeks rudely bisected by the hard lump within. He begins to finger me, lazily, while the four of us continue to watch me getting buggered on the screen.

Dimitri in the film is all the way up now. I try to recall the feeling: stuffed to bursting, stretched and a little sore, wondering if he had gone too far, but also revelling in my filthy sluttiness, loving that I was caught on camera with a big fat cock up my arse. He draws back – that part felt so strangely wrong that I began to wring my hands, which looks quite comical on the film – then slams, hard, so that his pelvis slaps my bum cheeks with a resounding crack. I cry out.

The audience laughs. Dimitri's fingers twiddle my clit and my nipples simultaneously. I wriggle on his rock-hard cock. We carry on that way, watching me get sodomised, the cock in, the cock out, my face, his face, fingers up me, on my clit, everywhere, his stiffness between my bum cheeks, in, out, in, out.

The woman in the film comes first, the camera catching that shameful rapture in its full no-holds-barred glory; then film Dimitri whips himself as quickly as he can out of my arse and splashes his spunk all over my red rear cheeks, painting it on so it covers them. I am next, jiggling all over Dimitri's lap while Dale and India cheer and express their intention of going to the bedroom.

'Good,' says Dimitri, no longer interested in the fucked-out couple on the screen, collapsing down on the sofa. 'Get on your knees on the floor. I'm going to fuck you again.'

It was worth every penny. I have my lovely secret tape to watch whenever I like now. Dimitri asks me now and then to star in one of his films, but of course, I can't say yes to that. There have been a few more private productions since then, though … Jazzy Jewel has gone on to more mainstream porn fame now. When she is interviewed in *Forum* or *Penthouse* she always acknowledges the role Dimitri played in her career, and wishes him well with his new relationship.

Lucky Dip

'TELL ME AGAIN HOW long you left the email unread?'

'Three days, sir.'

'And tell me again *why* you left it unread for three days?'

'Because I got another one two minutes later, and it was from you, so I read that and just … forgot … about the other one.'

Charlotte screwed up her face. It was hard to think on one's feet, and even harder to think on one's tiptoes. Especially when cuffed and strung up by the wrists to a ceiling hook. With nothing on but a shirt and shoes and socks.

'And now,' Collins said again, magnifying the enormity of her transgression with the weight of disapproval in his voice, 'our customer has complained. Not only that, but she intends to withdraw the recommendations she has made to friends. And this is no ordinary customer, Charlotte, oh no. This is a very highly valued customer; a lady who has availed herself of our service no fewer than four times.'

'I know, sir. I'm sorry, sir.'

'Sorry doesn't pay the bills.' Collins ran the cold flat tip of his riding crop over Charlotte's undefended bottom cheeks. 'How many have you earned, Charlotte, in your estimation?'

130

Charlotte hated this part; having to guess how many strokes he would give her (for she was under no illusion that her hazardings were ever taken into final account when he calculated the total owing).

'Twenty, sir? Hard?'

'Twenty, hard. Hmm. I'd say that was the minimum. Let's start with ten medium and then work up to ... thirty. Hard.'

Oh dear. This was the worst tally yet – though Charlotte had not, thus far, committed any transgression more serious than forgetting to order new stationery, so that was hardly surprising. Lady Markham was extremely displeased, judging by the tone of her follow-up email, and Collins was correspondingly incandescent.

The medium ten were bad enough, stinging and inescapable as she struggled to keep her tippy-toes on the ground, but once he started to put the full strength of his arm into them, Charlotte knew she would not get through the first dozen without some pleading and bargaining. Pleading and bargaining never worked with Collins though. Bryant could sometimes be persuaded, but Collins was made of resolution and utterly unswerving once his course was fixed.

The cuts came hard and fast, which was one scant mercy – at least he did not draw out the agony – and pretty soon, Charlotte was almost spinning in a twisty dervish-dance, swinging on that hook like a punch bag buffeted this way and that. No matter how she tried to position herself, Collins found her bottom with the deftest, surest flick of his wrist and each stroke of the thirty found its target with ease, until she was striped and tight, burning all over from the disciplinary attention.

'Now,' said Collins quietly, cupping her punished globes with a considering hand, 'I am going to uncuff you and you are going to sit on that hard wood chair and take dictation for me.'

Charlotte breathed in deeply as the cuffs clicked and she was reacquainted with her heels. Sitting on the chair was not comfortable, but at least the worst of the whipping was past and she was free to redeem herself.

'Dear Lady Markham,' opened Collins, standing by the window and looking out while Charlotte commenced typing. 'Please accept my humble apologies for the oversight regarding your most recent email. My slapdash omission was inexcusable and you will be pleased to hear that I am sitting on a very sore bottom as I type this, having been soundly whipped by an irate Mr Collins. He has asked me to tell you that, if you feel my punishment insufficient, he is very happy to add to it.'

Charlotte lifted tragic eyes to her employer at this juncture. Surely this was humiliation enough? But Collins slight half-smile conveyed pleasure in her abasement, so she was sure any protestation would meet with short shrift.

'I hope you will feel able,' continued Collins, 'to continue with the arrangement you sought to make in your preliminary communication. I would be very happy to offer you the scenario you outlined at fifty per cent of the usual price, for the sake of continuing goodwill. I will personally make up the shortfall by working overtime and taking on a more hands-on role from time to time. I sincerely hope this will be agreeable to you, and look forward to your reply. Abjectly, Charlotte Steele.'

'A more hands-on role,' said Charlotte nervously, looking up at her employer. 'What did you mean by that, please, sir?'

'I mean, Charlotte, that when a female player is

required in these fantasies, you will have to take that part. It will save me a good deal of money. Money I cannot afford to lose.'

'Oh, I see.'

'Good. Now come and sit your sore behind on this windowsill and show me your contrition in the usual manner, Charlotte. I haven't got all day to deal with your misdeeds.'

'Lady Markham isn't quite sure how she wants this set up,' Bryant explained, leading Charlotte and Collins through the Harley Street rooms, deserted at this time of night, but giving exactly the right atmosphere. 'I gather from Charlotte that she is keen for some kind of quasi-medical consultation, with her as the submissive, brought to an appointment with a doctor by her exasperated husband or employer. What do you think, Charlotte? Husband or employer?'

'I think husband,' said Charlotte. 'Then it's clear that he already has a sexual relationship with her. A boss is good too, though … I don't know.'

'Well, you need to know,' said Collins impatiently. 'You're the submissive on the payroll. This is what we pay you for.'

'Maybe a husband then. He is taking her to the doctor to find out why she is so temperamental and disobedient. The doctor examines her … y'know … and makes his recommendations. And perhaps demonstrates a few.'

'Good,' said Collins. A doctor, a masterful husband and a wife who needs to be brought to submission. I like it. I think Lady Markham will like it too.'

'It's funny, isn't it,' said Charlotte, 'how an amazingly powerful woman like Lady Markham, who has made policies and everything, likes to get spanked and ordered about. Weird.'

'Not weird really,' smiled Bryant. 'I suppose it's a release for her.'

'I suppose so.'

They came to the top of a flight of stairs and entered a large, airy, plant-filled consultation room.

'Well then.' Bryant switched on the lights and drew the blinds. 'I think this will do rather nicely.'

Collins slid himself into position behind the substantial walnut desk and took out a clipboard and fountain pen. 'Notes,' he explained tersely. 'You'll find my waiting room next door, Mr and Mrs ...'

'Masterton,' supplied Charlotte.

'Perfect. Well, then. Go and wait for me to admit you.'

Charlotte and Bryant walked through to an equally spacious room amply supplied with comfortable chintzy seating and copies of *Country Life* on the expensive antique occasional tables.

'Well, my dear,' said Bryant, getting into strident role, 'I'm told that Dr Collins is the leading authority in this area. I certainly hope he will be able to help us.'

Charlotte lowered her eyes to the floor, shifting uncomfortably in her armchair. 'Are you sure this is necessary, darling?' she muttered.

Bryant smiled, perching on the armrest and clapping a hand of reassurance on her shoulder.

'If you want this marriage to work, dearest Charlotte ... and I know I do.'

Charlotte, momentarily transported to an alternative reality in which she was Bryant's wife, could only stare at him, mute with the possibilities such a situation would have to offer.

'If it's what you want ... then I will go along with it,'

she finally faltered.

She was re-anchored in the present by the click of the consulting room door and the sight of Collins's head, spectacles lowered to the bridge of his nose, peering severely at his clients.

'I'm ready for you now, Mr Masterton,' he said, ignoring Charlotte and turning his back on them to return to the desk.

It was an impressive, expansive figure who greeted the couple, fingers knit in a steeple, head cocked to one curious side.

'I note from your referral,' opened Collins, glancing at some hastily-scribbled papers, 'that you have been experiencing some marital difficulties. Please could you expand on these for me, Mr Masterton.'

'Of course,' Bryant opened enthusiastically. 'When Charlotte and I became engaged, we made certain agreements – a contract of sorts – as to how the household would be run. She accepted that I would be master of the house in every respect and that I had the right to demand her absolute obedience. However, it seems that she was … less than honest with me when she made that agreement.'

'Oh really?' Charlotte felt a trickle of excitement in the face of the hard stare Collins was now subjecting her to. She shifted in her seat, causing Bryant to grasp her hand and hold it tightly.

'Sad but true,' continued the disappointed husband. 'She is consistently disobedient, lazy around the house and has even begun to withhold her body from me, in direct contravention of the rules we established together.'

'Separate beds?' snapped Collins in disgust.

'Upon occasion, I regret to say …'

'But do you not insist?'

'I have insisted. I have threatened. I have begged.'

'Enough!' Collins, his eyes now hardened flint, held up a hand. 'You must *never* beg. She will laugh at you.'

'Then what can I do, Doctor?'

'Watch,' said Collins, his voice a purr of menace, 'and learn. I can restore to you a pliant and submissive mate who will open her legs for you at the merest suggestion of desire on your part – but you must observe and follow these techniques to the letter. Are you prepared to do this?'

'Oh yes.'

'And you, Mrs Masterton?'

Charlotte pursed her lips, her chest already heaving in anticipation of the dread delights to come.

'I ... oh ... if it will save my marriage ... then yes.'

'Good. Masterton, ask her to do something for you. Let me see how she behaves.'

'Very well. Er ... would you care to suck my cock, darling?'

Charlotte forced the laughter down and retorted, 'Certainly not! I'm not some whore, you know!'

'I see,' said Collins icily. 'We have much work to do. Mr Masterton, may I ask you to place your chair against the wall, somewhere that will give you the optimum view, and observe how I would deal with this kind of insubordination.'

Bryant, nodding, moved away from the desk and sat, legs crossed and arms folded, ready to enjoy the spectacle.

'Now then, Mrs Masterton, let's try that again.' Collins rose from his desk and came to loom behind Charlotte, his hands braced on the back of her chair. He bent and put his lips close to her ear.

'Suck my cock,' he hissed.

'No!' yelped Charlotte, bolting forwards until she almost fell off the chair, but Collins had closed his hand around her upper arm and was dragging her up and out of her seat, whisking her briskly out of the way so he could take her place and then pull her, so seamlessly that it was like a perverse ballet, back down across his lap, head and legs dangling and tight-skirted bottom vulnerable to attack.

'I'm not sure I heard that right,' he said, patting a hand against the swell of her buttocks with dangerous intent. 'Did you say no?'

'Ohhhh,' moaned Charlotte, fully aware of her precarious position.

It seemed that Collins did not really require an answer anyway, for he addressed himself to Bryant instead.

'My advice to you,' he said, 'is to put a system of consequences for disobedience in place as soon as you can, and to stick to it. This is just a suggestion – you can use other sanctions as well as, or instead of, corporal punishment; but once you have decided on your system, you must be firm and consistent in applying it. And now, with your permission, I intend to give your wife the spanking she so clearly needs.'

'Oh, please, be my guest,' said Bryant and then Charlotte's squeals drowned his words, together with the salutary crack of Collins's broad palm against the tightly-skirted rear.

'You must judge for yourself how far and how hard you want to take it,' said Collins, smacking away with gusto. 'For instance, you may decide to stick to spanking her over her skirt or trousers. Or you may decide that these offer too much protection – I tend to go along with that viewpoint – in which case …'

Charlotte kicked her legs as the skirt rose up, trailing ticklishly along her thighs and revealing her high-cut French silk knickers.

'... You might try warming her behind in underwear only. These are very nice; did you buy them for her?'

'I did,' said Bryant – and it was true. 'They're from Agent Provocateur.'

'Oh, yes, a favourite haunt of my wife's,' said Collins, and Charlotte's buttocks clenched suddenly. 'No, Mrs Masterton, you do not clench for me, unless you want extra strokes.'

Charlotte both did and didn't want extra strokes; but what she definitely did not want was for Collins to be married. Was the wife real, or imaginary, constructed for the furtherance of the narrative? Not sure why she should care, Charlotte endeavoured to put the thought from her mind, and she was ably assisted in this by the renewed forceful application of Collins's hand to her silkily clad rear.

'Do you repent your ill-mannered disobedience?' Collins asked, whaling away. 'Can your husband expect the submission he deserves from you in the future?'

Charlotte knew that Lady Markham would be far from ready to throw in the towel at this point, so she shook her head and blurted, 'No, no.'

'Very well. Then I shall have to bare your bottom.'

'This can't be a medical technique! I demand to see the textbook!'

'My methods may be unorthodox, but they carry a one hundred per cent success rate.' Collins whipped the knickers down to Charlotte's knees and spent an agonisingly long time inspecting the state he had made of her bottom.

'These look like the marks of a riding whip,' he

138

noted, pressing a thumb into the fading bruises from the cropping he had given her in the office two days earlier. 'You have already tried this method?'

'Tried,' said Bryant. 'But I can't seem to make it sink in.'

'Are you consistent? Does she know that *any* unacceptable behaviour will result in these marks of punishment?'

Bryant sighed. 'No, I suppose I have let her get away with a great deal.'

'There you are. You must strengthen your will, Mr Masterton; you may find that you are spanking your wife ten times a day, but eventually, the message will get through. I know it will be … unpleasant for you, at first.'

Charlotte heard the mild snuffle of repressed mirth from her play-husband. Unpleasant! Yeah. Right.

'But it's necessary.' As if to reinforce this point, Collins began to spank Charlotte's naked behind with loud, percussive, stinging smacks that made her wriggle and yelp. Although he wielded canes, crops, paddles and straps with expert accuracy, somehow his hand had a uniquely painful quality all of its own, especially on bare skin. She knew she could safeword at any time without prejudice, but it was important to Charlotte to *do what Lady Markham would do*. And Lady Markham had been known to wear out a variety of professional Doms, both male and female, in the past. She was obviously some kind of super-submissive, and Charlotte aspired to her high tolerance of pain and humiliation.

'Even if your hand begins to tire,' Collins was lecturing Bryant as he worked, 'you must not end the punishment until it is very obvious that your wife is chastened. I see that Mrs Masterton is unusually stubborn, so she will require an unusually sore bottom.

Isn't that so, Mrs Masterton?'

'Ouch! Please stop! This is outrageous!' was Charlotte's dramatic response. She knew that her bottom was radiating serious heat now, and she imagined with some satisfaction the exact shade of red it must be. All the same, the sting was beginning to build to barely bearable proportions, and she wanted to pretend to relent. Surely Collins's hand must be swollen to about twice its natural size by now? How long could he keep this up?

'You agree with me, then,' he said smoothly. 'You need particularly firm handling and severe punishment. I shall mention this on your notes.' The scorching rain ceased for a moment of blessed relief. 'Come and look at her bottom, Mr Masterton,' invited the ersatz doctor. 'This is the kind of result you need to be aiming for.'

Bryant stepped over, placing a hand on the sizzling skin.

'Gosh, it's awfully hot. I don't know that I've ever spanked her as hard as that.'

'Well, that is where you are going wrong, I imagine,' said Collins grimly. 'And we aren't even finished yet.'

Charlotte moaned, but refused to say the words of surrender.

'Or are we, madam? Do you want to save yourself additional chastisement by promising to serve your husband in a fitting spirit of submission?'

'Oh … it's not fair …' she wailed ineffectually.

'She isn't ready yet,' Collins confirmed. 'In that case, I recommend that she spends some reflective time in the corner before we continue with the next phase of her punishment.'

Charlotte began to shift in Collins's lap, preparing to stand, thinking that a period in the corner, dull as it was, would give her bottom some recovery time. She thought wrong.

'Ah ah ah, not so fast, young lady,' cautioned Collins. 'I have something that might aid your reflections first. Mr Masterton, when your wife is in such an obstinate frame of mind that an over-the-knee hand spanking does not suffice, I recommend this little device to concentrate her mind during corner time.'

Charlotte did not know what Collins was taking out of his desk drawer, but she twitched with delicious dread, knowing it would be nothing trifling or ignorable.

'Oh! What an interesting idea!' Charlotte heard the poorly hidden glee in Bryant's voice.

'You think so? Good. Perhaps you would like to prepare her for me.'

Charlotte, so turned on that she could barely keep still, now that the spanking had ended and only its warm, fierce, arousing residual effects remained, writhed in Collins's lap, anxious not to dampen his smart trousers.

'Keep still,' advised Bryant, and then she stiffened as his finger, coated in cold, wet, slippery stuff, snuck in between the scorched buttocks and began to grease up her tiny hidden anal bud. Not an enema, she hoped. She hated those. She clenched her teeth and silently prayed for a butt plug. Surely it must be a butt plug. But how big? She knew Collins was not a fan of the smaller-sized invaders.

Bryant's forefinger was penetrating her ring now with a rude slurping sound and she was trying hard not to tense her muscles and let him prepare her most private passage for public violation by the doctor.

'She is not a virgin in this method of intercourse, is she?' enquired Collins casually.

'Oh no,' Bryant assured him with a laugh.

'Good. Another course I recommend is to restrict her to anal sex without climax when she is behaving badly. Forbid masturbation, obviously. We have special equipment you can purchase to make her own private parts inaccessible to her, if required. I'll show you our catalogue, while she is in the corner.'

'I would be very interested to see it.'

Charlotte let out a low cry as the slick bulbous silicone head of a large butt plug replaced Bryant's finger in her tender circle of muscle. At least she had escaped without an enema, she reasoned. But this plug was *big*, travelling slowly but inescapably up the tight channel, creating a burn that made her gasp and struggle fruitlessly, for Collins's hand was heavy on her back and Bryant was holding her thighs straight so that she could not kick or move away.

'Ohhhhh,' she moaned, as the widest part of the plug arrived triumphantly at her door, stretching her almost beyond endurance. 'No!'

Collins held it there, the sadist in him profoundly satisfied, for a full minute, before shoving the remainder up inside her and patting the wide flange that secured it in her bottom.

'How does that feel, Mrs Masterton?' he asked, idly twiddling the base of the plug to create a riot of pleasure-pain sensation inside his hapless client. 'A bit difficult to be rebellious when your bottom is packed full of your master's plug, isn't it? Have a good long think about that while you're in the corner.' He gave her one last hard spank for luck, the vibrations of it causing the plug to jiggle inside her. 'Off you go. Hands on head and spine straight, please, or there will be consequences.'

The two men spent a pleasurable few minutes of silence in contemplation of their colleague, waddling gracelessly across the room and then coming to rest, scarlet-bottomed and plugged in the corner, her long hair cascading down to the middle of her back, her arms arched pleasingly either side of her head.

'That's one of the finest bottoms in London,' commented Collins at last. 'You're a lucky man. Or, at least, you will be, once you can get her to behave herself.'

Charlotte, cornered and feeling as meekly submissive as she ever did, listened at first to their conversation, which revolved around plugs and whips and chastity devices; gags and clamps and heated lubricants. At least they had only used plain lube today, she thought gratefully, hearing Collins extol the delights of a lubricant made with chilli oil. On the other hand, this plug was so large and solid that one could never ever forget that it was lodged there, stretching and making her passage smart.

The degrading plugging, combined with her still-throbbing bum, and the way the men were casually discussing plans for her further humiliating use made Charlotte achingly aware of her wet, hot pussy and the juices leaking down her thighs. She would give anything to be allowed to sneak a hand down between her legs just now, oh, anything at all. She tried hard to maintain her posture, but she could not help a little snaky wriggle of her hips, squeezing her cheeks together to hug the plug even tighter and try to rub her lower lips against something, anything, just the merest touch of friction would probably make her come then and there in the corner.

The only thing for it was to try and take her mind off it, she realised. Concentrate, Charlotte! Think of something mundane, or unpleasant. Oh! A flash of the

143

earlier scene returned to her, making her feel deeply uncomfortable. The suggestion that Collins might be married had given her a real jolt, and she was still not quite sure why. Well, for one thing, she thought virtuously, she would not want to wreck some poor woman's marriage. If someone was lucky enough to be married to Collins, presumably she would want to stay that way and not worry about him fooling around with submissive little sluts like her. Or perhaps she had no interest in BDSM, knew all about his work-related activities and fully condoned them. Perhaps she had lovers of her own. Perhaps they were polyamorists. Perhaps she was a dominatrix! Perhaps she would like to join in the games ... Oh dear. Charlotte's attempts to douse the flames in her lower regions were simply making her even more excited.

Now look here, Charlotte, she enjoined herself sternly. *If Collins is married, it's none of your business. You have no claim on him. This is work, pure and simple.* But was it? Could she continue to work for these men without wanting more from them than wild kinky sex? And if she couldn't ... what then?

'... Have you ever tried tying her to the bed and bringing her to the brink of orgasm, then denying it, repeatedly?'

Collins's voice cut through the angst and Charlotte returned to the reality of her fantasy situation. Her arms were beginning to ache, so she must have been standing there for a good while. Her bottom was sorer than ever and she longed to expel the plug, which was sending waves of pain through her pelvic area now, though her pussy was even wetter than before.

'No, but I'd like to try it,' said Bryant. 'Her sex drive is high, but she seems to delight in locking me out of the bedroom and bringing herself off, noisily. I think she does it to make me angry.'

'Passive-aggressive,' said Collins sagely. 'Well, we can deal with that. I think she's served her corner time now. Mrs Masterton, please come back here now, and we'll deal with your defiance and disobedience.'

Charlotte both welcomed and feared her release from the corner. She knew she would be made to take more punishment, but after that, she was optimistic that she would be used hard for rough, assertive sexual release by both of her bosses. Her legs were stiff and her progress back to Collins's desk correspondingly slow. The plug was enormous inside her now and her legs seemed made of her juices, the skin of her thighs cold and glossy.

'I'm going to use a paddle next,' said Collins to Bryant, and Charlotte groaned inwardly. The one thing she hated on her bottom above all others was wood. She would have to give in fairly swiftly – but she supposed this was all part of Collins's plan. He must be impatient to move on to another activity. Well, that was fine with her!

She allowed Bryant to push her down until she was bent over a low footstool covered in rubberised coating. Presumably it must have some medical function, but she could not imagine what.

She waited, eyes screwed shut, for the removal of the plug – always somehow worse than its insertion – but it did not happen.

Instead, oval-shaped pats on her rear introduced her to the knowledge that she was about to be given a hard paddling with the butt plug still inside her.

'This will hurt, Mrs Masterton,' said Collins softly. 'But it's a necessary pain. Cruel to be kind. You must let me know when you've had enough by using the words "I surrender." I shall stop immediately as soon as I hear them. But you do understand that, once spoken, those words cannot be taken back, and you will signal your willingness to serve and submit to your husband. Now then. Let us begin.'

The first stroke was fierce and Charlotte wailed aloud, feeling aftershock pains tremble through the inside as well as the outside of her bottom as the plug was driven deeper. Only a few of these could be taken before she gave in.

She made it to eight, by a combination of gripping, lip-biting, foot-lifting and hip-wriggling, but her bottom was so hot it was almost cold, so sore it was almost numb.

'She's a stubborn little madam,' said Collins, rather fondly. 'But I'll break her.'

Charlotte heard the rustle of his shirtsleeve as he drew his arm back once more.

'I surrender,' she gabbled.

Bryant clapped, while Collins gave her burning cheeks a comprehensive feel with both hands.

'You have made a wise decision,' he said. 'You won't be sitting comfortably for a while all the same. Poor Mrs Masterton.' One finger hooked itself beneath the plug flange and yanked it out in a swift, unutterably painful move. Although its absence was a relief, Charlotte could feel her muscle flaring and contracting, confused by the sudden extraction.

'Your punishment is over,' said Collins soothingly. 'But we must still address another matter.' He pulled apart her bottom cheeks, inspecting the gaping hole between them, then took hold of her arms at the elbows and helped her to stand. 'Look at your husband. Look him in the eye.'

Charlotte, always in a small, tight space of beautiful submission after being dealt with by Collins, found it difficult and shaming to make eye contact. But she managed to lift her gaze to meet Bryant's kind blue eyes and held them, blushing furiously all over while Collins removed her skirt for good.

'Do you find him attractive?'

'Yes,' she said, her voice husky, throat uncleared. 'Yes, I do.'

'Is he a good husband to you?'

'Yes, he is. He is never angry or mean or rude or sulky.'

'So he is a good man; the man for you?'

'I … think so.' Bryant looked as if he was accepting her words at face value. He looked somehow *moved*, as if he had forgotten that this was all part of a scene.

'I see. But something troubles me, Mrs Masterton. Your husband has told me that you are in the practice of withholding sex from him. Why do you do that, when you are so obviously a wanton little slut?'

Charlotte gasped. Collins's hand had made a lightning strike between her legs and he was fingering her soaked pussy with ruthless efficiency.

'I'm … not …' she said faintly.

'How can you deny it? You're extremely wet down here, yet all I've done is punish you. If you can be aroused by something as unpleasurable as a strange man's hand spanking your bottom, then how can you claim not to want a good fucking?'

'I …'

'You do, don't you, Mrs Masterton? You want a good fucking. You don't even care who you get it from. Could be me. Could be him. Could be both of us. Could be some passer-by off the street. Couldn't it?'

He homed in on her clit and she was beyond all resistance, leaning back against him, gyrating slowly on his fingertips, needing the release so badly, so very, very badly.

'Mmmm,' was her distant response.

Collins whipped his hand away, shoving the fingers with their sex-drenched aroma between her lips so she licked the evidence of her from them.

'I need to examine you,' he said curtly. 'Make sure you have … normal … physiological responses to sexual stimuli. From what I'm seeing now, you are abnormally hypersexual. I may want to study you at length, if your husband is amenable. Remove all clothing, please.'

Charlotte was left to take off her blouse and bra while Collins opened the door to a small anteroom and wheeled out a medical examination bed, upholstered in black leather with adjustable sections and restraints attached to the sides.

'Lie down on this, please,' ordered Collins. Bryant gallantly stepped forward to help her up, lovingly strapping her wrists above her head and her ankles high up in a set of stirrups while Collins fiddled with the settings until she was half-sitting, half-lying, thighs wide and high, almost straining, everything on full show for the doctor and his client.

Collins, frowning, pulled the stirrups higher until Charlotte's aching bottom was half-off the leather, cheeks parted and vulnerable to further rough manipulation.

'Good,' he approved, one finger pressed contemplatively to his chin. 'This little slut can't hide a thing now, can she? Do you mind awfully if I call her a slut, by the way?'

'Be my guest. It's what she is,' said Bryant, beaming

148

gently at his 'wife'.

'Now, I would like you to kiss her. Go on. With tongues, if you wish.'

Bryant hesitated for a moment, then stood by Charlotte's head, twisted down and put his lips to hers, engaging her in a long, slow, sensual French kiss.

Charlotte, taking his tongue inside her mouth and shutting her eyes in helpless pleasure, almost bit down in shock when she felt a cold invasive pressure around her clit, then inside her vagina. What was that?

'No need to tense up, Mrs Masterton,' she heard Collins say. 'It's just my finger. I've put on some surgical gloves for this exercise. You are well lubricated, by the way. You enjoy being kissed and tongued, hard and deeply, don't you? You needn't answer. I know it's rude to speak with your mouth full.'

Charlotte's mouth was indeed very full, and she was perfectly happy for it to be so but, to her regret, the order came for the kissing to stop, and Bryant's tongue was retracted with a sigh.

'Fondle her breasts, Mr Masterton.'

Bryant obeyed with a will, rolling nipples between finger and thumb before applying the tip of his tongue and squeezing the soft flesh that surrounded the hard nubs. Once more, Charlotte felt Collins's fingers, swirling and pinching her intimate lower areas.

'I am going to take your temperature,' he informed her, inserting a slim glass rectal thermometer, to Charlotte's considerable shock and shame. He held the thermometer in firmly, continuing his digital manipulations of her pussy all the while, before withdrawing it and taking a reading.

'Temperature – elevated,' was the verdict. 'You are hot, Mrs Masterton. Extremely so. Well, Mr Masterton, I

149

doubt she will refuse you now. All the same, I have one final test for her. I need to time the period from first sexual contact to orgasm – first I need to lower her arousal levels a little. Could you hand me those wipes?'

Charlotte shivered as the antibacterial wipes were applied to her nether regions, sopping up the gush. Somehow she couldn't help feeling that Collins was setting himself too tall an order, though, if he expected her to calm down now. She was right on the edge of that heightened consciousness he often brought her to; tense with need, unable to come down until one or other of her skilled employers arranged her release.

'Hmm, well, her nipples are still erect, but perhaps we could attribute that to cold,' mused Collins. 'Here, Masterton.' He handed Bryant a sleek metallic vibrator. 'Which of her orifices will you commandeer?'

'Oh, I think I'll work on her cunt,' he said. 'This vibrator has a clitoral stimulator, does it? I'm not sure we'll get an accurate reading without one.'

'Oh, yes, I do beg your pardon.' Collins replaced the no-frills vibrator with a more complicated version, complete with clitoral attachment. 'I shall use this one in her more private passage. If I might venture a personal disclosure, I'm more of an arse man myself anyway.'

'Please be my guest,' said Bryant formally. 'Now, do you want me to stand at the right or left side of her?'

'Oh, you take the right, I think.'

So it was that Charlotte was brought to a state of full submission, by way of intense, double-plugged, overstimulating, tear-streaked and red-faced orgasm. She was made to watch as Collins and Bryant, still impeccably suited and booted, stood at either side of her hips, lazily swivelling and thrusting inside her with their humming tools, waiting for her to reach a panicked fever

150

pitch, then smiling and clucking encouragingly as she tipped over her edge, flailing and desperate, into a black hole of deepest, most heartfelt surrender.

'Goodness,' remarked Collins, checking his stopwatch. 'Only three minutes from start to finish. I think your wife needs taking firmly and frequently, Mr Masterton, if you want her to stop masturbating all the time. She seems quite unable to control her sexual urges. You need to take them into your control. If you cannot fuck her as often as she needs, perhaps we can come to some kind of clinical arrangement …'

'What an excellent idea. Shall we say, home visits, three times weekly?'

'I would be delighted to assist.'

Later, after several more orgasms on everybody's part, the trio found tea-making facilities in one of the rooms along the corridor, and they sat together in the office, drinking and recovering their collective breath.

'That examination couch is really rather remarkable,' said Collins, caressing the stirrups. 'I would like one myself. I wonder who makes them?'

Bryant shrugged, smiling as Collins stood and wheeled the bed back into its allotted space next door.

Charlotte took advantage of the absence, leaning towards Bryant to whisper, 'Is he really married?'

Bryant raised an eyebrow. 'Why would you ask me that?'

'He said … his wife liked Agent Provocateur underwear. Is that true?'

'Charlotte, I have no idea what anybody's wife likes to wear under her skirts. Well, maybe *some* people's wives,' he amended.

'Yours?' Charlotte was struck again. 'Are you

married?'

'No, Charlotte, I am not.'

His face, so amused and playful seconds earlier, suddenly darkened, eyes seriously intent.

'Lady Markham would have enjoyed that,' she said, changing the subject awkwardly on Collins's return.

'She most certainly would. And she will.'

'Will you be the doctor for her?'

'Oh no,' said Collins, seemingly appalled. 'I don't mix business with pleasure!'

Charlotte laughed, stunned. 'Um ... what was that then? Just now? I mean, I thought it was research, so business, no?'

Collins looked vaguely annoyed for a second or two, as if caught out.

'You're special, Charlotte,' he said. 'We knew that from your very first email.'

She knew she was glowing; she felt golden and she could not stop smiling at Collins, until she heard Bryant cough and replace his teacup with a clatter.

'It's late,' he said brusquely. 'We'd better wash these up and go. Dr Mahmood wanted everything left the way we found it.'

But all the way back in the cab, her bruised bottom bumping over the potholes and her orifices raw with overuse, she heard those words – 'You're special, Charlotte' – and the lights of the lonely London early morning seemed like magic lanterns.

Lady Muck

I RARELY SEE THE women whose houses I clean; for the most part, they leave early, come home late, and leave me a wad of banknotes on the granite, or Corian, or quartz kitchen counter at the end of the week. I do, of course, know what they look like, from our initial hiring meeting, and from the large glossy portraits of them, in wedding dresses, or graduation robes, or accepting awards at some industry dinner or other, all over the walls and mantelpieces. Their personalities sometimes come through in the messages they leave me.

Mrs Redvers, a sleek brunette corporate lawyer, often complains that the refrigerator shelves are left in a mess, and I have explained over and over again that this is because young Jonquil and Reuben run rings around the nanny and are constantly raiding for illicit snacks. Her notes are terse; she is time-poor, as they say, and the subsequent need for economy seems to be carried over into her manners.

Ms Livesay is a television producer, a slightly manic-looking blonde. Although she is nearly thirty, she still lives like a student, and of all my houses, hers is the most labour-intensive. Bottles and cigarette butts in the sink, clothes flung everywhere, a leaning tower of magazines and CDs piled high on the coffee table. She is thoughtless, but usually quite effusive in her notes.

'Thanks, darling, you are a lifesaver,' she will sometimes scribble, with an extra fiver on top of the wage if the toilet was pebble-dashed with vomit or there was a particularly heinous stain on the sofa.

My final lady is a Lady. Lady Markham's London pied-à-terre is only occupied when the House of Lords is sitting. I must admit I used to have a crush on her, when I started cleaning for her. She is a stunning woman in her forties, with a look of Honor Blackman in her 1960s heyday, and the accent to match. She is, I suppose, quite patronising, but she patronises me so graciously and with such charm that I fall for it every time. She is habitually tidy, which makes the job easy, and she has beautiful, elegant taste, so that spending time among her knick-knacks is a pleasure. I do wonder about the little room – a walk-in closet really, I think – tucked to the side of her bedroom that is always locked and strictly off-limits, but it pleases me to think of Lady Markham having her secrets, just like I do.

I clean these houses in St Johns Wood every day, then I go home to my own tiny flat on a rough estate – just a stone's throw from their mansions – and clean up all my mother's clutter before cooking her supper. It isn't the life I dreamed of when we came here, but it is a life, of sorts.

Well, it *was*, until that awful Thursday at Mrs Redvers's house. It was a school holiday, so Jonquil and Reuben were underfoot all day, pretending to blast me with their space guns while I vacuumed. A tiny plastic alien I had not seen when picking up the toys earlier was sucked up into the tube and Reuben began to shriek and wave his arms like an alarmed octopus.

'What is wrong, Reuben?' I asked, clicking off the drone of the hoover.

'You've just hoovered up Floople, you bitch!' he shouted.

I might not be a rich or well-respected woman, but I was not taking this from an eight-year-old.

'How dare you use that disgusting language to me! I will tell your mother!'

'She won't care! She thinks you're a stupid foreign bitch as well!'

'It's true,' drawled ten-year-old Jonquil from the doorway. 'She'll freak if she hears that you've been telling us off. Who the hell do you think you are? The hired hand is all you are.'

'Yes,' I hissed at her, 'I am just a cleaner. But I used to be a lawyer, just like your mother. Would you like somebody to speak to your mother like that?'

Jonquil's reply came in a V-shape. Reuben, effing and blinding hysterically, was trying to dismantle the vacuum cleaner, sending a cloud of dust billowing into the room. I reached out for the tube.

'Mummy, mummy!' I heard Jonquil screaming, 'she's gone mental, she's trying to hit us!'

Mrs Redvers walked in to the room to find me wrenching the vacuum cleaner from a howling Reuben while particles of refined St Johns Wood dust darkened the air like storm clouds.

'Sack her! She's killed Floople!'

'What on Earth is going on? Why are the children so upset? I think you'd better give me an explanation, Krysztyna!'

I stood up, coughing, and looked Mrs Redvers in her icy eye.

'Your children have insulted and sworn at me, Mrs Redvers. I think they had better give me an apology.'

'My children … they do not swear! Oh, you must be

155

lying! I think you had better get out before I say or do something I regret!'

So I got out. I walked the three streets to Ms Livesay's chaotic terrace and let myself in. There was a terrible smell in there, bad enough to turn my stomach. I couldn't face it; not just then. I doubled back to Lady Markham's mansion block, found her beautifully comfortable sofa, sat down in it and cried until I thought my heart had broken.

'I say, Krysztyna, whatever's up?'

Lady Markham was up, standing in the hall with an aghast look on her face. I leapt off the hand-embroidered cushions.

'Oh, Lady Markham, I am so sorry! Please do not be angry – I have had some bad news, is all. I will start cleaning now.'

'Dear girl, please sit down! I'm not an ogre, you know. You look as if you could use a brandy – let me pour you one.'

I remonstrated, but she was insistent, and the mellowest, fruitiest, fieriest brandy I had ever tasted burned a sweet path to my stomach, calming my angst and bringing the old Krysztyna back to the surface; the girl who had laughed and loved, not the woman who mopped and scrubbed.

'What do you do for fun, dear girl?' asked Lady Markham, once she had extracted my full confession about the horror at Mrs Redvers's. 'You seem to work terribly hard. When do you play?'

'Never,' I said with a bitter little laugh.

'You have no lovers? You are an attractive woman, you know.'

I looked away, blushing, wanting to tell her, feeling she would understand ... but what if she didn't?

'No,' I said simply.

'Darling, there are so many men in London who would simply adore a gorgeous thing like you on their arms. I can think of at least twenty offhand. Most of them are terrible old roués, mind you.' She chuckled and rubbed my arm. I drew a deep breath. I took the plunge.

'Men … I'm not so interested in …'

She sat back a little, regarding my face with a look of amused surprise.

'Oh, Krysztyna! I should have guessed! I'm usually so good at guessing that kind of thing!'

'Are you shocked?'

'Good Lord, girl, no, why would I be shocked? I'm just shocked that you haven't taken yourself out to one of the very many lovely gay bars and clubs in this City and scored yourself a nice young lady.'

'I live with my mother. She is not well, and she is a very devout Catholic. I have never told her, and I never will.'

'I see.' Lady Markham sat, pursing her lips, intent in thought for some time. I did not like to break the silence, and there did not seem to be much I could say, anyway.

'Listen, Krysztyna. I'd like to give you a gift. I think you deserve this gift, and I think you would know how to use it. If you do not wish to, then that is your prerogative, but I rather hope you will.'

'I would never ask for anything …'

'Hush, hush, dear, I know you wouldn't. That's rather why I'm giving it. But it must remain strictly – and I mean strictly – *entre nous*. You must never breathe a word to anyone. Can you promise me that?'

'I can keep secrets.' I was too intrigued to deny her this mysterious offer she was making. Even if it turned out to be something I could not use, I wanted to know what it was. Was she going to let me into her private room?

In the event, she did not. But she let me into another secret; a wonderful and decadent secret. A secret I intend to keep for the rest of my life.

Thus it was that I found myself looking through portfolio photographs with a friendly young woman in a top-floor office.

'How many pleasure slaves did you have in mind?' asked the woman, whose name was Charlotte.

I remembered Lady Markham's words: *I insist that you spare no expense. If the bill runs into millions, I shall still cover it.*

'I would like perhaps half a dozen. And all female, as I mentioned in my email.'

'That shouldn't be any problem at all. Do any of these appeal to you?'

I shuffled the photographs, searching for the types I wanted.

'This one,' I said. She was tall, angular, well-groomed, with sleek chestnut hair and cruel eyes. She looked just like Mrs Redvers.

'OK.' Charlotte ticked a box on her computer screen.

'Oh! Yes! Her!' A cheery-looking girl with blonde dreadlocks and a nose ring who could have been Ms Livesay's sister beamed out of a photograph, begging me to choose her.

'As for the rest ... well ...' Now I was free to just pick the girls I fancied, and I did so with alacrity, imagining them oiled and ready for me, pouring my wine and licking the stray drops from my lips. This might be my one and only chance to achieve sexual nirvana, and I was going to seize it with both hands.

What does the mistress of a fleet of pleasure slaves

wear?

This had been my quandary all day, and as the evening approached – The Evening of Evenings – I was still undecided. I knew what my slaves were wearing. The Mrs Redvers lookalike would be sporting an abbreviated French maid's outfit, cut low at the bust and high at the derrière, together with uncomfortably high heels, padlocked on at the ankle. Ms Livesay Mark 2 would be in nipple tassles, a diamanté thong and very little else. She was my toy for the evening. The other four girls would be dressed in various underwear combinations, chosen from the agency's exclusive catalogue. Lovely, silky, scanty things – tiny panties and severe corsets; teddies and camisoles and boned suspender belts, all frothy with lace and sheeny with satin. The anticipation of all that prettiness and sexiness at my command was making me feel giddy.

I was at the door of the hired town house in a smart London Square before I made my final wardrobe decision, and when I ventured out of the dressing room and down towards the banqueting hall where my minions awaited me, I was draped in a diaphanous sequinned gown that loosely covered my curves, but left every place of interest comfortably accessible. My shoes were high and clacked unforgivingly on the wooden floors, and I felt like a Queen, like Nefertiti or Cleopatra, high on the charge of my sexual power.

The double doors to the banqueting hall were flanked by two of the pretty girls in underwear. Each one dropped a deep curtsey and I gave them my arms, escorting them inside. The table was laid in magnificent style – I had worked a few shifts as a silver service waitress in my time, and I knew a good table setting when I saw one. This one seemed to shimmer, its opulence almost beyond the bounds of good taste, yet working well in the lavish surroundings. Another barely-dressed nymphet pulled out my chair – a kind of throne – for me, and waited until I was seated. The four underwear girls, who were to be my waitresses and general handmaidens, ranged themselves around me, dropping to their knees and demurely hanging their heads.

At one end of the room, on her hands and knees, panting and puffing as she applied wax to the floor, was Mrs Redvers. The stiff nets under her tiny black skirt rose over her pale bottom as she worked, exposing it rudely with its strip of black latex thong between the cheeks. She looked completely humiliated and a little hot and bothered. I sat back, enjoying the sight, before noticing that the banquet centrepiece in front of me, with its elaborate abundance of flowers and fruit, was actually Ms Livesay, lying flat on her back, breasts and belly overspilling black grapes and posies while a solid silver candelabra was lodged between her thighs. Like her real-life counterpart, she was a bit of a mess, and would doubtless be even more so before the evening was out.

'How charming,' I breathed, unconsciously imitating Lady Markham's voice and accent. I reached out to touch Livesay's thigh, around which was wrapped some twine with little buds of flowers attached. The candelabra blocked my immediate view of her pussy, but that would not stay the case for too long. Livesay twitched, very slightly, but was not able to speak, because she had a peach lodged in her mouth. 'You do look edible, Livesay,' I murmured to her. 'I shall certainly be enjoying you later.'

Beyond the end of the table, Redvers was still polishing effortlessly, her tight backside wriggling in a fury of industry.

'Redvers! Stop that and come here.'

It was not easy for her to rise gracefully in those sky-high heels, but she did her womanly best, tottering over to the table with a blank, sulky look.

'You can take that sullen look off your face,' I told her. 'Come here and wipe the table in front of me.' I pushed my chair back so that she could bend right over and apply that duster with the maximum of elbow grease. Her pretty arse was within my reach as she huffed and toiled. I reached out and touched it, cupped it, rubbed a thumb over its softness. She did not miss a beat, polishing on, swaying on those ridiculous heels.

'Do you know what, Redvers?' I said, stroking the back of her thigh, right down to the hold-up stocking top. 'Later on, you are going to polish me. I am going to work you so hard … I won't let you stop work until you have cleaned me right out.'

Redvers said nothing but 'Yes, ma'am,' and continued her buffing until the wood shone, at which point she turned around and curtsied, so beautifully. I had never seen a sexy curtsey before, but this girl had the knack.

'Keep those knees on the floor and that lovely bum in the air, Redvers,' I instructed, pointing to the floor immediately to my right. 'Carry on cleaning until I have finished eating. I expect perfection, or I might have to spoil that gorgeous arse of yours with a spanking, do you understand?'

'Yes, ma'am,' said Redvers, slightly throatily. Oh good. This was making her horny as well.

I turned my attention to the feast at the table, clicking my fingers so that two of my oiled beauties hurried either side of me.

'You! Pour me some wine. You! Feed me some of these lovely foods.'

Beauty #1 put the crystal glass to my lips, alternating with Beauty #2, who fed me scallops, morsels of sweet flaky pastry, Parma ham, grapes, cubes of French cheese, in loving succession.

'This is delicious, but I need some entertainment as well. You two!' I clicked my fingers again, and the remaining two girls flitted up to the table. 'I would like to watch you make out. You know what I mean? Kiss, touch each other, perhaps, if you have time, bring each other off. Can you do that.'

They nodded eagerly and I smiled to see their curves meld and their shining skins slide together as they kissed, sweetly at first, then more deeply, more passionately, the tongues colliding, the dainty hands grabbing and pawing while I ate and drank my fill.

Livesay's sumptuously ample body was losing its coverage as Beauty #2 continued to ransack it for my meal; here and there a clutch of grapes disappeared to reveal a swell of breast, or the prawn ring around her navel developed gaps, showcasing her white, soft belly. I was beginning to want to lick it. But I waited a little longer, enjoyed the feeding fingers and solicitous lips of my handmaidens, who were now transferring the wine to my mouth from theirs, and swapping slivers of meat from between their pearly teeth. We began to kiss each other as we fed, tasting the lips and tongues as well as the salty-sweet food combinations, all three of us dropping scented kisses on to faces and collarbones and earlobes, breathing each other in and sighing as we satisfied our senses. My hands – the only ones permitted to wander – found their dewy pussies and investigated them as we disported ourselves. I lay back in my throne, allowing one girl on to my lap while the other stretched herself backwards over my belly from the arm of the chair, and all the bounty of female flesh was at my disposal, the whole world of woman lay before me.

'Have you had enough to eat and drink, ma'am?' one of them whispered, and I snapped back into consciousness, looking over their heads at my Entertainers, who were now writhing and twisting on each other's fingers, biting and sucking each other's necks, butting up against each other with aggressive arousal, almost at the point of release.

'No,' I whispered. 'I don't think I have. Stand aside.'

The Handmaidens fell to their knees on either side of the throne, and I stood – a little shakily – to inspect the state of my pretty, ravaged centrepiece. She looked a poor display now, all sticky and patchy with juices, her edible veil half-wrenched away from that lavish body, but I preferred her like this. The candle would have to go though, and I removed it, seeing the part of her that had been concealed for the first time, in a split-crotch diamante thong. Her legs were parted and her little red clit peeked out between the paste jewels like one of the berries that topped her nipples, ready to be anointed with cream and then licked and eaten until the remnants stained my face. Oh yes, that would have to be done. But first …

I was dimly aware of the Entertainers wrestling on the floor, grunting and panting and bucking like rodeo horses, but I had lost interest in them, and just wanted a bite of my Livesay, my living banquet. I climbed on to the table and positioned myself between her thighs, bending over to take the remaining fruit into my mouth, licking each bared portion of flesh, sweeping it with my tongue, before chewing and swallowing the food. I sucked up the raspberries from each pert nipple, slowly, nipping with teeth, until they were licked into paste and she was moaning quietly, as if begging me to stop, or carry on. Then I moved down her body, munching a narrow trail around her belly button, licking the smoked salmon mousse from her shaved mons before arriving at the crowning delicacy – her unseasoned, unsauced, perfectly fresh pussy.

'Hmmm,' I pondered. 'As it comes? Or with cream?'

'Ma'am?' Beauty #2, tremulous and eager to please, handed me the vacuum can of squirty cream, making the decision for me. I depressed the button and sprayed the stuff generously between the split of her lips until she was covered and smothered in frilly white, ready to be licked clean.

I swooped into action, scooping up the melting substance with my tongue, careless of how much of it covered my chin and cheeks, hunting down that hidden clit like a pig hunting a truffle. I curled into every crevice, lapping and licking, exhaustive and ravenous, until she was clean and her sweet, fat jewel cried out to me for attention. I gave it; I sucked that little morsel until she began to cry out. Then I took the aerosol and repeated the process all over again.

'Messy, messy girl,' I crooned, when, after the fourth version of this procedure, I finally allowed her to come. 'Always such a mess, Livesay.'

I sat back on my heels, looking at her, all purple and orange with fruit stains; the leftover foodstuffs jumbling across her skin.

'Girls,' I said to the four lissom beauties, who had been watching the performance raptly. 'Dinner time.'

It was a wonderful sight; the four sheeny-skinned nymphs devouring what was left of the banquet from

Livesay's flesh; Livesay, tossing and squealing as if being tickled to death. They plunged their mouths into her pussy and over her breasts, squeezing and suckling until their pretty faces were smeared with the evidence of their depravity.

I caught Redvers in a longing over-the-shoulder look and pushed her bottom with my foot, forcing her back to the scrubbing.

'You don't get treats, Redvers, you nasty little slut. That's not what you're here for. But actually, while the others are busy, perhaps I can find another use for you. Why don't you kneel down here and show me how good you are with your tongue. Not talking – I don't want to hear you talk. You know what I mean?'

Slightly abashed, she nodded, but she was so relieved to be taken off floor-scrubbing duty that she scrambled between my knees without further bidding, lifting up my gown – underneath which I was naked – and bringing that smooth, lovely face up between my thighs, which she kissed shyly as a rather charming and submissive preamble.

'I like that,' I approved. 'A little initiative can be a good thing.' Redvers – the real Redvers – had said those very words to me on occasion, the condescending bitch. I patted false-Redvers's head and shifted my thighs, the better to accommodate her darting tongue. I leaned back, watching Livesay yield to the eight fluttering hands and four greedy mouths of the Beauties, while Redvers attended to my pussy with such finesse and sensitivity that I had to think she must be a professional.

My words, when they came, brokenly but forcefully, were in Polish, while my spendings flowed into Redvers's grateful face. She bobbed back and looked up at me, a little fearfully, as if she was worried that I might be cursing her in my mother tongue.

'No, Redvers,' I panted, pitying her for that brief moment. 'That was good. Thank you.'

Livesay was now stripped of all edible matter, her body gleaming with the combined saliva of the diners; that well-licked clit all swollen and stiff between the sparkly strands of the split-crotch thong.

'Let's take a little break,' I suggested, drowsy after the good food and better orgasm. 'Some of you girls can dance? I did order some music, I think.'

As if by magic, from a gallery to the side of the room, a string quartet struck up some gracious music from times past – waltzes and foxtrots – while the four Beauties coupled up and took to the floor. Livesay lay on the table, almost asleep, while Redvers was permitted to bend over and watch the display while I fondled her magnificent backside, making plans for it which grew wilder and lewder as the dances mutated from respectable ballroom to lascivious tangos and lambadas, the girls pressing closer, spinning and wheeling each other around the room in poses that stopped only micromillimetres short of sexual penetration.

'Redvers,' I whispered eventually, my senses reignited by the behaviour of the girls on the dance floor. They seemed to have turned the dancing into some kind of Roman orgy, and were kissing and caressing in a big scrum at the centre of the floor, all arms and legs and tiny scraps of lacy silk. 'Fetch me my whip and my strap-on.'

With careful consideration of her padlocked ankles, Redvers rose to her feet and went to a cherrywood chest in the corner of the room, withdrawing from it a martinet whip and a large dildo attached to a leather harness. Eyes downcast, she bore them to me, not even glancing sideways at the gasping ball of womanhood that rolled around the centre of the floor.

'You, Redvers, need to be punished,' I told her, my eyes narrowed, head full of a flashback to that awful Thursday morning at the Redvers abode.

'I know, ma'am,' she said meekly.

'Bend over the end of the table.'

I snapped my fingers at the bawdy quartet, and at the recumbent and half-asleep Livesay, all of whom awoke from their stupors of lust and sloth to focus on me once more.

'More play to come later,' I promised. 'But first we must all take turns to punish Redvers here. She has been a very, very bad and nasty girl, and I want you all to give her ten good lashes with the whip. It isn't a very terrible whip – you won't damage her. But you can lay it on as hard as you like. I want that bottom bright red by the time we've finished with her. Livesay, you may start.'

Livesay, her nipple pastes sparkling, clambered from the centre of the table and took the whip in her hand, frowning at it as if unfamiliar with its design – which she possibly was. All the same, she took her station at Redvers's rear and began to flip it through the air, laughing with exhilaration as each thin strip of tail caught the unfortunate maid's bum, flecking it with pink. The Beauties, sniggering and nudging one another, queued up for their turns behind Livesay, who had an unexpectedly powerful arm and was opening the batting very creditably, causing Redvers's breath to hitch and her fists to curl and uncurl.

It was lovely to watch, and as each girl wielded the whip hand, the beautiful slut-maid twisted and turned, growing increasingly uncomfortable, but knowing that she had no other option than to keep that pert bottom thrust out for more stinging kisses, until my pleasure was satisfied.

Once all five girls had had their chance of whipping poor Redvers, I stepped up, first taking a little time to feel the heat and tenderness of that abused flesh.

'How sore that must be,' I said soothingly. 'Is it very sore, Redvers?'

'Yes, ma'am.'

'Good. And it's about to be sorer.'

I did not stop at ten strokes. I kept on until I had lashed the need out of me. Redvers was a good submissive – perhaps a true masochist – and although she wailed and begged, she did not use the safeword, but let me have my way until her arse was red and hot as flame, tight and swollen to the touch.

'Good girl, Redvers,' I finally managed to breathe, exultant and almost giddy with the power of my emotion and my lust for her. 'You have done well. Livesay, hand me the strap-on.'

I donned it with fleet fingers, wanting to plunge into her, to violate her in every way, and I wasted no time in penetrating her to the hilt while she thanked me, over and over, in her breathy, hoarse voice. I gave her first a few hard thrusts, then I unbuckled myself and passed it over to the next girl.

'You may all fuck her with this,' I told them. 'When you have given her as much as you can, come to me.'

I took the candlesticks from the candelabra while Livesay bucked and surged into Redvers's juicy pussy.

'Come on, Livesay,' I ordered her, lying myself down on the table on my stomach, so that I faced the bug-eyed, puffing Redvers and could watch her expression as she was fucked with the strap-on. 'Come between my legs and do your worst with one of those candles. If you can eat my pussy at the same time, I'll give you a five-star recommendation on my customer feedback form.'

She did it too. I had to get up on my knees and bend forward, but she slid her artful little face down underneath me and clit-licked for England, while the candlestick sawed lazily back and forth in my pussy. Beauty #1 abandoned the strap-on and passed it to Beauty #2, leaving a vacancy. 'Come and fuck Livesay with a candle,' I invited, and so we went on, until five of us were arranged in a long line, all frantically fucking with candles apart from me, who enjoyed the receipt but not the gift, and was too busy making sure Redvers knew she was being watched in her humiliating position to bother with anything else anyway.

Redvers, exhausted and shagged to mush, her face as red as her arse, begged for mercy as Beauty #4 began to lose steadiness and grind to a final halt.

I had come three times myself, and could no longer support myself on my elbows, so I asked Livesay to put away her tired tongue and retract the candle, while we all took a long deep breath.

'How about a bath?' I finally suggested, once my brain was engaged once more. 'All of us together? There is a wonderful, huge hot tub in the next room.'

The girls, some still sprightly, some barely able to walk, followed me into the adjacent chamber and disrobed, joining me one by one in the fragrant milky waters, sinking with sighs into the bubbles.

I poured us all a glass of champagne and sat back for a speech.

'I would like to thank all of you for taking part in this. I have showed you a side of myself that rarely comes out – a side I am maybe not so proud of, but which needs its release now and then. Thank you for helping me to

169

achieve this.'

The girls all simpered responses of the 'it's a pleasure' variety.

'Really?' I asked, turning to Redvers. 'It was a pleasure? Even for you?'

'I work in a BDSM dungeon club,' she said, smiling, and her face looked calm and beautiful now. 'I wouldn't do it if I didn't like it. You would make a fantastic pro-Domme. Have you ever considered that line of work?'

'I don't want to whip men's hairy bums,' I declared, to general giggles and raisings of glasses. 'Not for a million pounds.'

'That's fair enough,' she conceded. 'I bet you could get a few private clients though. Lady clients. Wealthy lady clients.'

The way she put the emphasis on the word 'lady', coupled with the significant look, made me stop and think. She was trying to tell me something. What was she trying to tell me?

I did not know how to ask, so, once we were soaped and shampooed and towelled and perfumed and had done a little bit more kissing and light caressing, we parted company, well satisfied with our evening of debauchery.

At Lady Markham's apartment a few days later, she interrupted me in my vacuuming and invited me to sit down and take a drink with her.

'I hear a wonderful time was had by all on Saturday night,' she remarked, smiling from ear to ear, as she handed me a tumbler of gin and tonic.

'I can only thank you once more,' I said. In truth, it all seemed like a distant dream now. I had gone back to work as normal on Monday morning – not to the Redvers's, but to another similar family put my way by the agency. Bills needed paying, mother had a bad back, I was a single frustrated Polish lesbian not getting any younger.

'You deserved a wonderful escape from your routine, dear,' observed Lady Markham. 'I'm so pleased it was enjoyable. Penny tells me she was terribly impressed with you.'

I looked up sharply. Lady Markham knew one of my pleasure slaves?

'Oh, don't look so stunned,' she laughed. 'I'm rather closely connected with the whole operation. I more or less bankroll it. I put Penny their way – she works at a dungeon I sometimes like to visit.'

'You ... a dungeon? You visit a dungeon?'

'Strictly hush hush, my dear, you'll understand.'

'Of course!'

'I do trust you, Krysztyna. I think you're a good soul. A discreet soul.'

'Oh, I am. I have my own secrets ... as you know.'

'Yes. Sometimes, a secret shared can be such a weight off one's mind. Penny and I play scenes together on occasion, when I feel like a little submissive company in my suffering.'

'You're a ...?'

'You hadn't guessed? Well, I hadn't guessed about you being a marvellous Domme either, so perhaps that isn't surprising.'

'No.' I put my glass down, unsure what on earth to say next.

'The thing is, Krysztyna,' said Lady Markham softly, so softly I could barely catch the words. It wasn't like her to be shy at all. I leant forward, hanging on the words that dropped from her pristinely lipsticked mouth. 'Marvellous as the dungeon club is, all the cloak-and-

171

dagger creeping about round the back streets is such a bore. I constantly fear exposure. It would be disastrous for me, personally and professionally, if I were ever spotted. I've been thinking I probably shouldn't go there any more.'

'Oh. That's a pity.'

'There's the wonderful Mr Collins and Mr Bryant, of course, but they are so difficult to pin down. And the preparations take so long. Sometimes one craves the experience too intensely to bear a long wait. I'm sure you know what I mean by that.'

'I ... do.'

'I wondered if you ... might ... be amenable to a private arrangement.'

'A private arrangement?'

'I like to submit. You like to dominate.' She shrugged, almost fearful of looking at me, it seemed.

'Lady Markham!'

'Oh, do call me Drusilla. Call me anything you like.' She chuckled, a little desperately. 'Bitch. Slut. Slave.'

It was only when my chest began to feel unbearably tight that I realised I had not drawn breath for a long time. Beautiful, über-sexy Lady Markham wanted to be my bitch. This could not be real.

'Dare I hope ...?'

'I ... am, well, I'm sorry, this is such a surprise.' I laughed, a little hysterically. 'A lovely surprise, please don't look so sad! A lovely surprise, of course!'

'Then you'll consider it?'

I would have been mad not to, wouldn't I?

I still clean my three houses. I clean for the new Redverses – known as the Blackleys, similar in profile but infinitely superior in manners. I still clean for Ms Livesay, but she has buckled down a little, acquired a

172

boyfriend, and no longer leaves the flat in such a horrific state. Not since I threatened to quit, anyway. And, of course, I am Lady Markham's domestic Dominatrix.

If she arrives home while I am cleaning, I often hand the trug of cleaning products over to her without a word, sit back on the sofa and watch as she sprays and scrubs in her expensive twinset, pearls crashing against the windows when she enthusiastically wipes them down. She seems to get a strange kick from the menial nature of it, though she has told me many times that she would hate doing housework if I weren't there to watch and issue orders. It is one of her ultimate fantasies, apparently, to be made to submit to her cleaner.

Sometimes I only want her to take off my shoes and rub my feet or give me a massage. Sometimes we just sit and spoon and use fingers and tongues to take the edge off our longings. But when I am in the mood, she takes me to her secret playroom. I may dress her as a Roman slave or a schoolgirl; I may have her naked or trussed up to the neck in tight shiny restrictive rubber; I may whip her until she screams or I may tie her up and tease her until she gasps and begs for release. We do what I want – and what I want is always what she wants.

She has referred me to a City practice seeking a legal secretary – if everything works out, I may be able to resign from my cleaning jobs next month. Perhaps mother and I will be able to find a bigger, nicer flat. Perhaps I will find a proper girlfriend and live happily ever after. Even if I don't, I have my Lady, and my Lady loves to be my tramp.

Lucky Escape

'SO MR COLLINS IS busy tonight?'

'Like I said.' Bryant looked up from the syllabub, and Charlotte caught a defensive gleam in the usually reassuring blue. 'He has some business or other to attend to.'

'Family business?' Charlotte tried to keep the tone casual, neutral, but she held her breath until Bryant replied.

'I don't know. I don't know what Collins does in his spare time, not being his keeper, Charlotte.'

Charlotte felt suitably tongue-lashed. For whatever reason – and surely it couldn't be the one she was thinking – this was a touchy subject. Best let it go and take her head out of the gift horse's jaw. It wasn't every night she was taken to an expensive restaurant by one of her suave and handsome bosses – in fact, this was a first.

'So where's this club we're going to?'

Bryant relaxed, taking up his napkin from his lap and depositing it on the table beside his empty dish.

'Oh, it's just around the corner.'

'Really? In this part of town? I thought this area was all Dukes and sheikhs and movie stars. It's Swanksville!'

'Yes, and the members are some of its richest citizens.'

'Oh, I see. For some reason, I always imagine that

kind of stuff going down in seedy basements in Soho or Kings Cross.'

'Some of it does. Some of it doesn't. In swinging, as in real life, all types of people from all social strata are represented. You know, for a girl who gets fucked in bondage more often than she eats a hot meal, you're surprisingly naïve.'

Charlotte's ears burned – ludicrous as it seemed to take offence at a comment that was both true and probably well-meant, she was mortified at Bryant's crude remark. She did not mind how many fucks and cunts he came out with mid-scene, but to treat her like a whore while she was innocently eating her dinner and trying to be normal struck her as too cruel. Collins would never have been so crass, she thought. Or would he? Why would she idealise men who were, after all, when it came down to brass tacks, procurers? Pimps, that was all they were, she thought, with an inward toss of the head. Think of them as such and perhaps she could drive back all these … feelings that had been boiling up in the last few months.

'I'm not here as your submissive tonight,' she reminded him tightly. 'And actually, I'm not your submissive really. Not in any meaningful way. Am I?'

Bryant did a double-take, leaning in close to her and taking her hand.

'Charlotte – are you all right? Have I said something to upset you? If so, I'm truly sorry. I would never seek to … there must be some kind of misunderstanding. Really.'

'Oh, it's nothing.' Charlotte lost her nerve, smiling wanly at him. 'I just … sometimes I think you forget I have feelings.'

Bryant, as if made of stone, stared blankly at her for a

long time, only his compulsive squeezing of her hand giving away the ticking heart behind the expensive suit.

'I didn't think,' he murmured, as if to himself. 'I didn't think we could … oh, never mind.'

He asked for the bill and paid before giving his arm to Charlotte and escorting her out into the five-star Mayfair night.

'So what do you think about swinging?' he asked, leading her along the wide pavements, beneath the low-hanging branches of the trees that sheltered the street.

'I don't know much about it,' confessed Charlotte. 'I think of key parties, you know. People in kaftans, with pampas grass in the front garden. It all seems a bit Seventies/Eighties, if you know what I mean. Old-fashioned.'

'I must admit,' Bryant confided, 'I haven't really looked into this scene much myself. But when you passed on that email from the client, it struck a chord with me. I suddenly thought I ought to check it out. And I couldn't go alone. Thank you again for offering to come with me, Charlotte. Do you think you'll want to … partake? Or simply watch?'

'Is watching an option?' asked Charlotte nervously.

'I should think so. I imagine a lot of the people here are voyeurs. Hopefully the figures balance, and there will be just as many exhibitionists. Otherwise it might be rather a dull night.'

They arrived at a gracious terraced house and descended some steps to the basement entrance – all very respectable-looking, with two potted bay trees either side of the heavy black-painted door.

Bryant rang a bell and a burly gentleman in exotic silk robes and a pillbox hat with a tassel answered, raising an eyebrow at them. Charlotte had a presentiment that this was going to be anything but a dull night.

'Names please?' he demanded, consulting a clipboard.

'Bryant and lady.'

'OK. You're on the list. Please come in.'

He showed them through to a small anteroom, all crimson and purple with beaded curtains hanging across the arched opening. Erotic paintings hung here and there, and Bryant helped Charlotte down on to the low cushions that provided the only seating.

'Well, this is jolly, isn't it?' he murmured into Charlotte's ear, amused, while the doorman went off to do whatever procedure demanded. He slung an arm around her shoulder, sensing her escalating tension. Somewhere in the distance, music was playing. 'Relax, darling. You're so tense!'

On a low table in front of them lay paraphernalia relevant to various different recreational drugs. Charlotte found this ominous and tried not to look at it.

'Will everyone be stoned?' she whispered to Bryant.

'Those that need a bit of extra stimulation, perhaps,' he mused. 'Personally, I like my sex straight up – I don't need chemical distractions.'

'It's never occurred to me to try it,' said Charlotte. She shivered, now extremely nervous. 'I think I'm a bit scared.'

'I'll look after you,' Bryant assured her. 'We can leave if you really want. You can research things without experiencing them, you know.'

'Oh no. I need to know how these things feel – or I can't get the details right for the client.'

'I suppose so. I applaud your dedication, Charlotte. You're a rare girl.'

Charlotte was still wondering whether rare was good

177

or bad when the robed man returned, carrying a cloth bag which he set down on the table before them.

'OK, you are new members, so I have to give you the full low-down. This club is not to be discussed outside these four walls with anyone who you haven't met within them. I know you have taken tests for sexually transmitted infections, but until you get your updated results, you must use barrier protection for the first six weeks. You understand?'

'Yes.' Bryant nodded. 'I'm fully equipped.'

'And your lady?'

'I ... yes.' Charlotte's face flared. The man's dispassionate manner made her think she was preparing for a gynaecological exam.

'Good. Now, there are different events – usually once a week. Tonight it happens to be a masked ball. I have masks for you here.' He emptied the bag, disgorging two eye masks – one plain black satin, the other adorned with paste gems and feathers. 'Put them on, please.'

Bryant looked dashing in his mask, Charlotte thought, like Dick Turpin or Zorro. She wondered if hers conferred the glamour of days gone by on her, or if she just looked a bit silly. Everything felt transformed, mysterious, alluring through the almond-shaped eye slits. It was like taking a holiday from oneself.

'You notice that something else was in the bag,' the man prompted. Charlotte picked them up – two long chains with different pendants attached. One was in the shape of a heart, the other a lightning fork. 'For the lady, the heart.'

Charlotte put the necklace on. The heart was heavy, hanging low in her cleavage. Bryant took off his tie, loosened his collar and placed his own identifier around his neck.

'At the party, you will see that everyone is wearing a necklace. Mr Bryant, you are free to choose any of the women wearing hearts. If none of them appeal, of course, you have recourse to your lady here. In the same way, she may choose any man with a lightning pendant. If she does not like them, she may come back to you. If you are chosen by somebody you really feel you do not want – then of course you are free to reject him or her. However, should you do this, you will have to find yourself another club. The choice is yours.'

Charlotte and Bryant exchanged mask-concealed glances. Bryant seemed to be waiting for approval from Charlotte, which she gave with a near-imperceptible nod.

The robed man motioned them upward and they followed him along a corridor that led through the prodigiously sized basement until a curtained double door was opened into … well, it wasn't really what Charlotte was expecting from a ballroom. It was more like an underground bar or nightclub, low-lit, distorted music flooding from wall-mounted speakers, the furnishings reminiscent of an old-time bordello.

The floor was dotted with couples, swaying, smooching, some of them groping. There did not seem to be a uniform dress code, for some were in full eighteenth-century masquerade costume while others were in fetish-inspired underwear. Charlotte, in her short, low-cut cocktail dress and stiletto knee boots, felt positively conservative in comparison, and Bryant was one of only a few men in a business suit. Frilly shirts and britches were everywhere, interspersed with leather trousers and the odd bare chest. Charlotte was reminded of New Romantic music videos from the 1980s and rather wished for a pompadour wig and a ribboned shepherdess's crook so she could really feel part of the

179

scene.

'Well then,' said Bryant, after drawing a deep breath. 'Shall we mingle?'

Charlotte, feeling shy, looked for a space on the low, cushion-strewn divans that lined the large bunker, but most of them were occupied by writhing bodies. None yet were at the stage of full engagement, but a few weren't far off that happy state. Perhaps she could get herself a drink – where was the bar? She approached a rectangular gap in the purple silk wall, but there was no barman to be seen, merely bottle after bottle of champagne and a stack of glasses.

'You help yourself,' a male voice behind her said. 'You're new here, are you?'

She turned to see a squat figure dressed like a Civil War royalist, long curly wig and all, neatly-trimmed beard and … a pendant that was not lightning-shaped. She felt obscurely relieved. It seemed a bit early in the evening for claiming yet.

He reached and took her heart shape in his hand. 'Shame,' he said. 'Stars for me tonight. Ah well. Maybe next time. Enjoy your drink.'

She poured a glass of champagne and took a big gulp, leaning against the wall and watching the action in the room, trying to follow Bryant's movements as he danced with a succession of women. He did not seem terribly keen on any, though, as he continually ignored his partners in favour of scoping the room until he caught sight of her, holding her eyes through the double barrier of their masks.

Charlotte was suffused with a warmth that was not just down to the champagne. Bryant. He had always been the nicer of her two bosses; the more solicitous, the caring one. He was the one who fixed the things that went wrong in her flat or slipped her an extra fifty pounds here and there when he thought she was looking pale or thin. He was a wonderful lover as well, skilled and mature. She could do much worse than seek him out tonight and take him on to the divans.

But that was not the point. The point was that any man here – perhaps more than one – could take her and have her. What a dizzying thought that was. Charlotte tightened her fingers round the stem of the glass and shuddered with exhilaration.

'A heart!' A triumphant male voice awoke her from her reverie, and there was a man at her elbow – as dandy a highwayman as she had ever seen. 'And you may have mine, my lady!' he said gallantly, drawing her into the mêlée.

Charlotte, deciding that he seemed like fun, allowed the highwayman his will of her, blushing and smiling coyly when he brought her knuckles to his lips for an extravagant kiss, eyes low and gleaming behind that tight black mask. He manipulated her into the first position, as if about to start some complicated ballroom dance, but instead he held her there, against his chest, one hand on her hip, the other interlaced with hers at the fingers, as if accustoming himself to her particular shape, size and scent.

'Oh, you'll do very nicely,' he told her upswept hair, the warmth of his breath parting the strands until it reached her ear. He smelled of some brash old-fashioned cologne – perhaps Old Spice – but it mingled so deliciously with the smell of the leather strapped across his chest that Charlotte felt swooningly faint. If they'd had aftershave in the eighteenth century, she thought, perhaps the ladies would have fallen into dead faints even more often. 'You're a real find. New here, are you?'

'Yes.' She breathed in sharply as the highwayman's hand slid over her hip and rested on the slope of her bottom. 'What about you? Do you, er, come here often?'

'Oh yes. I'm a regular here. This is the place to come if you want to … um …'

'Come?'

'Quite.'

'And do you observe, or participate?'

The highwayman put sudden pressure on Charlotte's rear, forcing her pelvis to crush against the crotch of his tighter-than-tight britches. Unless he had an antique pistol in there, Charlotte had to concede that his interest in her was genuine.

'I participate, Milady. I can't ask your name, so do you mind if I call you Milady?'

'Milady – yes, I like the sound of that.'

'Good. You may call me Dick.'

His other hand dropped hers and slipped instead around her back, preventing her escape from this dance-floor prison. 'Are you a bad girl, Milady? I presume you must be, to be here at all.'

'Yes. I am bad. Very bad. And wanton. A wanton hussy.'

'Oh, that's good. A trollop. A floozy. A strumpet.'

'Yes, all of those.'

'Mmm. Let's dance.'

But the highwayman's version of dancing was certainly the least energetic Charlotte had ever encountered. He simply gyrated very very slowly, one arm around her neck to guide her after him, the other busy gliding down the silky skirt of her cocktail dress. Before she could speak again, he had swallowed her words in a kiss and, as he kissed well, Charlotte was inclined to let him carry on, let that hand lose itself in the cloud of chiffon petticoats, let it find the elasticated lace of her stocking top, let it touch the cold, smooth skin of her thigh.

The palm moved up the back of her leg until it met the curving cheek of her naked bottom and then he broke off the kiss, staring at her in delight.

'No knickers!' he crowed. 'You really are a wanton hussy, aren't you?'

'I didn't think I'd need them.'

'Such a practical girl. I like it. And it's quite true – you certainly don't need them. But I think the whole room needs to know just what a fast little slut you are, don't you, Milady?'

Without waiting for her reply, he flipped the black sparkly froth of petticoats up, exposing her soft white bottom with its frame of black suspenders to the company. Many were too absorbed to notice, but there was some clapping and whistling and shouts of approbation at the sight of the fleshy curves disappearing down to the unhidden mound of her sex. Dick, not wanting anyone to miss the sight, drew further attention to it with a loud slap on her cheeks, cracking out like a pistol shot across the heath.

'Stand and deliver!' he proclaimed. 'I think it's time I fucked you, Milady.'

Milady certainly wasn't going to argue, even if Charlotte might have done, and she allowed him to steer her over to the divans. En route another couple stood in their way – a tall man dressed as a pirate with a full face mask and his partner, a curvaceous blonde who seemed to be some kind of kinky bunny girl in tight PVC and black horns rather than rabbit ears.

'Excuse me,' said the bunny girl, putting a hand out

to touch Dick's chest. 'We've been watching you and we wondered if you'd like a foursome. Captain Masters and I are wearing the same pendants as you. I know it's a bit cheeky to ask, but …'

'Milady?'

Charlotte, determined to go with the flow, merely batted the question back to Dick, who laughed and smacked her bum again.

'I might have known, you racy little whore. Milady here will take on all-comers, it seems. Very well. But I want Milady first, and I want both girls at the same time. Those are my conditions. Do you accept?'

The pirate nodded resignedly, seating himself on the edge of a free divan and settling in to watch the show.

'Right then. Let's see. Bunny Girl, you can suck my cock while Milady here sits on my face. How's that for starters?'

Dick stretched himself out on the divan, unbuttoning his fly for Bunny's greater ease of access and stretching out his arms either side in mute invitation to Charlotte. Charlotte pulled up her skirts and placed her knees beside Dick's ears, lowering herself steadily until the tip of his nose caught the end of her sex lips and then his hot breath was circulating around her wet slit. He caught her hips in each hand and slowed her descent, making it a drawn-out tease, flicking the tip of his tongue around her outer lips and the crease of her thighs until she was ready to beg for a direct hit on her clit.

Dick laughed richly into her cunt, the vibrations from his chest making her rock a little back and forth. Craning her neck around, she could see Bunny's slick red lips wrapped around a thick column of cock – it looked hot, and she wanted to be part of the hotness.

'Please, Dick,' she muttered, working every muscle

from abdomen to knee to try and force her clit into his mouth. 'Please lick it, please.'

'A gentleman never refuses a lady,' he growled, allowing her finally to crush those hot wet petals against his hungry lips and tongue.

Charlotte, looking around her, could see that they were a popular spectacle. Under the artificially roseate light, the crowds drew closer, enjoying this piquant variation on the *soixante-neuf*. It was not the first time Charlotte had performed for an audience, but it was certainly the largest group she had bared flesh in front of. Usually she was shy, enjoying the masochistic humiliation of it, but tonight the mask nerved her, and she let her exhibitionist streak run rampant. She ground herself on Dick's ravenous mouth, pushing her breasts up and together before wrenching down the top of her dress, so that they were visible to all. A cheer and some whistling greeted the revelation, so she continued the motion, keeping her spine straight, while Dick squeezed his fists into her rear cheeks before pulling them apart, making sure there was nothing sacred, nothing off-limits.

Suddenly he stopped and retracted his tongue, pushing her roughly off.

'Turn around,' he growled. 'I want you to watch Bunny there when she gets a mouthful.'

Obediently, Charlotte repositioned herself so that she faced the hardworking Bunny, whose cheekbones were hollow with all the sucking. Once again, Dick's mouth enveloped her dripping cleft, his tongue pushing harder now, a serious muscle probing every crack and crevice of her – but now he had added an exploratory thumb between her bum cheeks, pushing and circling, encouraging her to lean forward and stick her backside out further, to yield it to him. Charlotte gasped as the thumb broke through the border of her rear passage, beginning to jiggle and buck in earnest, her climax approaching fast.

The crowd were calling constant encouragement now; closer and closer they drifted until hands could reach out and touch her breasts and flanks. She saw a man come behind Bunny and twist the little fluffy tail around, so that it was obvious it must be a butt plug. Everyone wanted a handful, a piece of this action.

Bunny, her hands in their fishnet fingerless gloves around the base of Dick's cock, gave a final guttural sound and then Charlotte knew that she was sucking up and swallowing the highwayman's seed and the sight of it made her come hard on her temporary lover's tongue, the orgasm intensified by his spreading of her cheeks and thumbing of her arse. She fell forward, almost banging foreheads with Bunny, who was sliding her lips up the detumescing cock in triumph, her face landing on the billowy fabric of Dick's shirt, crossed diagonally with a leather holster-holder.

Dick, smiling roguishly with a glistening lower face and chin, allowed his handmaidens to dismount, sitting up slightly and leaning back on the cushions.

'That was most excessively diverting,' he drawled. 'But poor Bunny didn't get to come. Milady, I think you should help her out. Start with a nice kiss.'

Charlotte shuffled tentatively over to the other woman, wanting to ask her permission first, but feeling somehow that Dick would be disappointed if she did. Instead, they flung themselves against each other and lay down on the divan, engaging in a long and sensual kiss. Dick gave instructions at regular intervals, and they followed them without question. 'Squeeze her tits.' 'Get those fingers down between her legs … that's it.' 'Suck her nipples.' 'Milady, I think she needs you to lick her clit now.'

Charlotte went to work on the Bunny girl, snapping open her crotch zip and burying her nose in the damp, sweet delta that lay there. She was so busy discovering this new and underused talent that she did not notice Dick rousing himself from his languor and crawling over to the pirate. By the time she had licked Bunny to a squeaking, quivering orgasm, the pirate was well on the way to his own climax, courtesy of Dick's silver tongue and deep male throat.

When the pirate caught Charlotte's eyes upon him, he wrenched Dick up by the hair and flung him aside, then he fell upon Bunny, getting her on her knees and ready for rear entry.

'That looks so fucking hot,' commented Dick, rubbing his head where the pirate had pulled his hair so unceremoniously. 'But really, I could take offence at that. Are my blow jobs that bad?'

Charlotte, bemused, replied, 'I suppose I'll never know.'

'Wouldn't you like to? Wouldn't you like to know how it feels to have a cock? I often wish I could have a cunt for the day. I'd fuck as many men as I could, just to see how I could improve my own techniques. Don't you think that would be fun?'

'Er, maybe,' said Charlotte guardedly, never having considered this.

'Ah well, no point wishing for the impossible. Come on. Get on your knees, facing Bunny. Perhaps you two girls can snog each other while you're being fucked. I think the audience would like that. What a sight.'

It was indeed quite a sight, and Bryant, in the midst of the crowd with a glass of champagne, would have found it aesthetically pleasing. Two beautiful masked girls, their backs sloping and breasts dangling, their lips joined and their bottoms thrust up, getting fucked hard and fast by two handsome men, slamming and slapping into their presented hindquarters with furious intent. He would have found it aesthetically pleasing, at least, if one of the beautiful masked girls had not been Charlotte. As it was, his pleasure in the spectacle was strictly limited. Still, who could he blame? He had brought her here. If his calculation – that she would reject the other men with lightning pendants and look for him – had been inaccurate, then that was not her fault. She did not belong to him, after all.

A small female dressed like Madame de Pompadour appeared at his elbow, smiling up at him with gleaming teeth. 'This is the best night I've been to here. I've never watched such a hot foursome before, have you?'

He noted that she was wearing a heart pendant.

'It's my first time,' he confessed.

'Oh really? Your first time?' The woman put a kid-gloved hand on his elbow. 'I could show you the ropes if you like.'

He smiled at her, a little wistfully. 'You know, I hadn't planned any bondage for tonight.'

She tutted and tossed her head. 'You know what I mean, silly.'

'I think I'll just watch the rest of this show … and then think about my next move.'

'Do you mind if I watch with you?'

'Of course not.'

The woman moved into his side, pressing against him, and letting her hand drop, as if accidentally, down to his groin.

Back in the glare of full exposure, Charlotte

whimpered into Bunny's mouth, taking the final fusillade from her dandy highwayman, who gripped her hips and roared into her. The pirate, whom she could just make out if she rolled her eyes up and peered between Bunny's incongruous fluffy ears, was coming to a similar conclusion, though he was strangely quiet and none of the expected coarse oaths made their way through his heavy beard. When he had finished with Bunny, he withdrew without comment, re-laced his piratical trews and stood by the divan, watching Charlotte, it seemed, rather more intently than was necessary. Did he expect a turn with her now? Would she be able to take another partner tonight, or had the highwayman plundered all her treasures to the extent that she would prefer to hang back for the rest of the evening? She was not sure how long the foursome was supposed to last, or if there was some point of etiquette that demanded each partner have equal access to the available prizes.

She fell forward on to the sticky plush, her face finding it almost as sharp as Dick's stubble, while he set about the further divesting of his clothes. For him, it seemed, the evening was far from over.

'Phew, I'm melting,' he commented, and it was true that the underground room was humid and its air almost suffocatingly dense. 'Fancy a hot tub, Milady?'

Charlotte, flat on her stomach with her cocktail dress torn and disarranged around her naked breasts and bottom and her hard-used quim, thought it was an interesting proposition, but she lacked the energy to go anywhere or do anything just at that moment.

'She's beat,' said Bunny breathlessly. 'But I'll go with you. She can come in later.'

Dick took Bunny's arm and the nearly-naked man and

dishevelled bunny girl took their bows and their applause before cutting a path through their fans and out beyond a beaded curtain at the far end of the room.

'*Not even a kiss goodbye,*' thought Charlotte in confusion. '*Not even a "Thank you, ma'am" after all the whamming and bamming.*' Even Collins and Bryant at the height of their sadistic conspiracies were not so cruel or dismissive. It wasn't that she was against being used in public, it was just … oh, what was it? Charlotte had to accept that she didn't know what made her uneasy about the scenario. Something was missing. That was all she knew. And then she looked up to find that the pirate was looming over her with folded arms. Couldn't he see that she was rumpled, crumpled, ruined and stained? Couldn't he just go and let her sort herself out?

'You look fucked,' he said, and the voice was instantly familiar, low and caressing, with an undertow of velvety menace.

She scrambled instantly to her knees, wrapping her arms around her bare breasts, mouth wide open in shock.

'Mr Collins!'

The audience had drifted away, many of them into their own frantic couplings, and Charlotte and Pirate Collins seemed almost the only people in the room who weren't fucking – writhing bodies, vanilla and chocolate and coffee, filled the divans with heaving, throbbing lust in action as far as the eye could see. Bryant seemed to have wandered off the map, unless he was in the Jacuzzi, or one of the dancers – more like gropers now – on the floor.

'Don't say my name. We don't have names here.'

Charlotte had no idea what to say next. She felt obscurely ashamed, as if caught out in a misdemeanour, though heaven knew she had done all sorts of equally

190

depraved things with Collins either involved or observing.

'What are you doing here?'

'What are *you* doing here? Who are you here with?'

'Mr Bryant.'

Collins stroked his falsely-bearded chin for a moment. Something told Charlotte that he was angry, though he was not a man who ever betrayed outward emotion.

'He had no right,' he said at last, so tightly that Charlotte felt frightened for her other employer.

'It was research,' she whispered. 'For a client.'

'That's what I'm here for. It's too bad. Bryant has gone too far. I know what he is planning, and I won't stand for it.'

'What do you mean?'

'I mean, dear nameless tart, that Bryant is greedy and doesn't like to share.'

'Share? Me?'

A nod was the terse rejoinder.

'That's absurd,' said Charlotte with a near-hysterical laugh. 'If he doesn't want to share me, why would he take me to a swingers' club?'

'I suspect he planned to keep hold of you. Perhaps put on a show with you while the others watched. Or perhaps not take part at all – just watch with you and then take you home. To bed.' It sounded, for all his blank delivery of the words, as if there was a volcano boiling up inside Collins, and Charlotte was a little nervous of being there when it erupted.

'Why …' Charlotte tried to phrase it delicately, then gave up. 'Why shouldn't he?'

'Have you all to himself? Is that what you want? Do you want a lovely little romance with our Mr Bryant?

Hand-in-hand down the Strand? Flowers and dinners and visits to galleries? A little house in Barnes or Putney? Marriage, children, pensions?'

'You talk as if all of these are bad things. They aren't. Why do you think they are?'

'They aren't meant for you, or me. They probably are for Bryant though. He's so dreadfully suburban at heart.'

Charlotte was shocked at the naked animosity in Collins's words, and yet she was excited by it too. Excited by the clear signs of jealousy it displayed.

'You think he's your … rival?'

'He is my rival.'

'I thought you had a partnership.'

'We did. And now he is my rival. He has made himself so, by bringing you here, in secret, without my knowledge.'

'But you came here in secret without his knowledge too.'

'With Lady Markham.' Collins waved a hand in disgusted dismissal. 'She is getting rogered by some person done up as the Marquis de Sade. She is quite happy. Bryant would neither care, nor want to know about that.'

'Whereas you do care, and you do want to know, about him coming here with me?'

'Precisely.'

'Why?'

'Why do you think?'

'I think you should tell me.'

'I think we should go.'

'I don't want to. I want to find Bryant.'

'Then it is him that you want?'

'No, I didn't say that! I just think … can't I want you both?'

'Not any more.'

Collins turned to leave. Charlotte leapt up behind him, pulling on her heels, reluctant to let him leave thinking that she had somehow rejected him.

'Please! I don't want to … split you up.'

Collins turned to her, and his eyes behind the mask glittered venomously.

'We aren't lovers,' he said.

'I don't want this! I don't want … what we have … to be disturbed. I don't want you two at each other's throats.'

'So what *do* you want, Charlotte? Or, more to the point, *who* do you want?'

'I want what I've got! What I had! I think.'

She stopped abruptly. Was that true? Wasn't it the case that a seed of resentment had been creeping into flower inside her – nagging worries about her lovers' near-anonymity, about their intentions, about never knowing where they lived or with whom. She did want more, if she was honest. But how much more? And with both of them, or just one? The questions tangled in her head like thorns, and she could not say any more.

'You think? Better be sure, Charlotte. Because nothing stays the same, you know. Change is part of life. Are you coming with me?'

'I can't leave without … wait. Let me just tell Bryant I'm leaving.'

'No. Come with me now, or don't.'

The split second of hesitation was enough to give Collins his chance to turn on his heel and disappear through the bead curtain, towards the Exit.

The distorted music was too loud now, and the club smelled of sweat and rancid perfume. Everywhere people gyrated, whether in dance or sex, in a manner that seemed to Charlotte now ludicrously overwrought. Nothing of intimacy or affection existed here, and she had lost the taste for it as quickly as a piece of gum has its flavour chewed out. She would find Bryant and tell him what had happened.

When she found him, he was sitting on a divan with a rather glum expression, being desultorily sucked off by an eighteenth century courtesan.

'Ah, Charlotte,' he said, seemingly able to converse effortlessly mid-fellatio. 'I thought you'd gone for second helpings with that pirate.'

'I, um, no. That pirate,' she said, unsure how to broach the subject, especially with a man who had his cock in some woman's mouth. 'Sorry, sir, but I think we should talk. It's important.'

'Important, eh? Sorry, dear.' He tugged his cock out of the woman's mouth, leaving her to splutter indignantly. 'Thank you so very much, but something's come up. Please don't take it personally. You're, ah, a highly accomplished woman. Good evening.'

Outside, in the cool fresh air, Charlotte walked with Bryant over to the neighbouring park, finding a secluded bench in the thick of the bushes, which rustled with nocturnal activity.

'Why have you brought me to the local cottage, Charlotte?' asked Bryant, bemused. 'If you wanted to watch me with another man, there was provision for that in the club.'

'Would you have done it?' asked Charlotte, momentarily intrigued by the scenario to the extent of forgetting why she was there.

'Would I have? I have done. Not with Collins. His tastes are too close to mine. But certainly with other men, particularly when I was younger – mostly letting

194

submissive young men suck my cock, though I have gone … further. On occasion.'

'I didn't realise.' Charlotte put a hand on Bryant's thigh, expecting him to cover it with one of his own, but he was unusually unresponsive. 'Did you … enjoy your evening?'

'Honestly, Charlotte? Not really.'

'Why not?'

'Not as much as you did, at any rate. You and that highwayman …'

'Are you jealous?' Charlotte could suddenly see the truth in all that Collins had said; it was like sands shifting. Everything was different. How had she not seen this from the start? 'You are, aren't you?'

'You're precious to me, Charlotte.'

'So why … don't you show it? Or tell me? Or something?'

'Why do you think?'

'Collins.'

'Yes. Got it in one. Collins.'

'You know … he was there tonight. He was the pirate.'

Even in the darkness, Charlotte could see that Bryant paled.

'Are you joking? Please don't joke about Collins.'

'I'm serious. He was the pirate. And … he's quite angry. That you took me there, without letting him know. I'm sorry. I don't know what it is that makes it such a big deal but … I don't think things are going to be the same any more.'

'No,' whispered Bryant, staring straight ahead. 'Things can't be the same any more.'

Mechanics

IT HAPPENS EVERY TIME I smell engine oil, which makes taking the car for its MOT more hazardous than you might think. I have to inhale it deeply, and the corrosive petrochemical tang makes my heart sing and my clit grow fat. Everything in the garage makes me think of sex, from the jacks to the girlie calendars to the filthy rags, and once we come to the man in dirty overalls ... well. Strong stubby fingers coated with black, greasy oil; biceps taut and gleaming underneath the heavy-duty material; big clumpy work boots; hair greased back out of the way; smudges on his honest, sweaty face. There is only one thing better than that for me, and that is a man in motorcycle leathers. Both would be ideal, but either would do. Either type of rough and ready, no-nonsense, straight on the level shag partner would fit my bill. But I seem to attract rich, ambitious men. Men in suits. Men who buy flowers and dinner. Never a man who flips me over the bonnet and ploughs right in, knowing what I need, knowing the shortcut that leads to split thighs and grunting, melting orgasms. I have tried to broach the subject of purchasing a motorcycle with a couple of past boyfriends, but both blanched and wittered about the danger and the expense. When I tried to set them on the path to discovering their inner macho brute, they were diverted by theatre tickets and champagne picnics.

What can a girl do? I've tried fabricating ridiculous problems with my car – but the mechanics at my local garage are such gents, and the one I usually deal with is older than my father. I've tried hanging out at the local bikers pub, but my friend said the smell of rancid scrumpy made her feel sick, and I did see her point. She thinks I should get a bike of my own and join some chapter of something – but I don't want to be some Hell's Angel's 'old lady'. I don't want a 'scene' to join. It would be ruinous for my future career, for one thing! I just want an honest, hard shag from a hot man in leather. What on earth is so strange in that?

I suppose The Honourable Lucinda Ffolkes-Worthington is not supposed to have such appetites. But let me tell you now, no Eton boy in a Gieves & Hawkes suit is going to hit that sweet, secret spot at the core of me. I am out for a rough man or two, and I mean to get them.

So thank heavens for cousin Drusilla! She has saved the day by introducing me to two fellows that she supposes can help. And Mr Collins and Mr Bryant do seem to understand what it is that I propose. Dru swears that they are the very souls of discretion and nothing will ever get out – and I certainly don't need a scandal, in advance of my possible selection for Great Gatherington at the next election.

So here I am. Primed and ready. I have driven to a remote and obscure town where nobody could possibly know or recognise me, and now I am in the car park toilets, dressing for the downest and dirtiest day of my life. Discarded on the floor lie my Jack Wills striped shirt and sensible pencil skirt, my tan tights and ballet flats. And, if I'm going to carry out this brief to the letter, I really need to take off my bra and pants set too.

God, can I really go through with it? The garage is only a short walk down the main street of this one-horse town, but all the same ... *people* will see me. Daytime people, I remind myself, seeking courage. Not working, city people who matter. Just old men and young mums and people on benefits in a distant town I'll never revisit. Nobody, really. Besides, I'm not going to look like myself. Even if they do see me on *Question Time* one day, they won't recognise the soignée, elegant woman on screen – what they will see today is a trampy piece of trash, signalling the generally available state of her genitals no less blatantly than if she wore nothing at all.

So off comes the underwear, and on slides the tight white lycra bandeau that calls itself a skirt until it stretches so perilously across my rump that the crack of my arse is almost visible beneath the thin second skin. There is no question of bending over in this thing without flashing my lady parts to all and sundry; I am going to have to watch how I walk. Over my bare breasts, I put a wholly inadequate thin white vest top with spaghetti straps. It outlines my tits with unforgiving accuracy, and the slightest chill leads to nipple-shaped dents in the well-worn fabric. I buckle a hideous purple vinyl belt, almost wider than the skirt, around my waist to make it clear that, just because I'm wearing white there is no need to associate me with anything pure or virginal. I cinch it in tightly, then I go for the finishing touches. It took me ages to decide which looked cheaper – stilettos or white gogo boots – but in the end I had to go for the boots, since the combination of white boots and pale bare legs is such a classic of tramp style. Now I need to brush out and back comb my hair from polished blonde chignon to wild porn-star shagginess, apply buckets of red lipstick, blusher and nail varnish, and I'm all set for my promenade.

I poke my head out of the door – the toilet block is a dismal cement bunker at the back of a cinder car park. Nobody else is around, so I begin to crunch my way across the expanse, over to the misleadingly-named High Street – at this point, I realise the wisdom of rejecting the stilettos, for the ground is rough and bumpy and would have made the walk tricky. All the same, I rather dawdle across, dreading the moment I might meet another face, wondering what its reaction will be to this human version of a blow-up doll in clothes that make the word skimpy look like an understatement.

I don't have to wait long to find out. Two teenage girls, playing hooky in their vamped-up school uniforms, stare at me unabashedly, forgetting to swallow their mouthfuls of Diet Coke in the stunned moment.

'Who the fook does she think she is? Lady Gaga?' I hear one of them say before they both burst into wild giggling fits behind me. I have no time to process my slightly flattered reaction to this – Lady Gaga is rather *popular*, isn't she? – before I am caught in a hard rain of wolf whistles, coming from the workmen digging up the other side of the road.

Oh. I stop and smile back at them, noting their dirty hands and their brawny forearms. Shame those high visibility jackets are so very anti-sexy. All the same, I feel now that I have got the look right and, where The Hon Lucinda might have marched over and castigated their shameful objectification of women, Tart Lucinda puts a hand on a hip and tries to perfect her bottom-wiggle as she moves away from them. Only three hundred yards to the garage. Nearly there.

I pass only an elderly gentleman on a mobility scooter and a pair of pushchair-pushers on the remaining leg of my walk of shame. I worry about the elderly gentleman's cardio-vascular health, though he seems to take me in his stride; indeed, it is the young mums who seem affected the most, pursing lips and clicking tongues. I want to defend myself. It's just sex, darlings, the very same thing that filled those pushchairs for you.

'It's eleven o'clock in the morning!' one of them exclaims in my wake. *Much too early to be on the prowl. Only the lowest whore would be walking the streets at this time.* The thought pleases me. I am the lowest whore. And here is the garage.

A sign, rotating in the wind, declares that the place is closed, but I know better. I knock on the side door, breathing in the acrid fumes, already feeling that tingling below. My nipples harden beneath the thin vest and I fluff up my hair, probably more nervous than I planned to be, but determined to carry this off like a pro. Lucinda Ffolkes- Worthington does not let silly things like nerves stand in her way. Not at the party conference, not in a garage full of sex maniacs. Nerves are for little people.

The door is opened and a tall, bronzed man in a stained white overall towers in its frame. I think I actually lick my lips. Just what I ordered: a strapping lad with the shoulders of Atlas and the face of a Michelangelo sculpture, in dirty work gear. I bow to the genius of Collins and Bryant, and simper up into the man's handsome face.

He raises an eyebrow and his smile is distinctly salacious.

'Hello,' he says, looking me up and down. That is what they call a frank gaze, I suspect. He addresses my nipples, asking them, 'How can I help you?'

'I'm afraid my car has broken down,' I lie, leaning a hip on the door jamb, suggestively I hope. 'I'm all alone in a strange town and I've no money and no idea what to do to fix it. Please, I'll do anything if you'll help me out.'

And I will. Anything at all! It's all I can do not to lay my hands on him then and there. Behind him, lurking behind various broken vehicles and pieces of machinery, I spy two more mechanics, both looking on with lustful curiosity.

'Come in,' says Mr Handsome. 'We'll talk terms.'

He ushers me in and I cross the concrete floor to a doorless car one of the mechanics has been spray painting. 'Mind that, the paint's wet,' he cautions.

'I bet that's not the only thing that is,' says his friend slyly and they chuckle, making no attempt to be polite. Instead of leading me to a chair, Mr Handsome makes me stop dead in the centre of the floor while he leans back on a plywood desk at the side of the room, checking me out from head to toe.

'So you want us to help you, but you can't pay us?' he says eventually, once I feel that I've been comprehensively pawed and felt up by their three pairs of eyes.

'I haven't got any money,' I reiterate.

'You've got something else you can use as payment though,' says Mr Handsome, brutally honest, making me gush between my thighs. 'You aren't some vestal virgin, are you, dressed like that?'

'Do you mean …?' I stage-gasp.

'You know what I mean.' He beckons me with a finger. 'Come here. Let me have a proper look at the goods.'

'You want me to …?' I do as he says, standing close to him, my bare knees brushing his rough serge-clad ones.

'Come and take a look, lads.' He calls his minions over and they crowd me, three hungry men slavering over their lunch. 'Don't tell me you don't want it,' he scoffs, and his hand, big and meaty, cups a breast, squeezing it, getting a smudge of oil on my white top. 'You'd love it, wouldn't you? Three big men at once. You look like the type.'

'What do you say, luv?' breaks in one of the others, a curly-haired gypsyish-looking man with a silver crucifix in one ear. Mr Handsome is stroking my stiff nipples with his thumbs and my knees are beginning to give. The gipsy-man puts a hand on my bottom and rubs it. 'You want to swap parts and labour for your pussy? It's wet already, I can smell it. It needs a cock, doesn't it?' He holds me against him with a sinewy forearm pressing into that ugly purple belt. I feel how hard he is beneath the uniform. There is going to be no dainty foreplay or delicate courtship here. I am revved up, almost ready to go already. It has taken so little! I feel I ought to slow it down a little, but how?

'It needs three cocks,' says the third man, a pretty blond thing who seems to model his look on David Beckham. 'Don't you reckon?' He joins his friend at my rear and puts his mouth on my bare shoulder, sucking and nipping at it, moving up to my neck. Slowing this down won't be an option. I see that now.

'It's a deal,' I say faintly, and the three pairs of hands set to work on me, pulling down my vest front, letting my tits loose in the petrol-laden air. My skirt – such as it is – is harshly yanked up over my knickerless bottom and pussy, so that hands can forage and fumble and explore to their heart's content. I am able to stand only because I am surrounded and propped up by three overalled bodies, pressing into me, three hard cocks denting my nude flesh, six hands plucking and probing, three mouths biting and marking me. I know my legs are split wide, held apart while some of thirty fingers take a slide up inside, adding my juices to the grease. My nipples are sore now, pinched and licked and cold and throbbing and my backside is being pummelled by great fists and hands, used as a kind of stress ball, helplessly mauled this way and that with strength much greater than I would ever be able to resist. I am helpless, completely helpless, yet wanting no help, just losing myself in this enormity.

'She's ready,' says Mr Handsome, who seems to be in charge. 'I'll go first. Bend her over the bonnet of the Honda and spread her legs for me, Sean.'

Sean, the blond, supports me over to a bright yellow car – not the recently painted one – and lets me fall gratefully over its bonnet, my breasts squashed into the cold shiny surface. He nudges my feet apart with his, taking the opportunity to run his hands up my damp thighs and give my clit a little tweak. 'She sure is ready,' he confirms with a laugh. 'Horny fucking slut. Go to work on her, boss.'

Sean and the gipsyish man gather round to watch while Mr Handsome appears behind me, unzipping his overall and letting it drop around his ankles, then adjusting whatever clothing he was wearing underneath before I feel his legs, hard and hairy, take their position between mine. His hands alight on my arse, kneading it, spreading the cheeks, giving him the optimum view of what is waiting for him in payment. 'You're going to get it hard,' he warns me. 'Brace yourself.'

He is in me before I can count to three, his hot length filling me to the hilt in a single stroke. Now I am here, in the heart of my fantasy, bent over and fucked in a garage while hot men in overalls look on and clap and shout encouragement.

I do my best to savour the moment, but Mr Handsome is intent on putting me through my paces, thrusting with sharp, swift urgency, as far and as fast as he can. He grunts with each thrust and his broad hands fall on my rump, hard, causing it to warm up and glow along with my well-worked pussy.

'This what you wanted, hmm? Coming to my garage looking like a two-bit whore? This must be what you wanted?'

'Yes, yes,' I confess, each 'yes' a puff of winded breath as I bump and grind on the car.

'Getting fucked now, good and proper. And my mates are waiting their turn. You'll be walking like John Wayne when you leave here, babe.'

He grasps the inside of my thighs and pulls them upward, finding an angle that hits the g-spot with frictive precision. One hand finds my clit, strumming in time with each hard hump. 'Watch her, boys, she'll be coming any minute now. Watch the dirty slut come for me.'

His cock finds its target and I begin to wail, not wanting it to end now I'm finally here, but knowing there is much more to come, and grateful for that. A few big slams up into me bring me to that crowning moment and I lose myself underneath that glorious male body, impaled on his triumphant weapon, brought down to my true level by my own base lusts. He empties himself inside me and dismounts straight away, mindful of my instructions in the brief I sent the agency. No billing. No cooing. Just predatory, animalistic sex in the dirt.

Still bent over the bonnet, I try to catch a breath or two, feeling his cockload trickle down my thighs for all to see.

Sean barks a laugh. 'She is fucked, man,' he says. 'How was she, Big Guy?'

'Tight. But she won't be by the time we've finished, I guess. And really, really wet. Wettest snatch I've had in a long time. She loves it. Give her a minute and you can have a go – make up your own mind.'

'I want her to suck me off,' says Sean.

'How about she sucks you off while I'm fucking her?' suggest the gipsyish man. 'I don't know if I can wait much longer.'

'Deal,' says Sean. 'Shall I get the rug from the office?'

'Yeah. And a few cushions. Let's have her on the floor next.'

'Sounds like a show,' says Mr Handsome, taking a seat at his desk and leaning back, now all cleaned up and zipped again. 'You ready for that, princess? A nice long fuck with your mouth full?'

'I ... think so,' I say warily. My strength is slowly returning, but these two will have to take it a bit easier than their boss if I don't want to be red raw before lunchtime.

'Right. Can you stand up? Walk? Eamonn, do you want to get a bit of tissue and clean her up before you put yourself in there? She's dripping.'

I am subjected to the curly-haired Eamonn's tender attentions to my coated thighs and pussy with a length of kitchen towel before he helps me to my still-booted feet and walks me slowly over to a tartan wool rug festooned with various dusty old pillows.

'Now, I'm going to get comfortable here, Princess,' he tells me, lying himself down on the pillows. 'And when I've done that, you're going to get my hard cock

205

out and take a ride on it. A good, long, hard ride. Are you ready for that?'

'Yah,' I say, a little dizzily, still feeling the after-effects of Mr Handsome's brisk technique.

'And when you're in the saddle, all ready for a good canter, Sean here is going to kneel down and feed you your oats.'

I rather like this equine analogy. It is turning me on more than I imagined such talk would. I am a filly, a mare, to be put through her paces and stabled, steaming from the gallop, afterwards. I want to whinny. But I restrain myself, opting instead to crouch down and unzip Eamonn's overall to the crotch, pushing up the faded T-shirt underneath so I can see a chest scattered with wiry black hairs. His boxers cannot conceal the towering erection beneath, so I skim the elastic over it and take a good look. If I am going to be a horse today, it's just as well that my partner in pony play is hung like one.

'Gosh!' I say.

He laughs heartily. 'Gosh, you say. Well, I'll take that as a compliment. Now get on board for your second hard fuck of the morning. What are you waiting for?'

I straddle his still-overalled legs, feeling the rough material chafe my calves, and lower myself carefully down. I need to take this first bit slowly, and I wince a bit when the broad bulb of his cock tip makes its entrance inside my once-fucked passage.

'Nice,' he gasps, putting out a hand to steady my hips. 'Nice and tight still. Get down, then. Right down.'

I shimmy down the pole, easing him in, feeling every inch spread and broaden my poor penetrated channel. He is very thick and long, and it seems to take a long time to accommodate his full dimensions. Once I eventually reach his root, I feel almost unable to move, so split and filled I need a minute to get used to the strange satiety of it.

'Got you now,' he crows, in a strained voice. 'You're going nowhere, lady, except up and down on my big fat cock. Now get to work.'

I try an experimental jiggle, and it doesn't kill me, so I go further, grinding my pussy into his crotch, rocking back and forth, moving up only a little, but still getting a whole world of penetration sensation from my small circlings.

'You're so very huge,' I explain, though I know he didn't ask me to. 'I can only just …'

'You'll need to work harder than that,' Eamonn warns me. 'I want bouncing tits.'

'So do I,' says Mr Handsome from over on the desk, somewhere to our right. I squint over at him, seeing that his is licking the side of his mouth, intent with concentration on our humping manoeuvres. 'And get that arse up nice and high. I want to see you fucking yourself on that cock. Sean, fill her mouth. Perhaps you can give her the energy she's going to need.'

Sean strips eagerly, getting his overall all the way off before approaching me with cock drawn, pointing at me square in the face.

'Open wide,' he croons, dropping to his knees, and I obey, letting him guide his salty length into my waiting mouth.

'Now that looks filthy,' comments Mr Handsome, and I can just about see, blurrily, that he is getting hard again, his hand cupped over his crotch. 'I like it a lot.'

It is not the easiest of rhythms to establish – sucking on one shaft while another mines my pussy – but we manage to get up a pace we can all work with. Sean helps by feeding me, rather than making me hold his cock, while Eamonn wants me to use my hands to squeeze my tits. I get accustomed to his outsizeness in the end, and I start to bump, up and down, bending low, crushing my nipples into his face, then straightening up proudly, letting hair and breasts fly.

'Horny, this is horny stuff,' commentates Mr Handsome, his voice getting ever rougher and growlier. 'I want to bring myself off, but I have to save some for later. Fuck. I might have to go outside for a minute.'

He hobbles off, leaving the three of us to our base delights, Sean bobbing and thrusting into my mouth while Eamonn holds me firmly on his prong, keeping me exactly where I belong.

Sean, the younger man, is first to lose his self-control; abruptly and with a sulky moan of disappointment at not lasting longer, he pours his essence into my grateful throat and releases my mouth from its bondage. I continue my quest to give Eamonn satisfaction, giving my muscles an intensive workout, squeezing and stretching until I feel I am about to hit a wall, and then the sudden scrabbling of his hand on my clit gives away the closeness of his orgasm, and I let myself go, let myself fall and slump, twitching and groaning on his chest, racing to the finish line together while the steam rises from us.

'That's it, that's it,' he gabbles, clamping my hips and holding me down for the final rush. 'What a ride. Fuck me, what a ride.'

I clamber off, my mouth tasting of one man's spunk, while another's washes around my pussy. I feel utterly bad, the baddest of the bad, total trash. This is what I was after – this feeling. This self-obliteration. Now I have tasted it, I can go back and serve my country. But of course, it isn't over yet. I need feeding and watering, but there is one more twist in the tale to come.

Mr Handsome returns, a little shamefaced but no longer sporting the world's most obvious erection. 'I missed the money shot, did I?' he asks, frowning. 'Typical. Let's have a look at her.'

He comes and towers over my limp body. 'Get a mouthful, did you?'

I nod weakly. He crouches down, peering over one thigh to get a good look at my recovering pussy. 'Christ, you really got it, girl,' he says, awestruck. 'Great job, Eamonn. I bet she can't see straight.'

'Not on your life,' he says, sitting up and grinning. 'Jeez, man, I'm starving. Will we have lunch now?'

'Lady Muck here's already eaten,' says Mr Handsome with a cruel grin. 'Ah, no, I wouldn't do that to you. Sean, can you go over the shop and get us something to eat? And make it substantial. Some of us have an afternoon's work ahead of us.' He gives my thigh a light slap. 'Don't we, Princess?' He winks and I let my eyes shut, ready to sleep for a thousand years.

But a millennium of sleep is not to be given to me. Instead I get a cheeseburger, fries and a thick strawberry milkshake.

'You're going to need the calories,' says Mr Handsome. 'Speaking of which, I'd better get going. I have a costume change to organise.'

He kisses the top of my head and saunters off, leaving me to masticate my fast food in the company of Eamonn and Sean.

'Do you know,' I say lazily, 'I don't think I've ever eaten from one of these restaurants before. It's awfully salty, isn't it, but rather satisfying.'

Sean and Eamonn snort. 'Is that the food you're talking about?'

'Of course – oh! Gosh! Yes, that did sound rather rude, didn't it? Out of context, I mean.'

'Do you mind my asking,' Eamonn opens, 'what makes you want to do this kind of thing? You speak like a rich lady, but you want this down and dirty stuff.'

'I've never been allowed to be down and dirty,' I tell him, not wanting to give too much away to this complete stranger, even though I'm assured of the absolute discretion of everyone on the agency payroll. 'I suppose it's the appeal of the forbidden.'

'I suppose so. Me, I'm really a mechanic, in real life. So I like the idea of clean sheets and shagging in the shower. Perhaps there's something in that.'

'Is this not a turn on for you at all then? Getting down in the garage?'

'Oh, I wouldn't say that. You're a fine-looking woman and all. But I suppose I'd rather do a thing in comfort than not.'

'Well, yes. I'm not averse to a comfortable bed either. It's just that this is my fantasy. A marvellous fantasy. I'm thoroughly enjoying it. Even though I think I might need to rest my private area for a while ...' I smile to myself, remembering the last part of my orders. Resting the private area won't necessarily be a problem.

'Well, then, I suppose we'd better get on with it,' says Eamonn, zipping himself up and tossing the remnants of the food packaging into the bin in the corner of the garage. 'Come on, Sean. We've got to hose her down.'

Sean leaps up and grabs a length of rubber coiled on the floor while Eamonn heads for the taps.

'It isn't going to be too cold, is it?' I am suddenly rather fearful. I strip off my remaining clothes and take my place on the dirty concrete, ready for my DIY shower. A jet of water – thankfully quite warm – arcs

210

through the air and splashes over my shoulders, then moves lower to blast my breasts and belly. I hop about, squealing and laughing beneath the heavy pressure of the water, letting Sean soak me, then letting him hold me still with one hand while he gives my pussy a vigorous cleansing.

'Ready for anything now, aren't you?' Eamonn hands me a towel and lets me rub myself dry. 'You're to get that hooker gear back on now and wait for our next customer. Why don't you sit on the desk with your legs nice and wide open, so he doesn't get the wrong idea.'

'Well ... he *will* get the wrong idea if I sit like that ... won't he?' I pull on the unforgiving lycra once more, knowing that my make-up is utterly wrecked and not caring a jot.

'No, he'll get the right idea – the idea that you're available for fucking, any time, any place, by anybody.' Eamonn helps me buckle my lurid belt, running his hands over my hips in the process. 'As I well know.'

I'm somewhat relieved that Mr Handsome, with his manageable cock, has taken responsibility for my final fling. I'm not sure I could manage Eamonn's monster again. Especially considering what I have in mind.

I take my position, sprawling on the desk in a most unladylike pose, while Eamonn and Sean don visors, pick up some metal thing or other and ... oh, what do you know ... they actually *are* mechanics.

They are still respraying the car when I pick up the sound of something revving furiously outside the front doors.

'Boys! I say, boys!' I try to attract their attention, but their sprayers are noisy and they don't notice at first, until I get up on the desk and begin to dance an energetic striptease number.

'Jesus, will you look at that!' Eamonn switches off the spray and stares. 'Was that in the script?'

Sean, slack-jawed and close to drooling, just shakes his head.

'Listen!' I urge them. The noise, like an angry beast waiting to break through the doors and slaughter us, persists. It is, of course, the happy, happy sound of a motorcycle engine. I revert to my original pose, my face wreathed in anticipatory smiles. This might be my favourite part of the whole thing.

Eamonn wrenches off his visor and opens the double doors to admit a sleek, shining bastard of a motorbike, driven by a sleek, shining bastard in neck-to-toe tight black leather.

It is all I can do not to whoop and clap my hands, but I maintain my thighs-akimbo stance, while the biker removes his helmet to reveal himself as, surprise surprise, Mr Handsome. I liked the overalls, but the leathers are even better, moulded to his body in second skin perfection. His backside is taut and smooth, curving in to a long straight back and broad shoulders. I don't care about the ragged state I'm in; I want him. Badly.

'Can I help you at all?' Eamonn asks. He is a bad actor, the lines coming out unconvincingly.

'Maybe.' Mr Handsome is better. He looks over at me and winks. 'I've come for a spare part for my bike.'

'Oh, right, what is it you're after? The bike looks in good nick to me.'

'The bike's fine, but what I really need is a dirty slut for the pillion. Would you happen to have one of those in stock?'

'Well, sir, I think you're in luck!' exclaims Eamonn delightedly. 'I've a top of the range model for you, if you're interested. Take a look and see if it'll do for you.'

He follows the line of Eamonn's outstretched arm, walking over to me, inspecting me with fingers stroking his chin. 'Looks rough enough,' he says. 'Looks second-hand, actually. Is this one used or new?'

'Used, I have to admit. But still in tip-top condition.'

'I'll be the judge of that. Can I take a good look all over?'

'Sure. Stand up, slut.'

I rise to my feet, hip thrust out, trying not to look sulky or combative, which is my surprising natural reaction to this scenario.

'OK.' Mr Handsome is thoughtful, his hands tracing my breasts, poking around the nipples. 'Nice rack. Turn her around; a good arse is my number one requirement.'

Eamonn shoves me around by the shoulder so that Mr Handsome can give my buttocks a comprehensive tactile examination.

'Outstanding quality,' he drawls, giving them a little pat. 'Can you bend her over for me. I just want to make absolutely sure.'

Eamonn makes me lean over, elbows on the desk, bottom up high so that the lycra strains around my thigh tops, easily revealing my pussy to anybody's curious view.

'Ah, yeah, I can see that she's used now,' says Mr Handsome, peering up the canyon of my thighs. He puts a hand at the slope of each bottom cheek and pulls them apart, nudging up the lycra. I can feel his thumbs press into the soft inner cheek, feel my tensed anus under close inspection. 'Not so much here though. This part looks almost pristine. I'm happy with it. I'll take it. How much do you want for it?'

'Well, considering the stretched state of the front hole, I'll knock it down to a tenner.'

'Hm, make it a fiver and you've got a deal.'

'Well ...' Eamonn crouches beside Mr Handsome, staring up at the pussy he fucked so diligently earlier that morning. 'OK. Five pounds. It'll last you ages though, and it can take all kinds of hard use. You've got a bargain there. I'm robbing myself really.'

Mr Handsome just laughs and hands over a crumpled banknote before slapping my backside and ordering me over to his bike.

'Come on. I've got plans for you,' he says, handing me his spare helmet. I struggle to fasten it, never having worn one before, and he has to help me, keeping one hand on my tight lycra-clad bottom while he fidgets with it.

'Right. Hop on. The bike, that is.' He winks, climbing astride the seat and waiting for me to arrange myself behind him. I have to spread my legs over the leather pillion and my pussy is all but open to the air; the skirt hovering around the crest of my bottom cheeks. Anyone driving behind will glimpse a strip of split flesh between the sleek black seat and the tight white lycra.

'You ought to be wearing jeans and a jacket, for safety, but I'll take it as slow and easy as I can,' says Mr Handsome, twisting his head round to me. 'Hold on – hang on to me round the waist if you want, or you can hold the handle behind you.'

I don't feel confident enough to hang on behind, so I place shivery arms around his waist. I have a feeling this is going to be a cold ride, despite the early summer warmth, and I half wish for a set of my own leathers, although that would negate the Ride of Shame element of my fantasy. Ah well. The practical and the fantastical rarely marry, and, so far, things have gone rather more swimmingly than I expected. A little discomfort won't kill me.

The engine surprises me, flaring into sudden life, and I squeeze Mr Handsome tight. The vibrations roar through me. Oh, I am going to hate this. And I am going to love it. I have my eyes shut when he begins to wheel the bike slowly out of the garage, and shut even tighter when he turns into the High Road, building up speed, but keeping it steady and the pair of us upright. I open my eyes for the last few yards and am gratified to see some poppy-out eyes and dropped jaws on the pavement, following our progress out of town.

The bike takes us down into the valleys, along the shining snake of a river, and, although I hate the hairpin bends that force us to lean sideways until we almost touch the tarmac, I do enjoy the straight bursts that make my neck want to snap back and the wind sweep all around me. I laugh. I am exhilarated. It is almost what I thought it would be, and I am always pleased when my expectations are borne out. Perhaps, after all, I have missed my calling and was born to be wild. Rather inconvenient, if so. I shall put the thought from my head and resolve to simply enjoy this interlude for what it is, rather than where it could lead – for it really can't lead anywhere.

Mr Handsome steers his monster off the beaten track and into coniferous woodland, finally coming to a halt in a pine-needly patch of makeshift car park, overhung by trees and completely deserted. It would be quite easy to believe that nobody had ever been here, if only the car park didn't make it rather obvious that they had.

'Here we are.' Mr Handsome removes his helmet and places booted feet on the soft ground, grinning at me. 'Enjoy the ride?'

'Actually, yes. It was super.'

'Good. I hope you enjoy the next one too. Get your helmet off and bend over the seat. Quickly!' The last word is a growl; he grabs my wrist and pulls me off the bike. Once again, I can't make head nor tail of the helmet, so he removes it for me, then nods, grim-faced, at the bike seat. I swallow. This is it. It is going to happen. I am going to be buggered over a bike in the open air, just as planned.

The trees swish and birds tweet. It's all so wholesome I can hardly bring myself to … but I do it. I fold my stomach over the leather, still warm where we sat, and attempt to get comfortable while also ensuring that my legs don't accidentally touch the hot exhaust pipe. So many things I hadn't imagined having to consider … but now we are here, and now it will be done, and Mr Handsome gives a very good impression of a man who knows what he is doing, so I will just let him … do.

I hear him behind me; boots on the soft needles, then his leather trousers nudge my nude thighs, and he is standing over me, hard crotch perched between my exposed bottom cheeks, looking down at the picture I make, laid in readiness for my sodomising.

I wonder what he is waiting for when he makes no move for a minute or two.

'You sure about this?' he says softly.

'Excuse me, I am the paying customer here,' I tell him. 'If I'm not sure about something, you can be quite sure I will tell you.'

My condescending tone spurs him into immediate action, as I hoped it would. He lifts the inadequate scrap of fabric over my bottom, unzips a pocket and uncaps something – I can guess what. I have guessed correctly, as the chilly drip of a gelatinous substance hitting the target between my parted rear cheeks is the next sensation. Mr Handsome's rough, stubby fingers dive into the splodgy lube, smearing it all over the back entrance, working it in, making me twitch and quiver, making me delirious with the knowledge that I have no escape, that I must just bend over and take it.

'Your arse is getting fucked,' he tells me, as if I needed to be told. 'And if I had my way, I'd be spanking it first, but you didn't put that in your list …' He trails off, waiting for a yea or nay, hopeful of the former.

'No, I didn't. I'm not into pain. Only humiliation.'

'Right. Humiliation coming right up.' His thumb spears me, easily sneaking through the sphincter and inside the back passage, where it jiggles for a while, as if measuring dimensions. I squirm on it, happily helpless, loving the sound of his leather trousers creaking downwards, releasing the cock that has already fucked me once today.

His thumb pops out and then there is something wider and heavier there, backed by pressure that would be far too strong to fight. Mr H's hands are beneath my thighs, holding my legs straight and still, clearing the way for his intent prick. It makes its first bold sally into the tight breach, half-opening me where I have sealed shut on the exit of the thumb. My body tries to resist at first, in its inevitable way, but I manage to still my reflexes and hold tight, pushing out while he inches in, letting this man who is a stranger further and further up the forbidden passage until I feel his balls swing against the curve of my cheeks and I am full. Uncomfortably full, it must be said. But gloriously, uncomfortably full.

'This is what you need,' he grunts. 'What you've been after all along. Isn't it?'

'Yah.'

He begins to thrust. He is not ceremonious or

217

sensitive about it. He gives me the hard, fast bangbangbang I dream of, pinning me to his machine, slamming me into the cushioned leather. It is a miracle that the bike stays upright, but somehow it does, all the way through, from the opening of my arse to the filling of it with hot cream, from making me feel the thrill of submission to making me feel the thrill of orgasm. The bike triumphs – I think it is a Triumph, actually – and I take what I deserve.

When I stop howling, the birds are still tweeting, the trees still swaying. It is comforting to know that the world is still the same. Mr Handsome is still pulling out, and my muscles are doing that strange, possessive thing, as if they want him to stay for ever, when I start moving on in my mind, thinking about what I have to do when I get home, and whom I need to call, and how my hustings speech is only half-written.

He straightens up, puffing, chuckling a little under my breath.

'Christ,' he says. 'I could do that all over again.'

I breathe out, then find the forest floor with the soles of my gogo boots.

'Awfully sorry,' I say turning and pulling the tight skirt back down over my sore backside. 'But it's highly unlikely that you will.'

'I know.' He smiles. 'I can't promise I'll vote for you, but I think I'll be getting a special feeling in my trousers every time I see you on the news. I wonder what your leader would say if he knew ...'

'Well, he won't know, will he?' I am irritated with Mr Handsome. I want to brush him off like a fly. He has served, and now he should just back discreetly away. If I could make his memory of today vanish with the flick of a switch, I'd do it.

I think he realises this.

'Hop on then, if you don't want to do post-shag conversation. I'll get you back to your car.'

'Fine. Thanks. Really, thanks for everything.' I soften a little; he is trying to be nice, after all. He smiles and winks, then does the honours with the helmet again, and before my legs have recovered, I am back on the bike, sailing through the highways and byways, back to that same cindery car park the day began in.

I think of the road ahead – a long, hard road. Late nights, early press calls, endless canvassing. But at least that dark edge has been taken off now and I can face the future: true to my country, true to my heritage. I might buy a bike though, all the same.

Lucky Strike

IT WAS DIFFICULT, ROLLING along the tracks from London to Colliton on a forlorn and foggy morning, not to remember the train journey that started it all off. Charlotte laid her head back against the dusty blue-black check upholstery and swallowed down a lump. Nobody shared the compartment with her this time – was it the very same compartment they had used, all those weeks ago? There was nobody to make her take off her knickers and sit with her legs spread wide while they tapped away at their Blackberries, careless of anybody passing in the corridor outside. Nobody would demand she remove her earpiece and discuss erotic literature with them. Nobody. She was alone again, just her and her kink, rattling around together in the remote English countryside.

'I should have known,' she murmured to herself. 'Should have known it was too good to last. Too good to be true.' Melancholy music on the iPod tuned in with her mood, and she thought back to that last heated exchange between Bryant and Collins: the one when they had threatened to disband the agency unless Charlotte chose one of them or the other.

An impossible demand, and she had chosen not to make it. So here she was, on her way … well, it didn't feel like 'home' any more. It felt like failure.

There were no Torture Gardens in Colliton; the most outrageous thing the town had to offer was a popular dogging spot in the forest. If Charlotte wanted to express her sexuality, she would have to trawl the online sites for somebody who didn't live too far away – and even then, they would probably turn out to be all wrong. It was too daunting to contemplate. She would try to get her old job back at County Hall; meet up with old school friends; forget about her metropolitan adventure and settle back into the monotony of Colliton.

At the employment agency the next day, a spotty youth asked her why she had left her previous job.

'Redundancy? Dismissal?' he asked nasally.

'No. Not really.' Charlotte looked away, studying the cards, with their felt-tipped invitations to be a chef de partie or a stenographer.

'Umm … why then?'

'Personal reasons,' she said.

'You won't get Jobseekers Allowance then.'

'I know. That's why I'm here.' Charlotte's voice was ragged, on the verge of angry tears, and the clueless boy took refuge in his biro, clicking it up and down to fill the awkward silence. 'You're meant to find me a job.'

'Economic climate … is difficult,' he mumbled. 'Will your previous employer provide a reference?'

Charlotte bit her lip. She had been wondering how to deal with this.

'I left rather suddenly,' she admitted. 'So … I'm not sure I want to ask them. I'm not sure I want them to know I'm here, to be honest.'

'Really?' The boy was intrigued. Charlotte suddenly had the horrible feeling he thought she had absconded with a large sum of company money. 'That's a shame. We can't really offer you anything unless we have a referee. Two, ideally.'

Charlotte clenched her hands. She couldn't ask her boss at County Hall – not after she had left without giving *them* notice either … but she needed money. She needed a deposit and a month's rent so she could get away from her parents' understated disappointment as soon as possible.

'OK. You could try giving them a call. Umm …' She gave the boy Collins's office number and sat back, tense in every muscle, barely daring to keep her eyes open, as he dialled the number.

'Am I speaking to Mr Collins? Hello. My name's Paul; I'm calling from the Colliton branch of JobsWorth … I wonder if I could take a few minutes of your time to ask you about a Miss Charlotte Steele …'

Charlotte let the boy's annoyingly ingratiating words drift over her, consciously shutting her ears, refusing to hear what he said. Only when the click of the phone handset filtered through did she lift the self-imposed ban.

'So I'll give you a call when I've phoned round some of our employers,' the boy was saying.

'Oh. He agreed?'

'Er … yes.' The boy shook his head. 'As you must have heard. He said you were an excellent worker – very conscientious and that you consistently went above and beyond the call of duty.'

'He got that right.'

'Good. So we can start to find opportunities for you, Miss Steele. I'll be in touch later today, hopefully. Good morning.'

Charlotte, thus dismissed, picked up her bag and wandered off into the High Street, her emotions high and not completely comprehensible. It was good of Collins to give her a positive reference, wasn't it? That was good. But no. It was bad. It was a formal farewell. It meant that he washed his hands of her and consigned her, happily, to her freedom. He could have asked to speak to her, but he didn't. He could have raged at the boy and said he was owed four weeks work and if she didn't get straight back and perform them, he would take legal action. That would have been a comfort. Well, maybe not a comfort. But it would have left hope ... The thought that his voice had been in the room, pouring into the boy's ears, the mellifluous majesty of it wasted on the cheap-suited drone, made her want to cry. And she did cry, in the porch of the county museum, until the sun came out and she decided to browse the National Trust shop instead of moping.

The next day, she donned the smartest skirt suit from her old work wardrobe, applied discreetly glamorous make-up and headed out of the house and towards the offices of Allder, Lewis & Allder, Colliton's oldest firm of solicitors, specialising – cannily in this town of rich retirees – in the preparation of wills. The sun was out again and, as she walked along the flower-bordered Ropewalk to the town centre, she felt a tiny gleam of optimism flash through the dark clouds. *It'll be all right*, she told herself. *I will survive this.*

She swung her handbag and almost skipped, pretending to be a girl in an advert for hair products, letting the warm sun touch her skin and prepare her for the process of rebirth.

'Wake up, it's a beautiful morning,' she sang, passing the employee car park of a frozen food chain, its piled-high waste bins and general grottiness signalling the end of the fragrant Ropewalk and the start of the seediest area of town. Shame there were eyesores like this in such a pretty town, she thought idly for the millionth time, and then all coherent thought stopped abruptly, with the shocking clamp of a hand around her mouth and a backward yanking on to the dusty gravel.

She tried to yell that the hand tightening around her upper arm *hurt*, but all her breath was forced back into her throat by uncompromising fingers. In short order, she found that her mouth was taped shut, eyes blindfolded and wrists bound before she was pushed unceremoniously into the back seat of a car. Her kidnapper, though, had enough regard for her safety that he seat-belted her in. How odd. Why would he let her sit upright, where she could be seen from passing vehicles? The windows must be blacked out, she thought. Her heart leapt up her gullet, making her want to vomit. She made herself breathe deeply – vomiting wasn't an option when you were gagged. Feeling the warmth of whoever it was hovering near her skin, she tried to talk, making those frantic stunted noises that are all the gagged have recourse to. He – was it a he? – said nothing at all, but he brushed a fingertip along her cheek, and she smelled his scent and … She stopped making the animal noises instantly. She recognised it. She knew who he was. And she smiled, forcing the corners of the tape upward into her cheeks.

Charlotte was in the car a long time, it seemed, but the driver's pleasant taste in classical music helped her along. Once or twice, she even came close to dozing off, sealed in her silent darkness, unable to move or do anything for herself. If only she could talk, she thought, she would ask the driver to stop off so she could take a leak. It was starting to get uncomfortable. She wondered if he would insist on watching her, if she did. Probably, knowing him.

Just as she thought she might have to stain the rather

comfortable seat, the car purred to a halt. The music stilled halfway through a crescendo; the front door clunked and then hers opened, allowing warmth to drift in and over her. The car must have been air-conditioned. The smell was … London. A city smell. Vague rumbling noise in the background was probably traffic, or even trains. Trains. How she loved the sound of trains.

She felt the seatbelt slither diagonally across her chest and stomach, returning to its origins, and then there was a hand on her shoulder, steering her along the seat and towards the open air. *Does he think I don't know it's him? He must do, or he would speak. His voice would give the game away immediately.*

He helped her to her feet, standing her on the ground with two supporting hands on her shoulders. Then one of them lifted and she heard his fingers clicking, loudly, just next to her ear, making her jump. Footsteps approached, and she was manhandled roughly out of her kidnapper's grasp by another man. *I don't know this one!*

Her feelings were confirmed by his voice, which was unfamiliar. 'Come on. Let's get you tucked up nice and tight and safe, shall we?'

He dragged her by the elbow across what she guessed was a yard – the ground was hard beneath her feet, like concrete or asphalt. When they stopped, she heard a heavy door being unbolted, then she was inside somewhere dark and airless, chilly and damp. Very carefully, they negotiated a staircase, then they were in a small room with a very heavy – metallic-sounding – door. Without being able to see a thing, Charlotte somehow knew that it was a cell of some kind. Her captor brought her across to sit on a small, not-very-comfortable bed while he himself remained standing before her.

'Right then, Miss, I'm going to leave you here until the master calls for you, but you needn't think you aren't being watched – I'm to guard you, and I'll be looking in through the grille in the door to make sure you're behaving yourself. The bed is there, and just here,' – he nudged something up to her toe, 'is your chamber pot. Not easy to perform with your hands tied behind your back, I know, but I'm sure you'll find a way. Any questions? No? Good. I'll be back when you're summoned.'

Charlotte had questions – scores of them – but none could burst through the sleek black tape that trapped her mouth. Besides, she was so relieved at the presence of the chamber pot that every other consideration had been temporarily driven from her mind. She waited the few seconds it took for the cell door to bang shut, then she stood up and worked hard at lifting her skirt and lowering her knickers with her tightly tethered hands, having to rub them up and down the small of her back to do anything at all. It was a struggle, but eventually she got the knickers down to her knees, with the aid of much wriggling of hips and bending of legs, and was able to drop down on to the pot with a muted sigh.

As the hot liquid clattered into the basin, she knew she was being watched – it was inevitable – but she was strangely serene. Her tenuously gathered wits told her that she knew what was going to happen. It was all written down and stored in a file on her old work computer. And so far, the script had been followed to the letter. All that remained for her to do was to sit and wait …

He made her sit there, beached on the chamber pot while her nether regions dried slowly in the cold cell air, for exactly one hour. Not that she knew this – to

226

Charlotte, it seemed like an endless void of time. She had pins and needles in her wrists and knew that the rim of the pot had impressed itself into her skin by the time the keys jangled in the lock once more.

She made a vocalisation, an incoherent 'Who's there?' her heartbeat picking up speed while her chest tightened.

'Just me again,' said the guard cheerily. 'You need to get on your feet, Miss Steele. The master is ready to see you.'

Will I be able to see him, though? Charlotte thought, feeling that she ought to be able to exchange a joke with this man – he was probably one of their agency people, on call to perform in various fantasy guises. They had probably spoken dozens of times over the phone or at scenes. They were friends, weren't they? Probably?

He was in role, though, and the casual chumminess disappeared from his voice, replaced by an official stiffness.

'You'll need to show a bit more willing, Miss,' he reproved, grabbing her by the elbow to help her, slightly awkwardly, to her feet.

She made an apologetic noise, blushing furiously, and tried to gesture downward with her chin, to her knickers. They were still bunched at her knees, plainly visible beneath the hem of her flippy skirt.

'I think the master will prefer you to keep them where they are, to be honest,' he said. *Oh, I know that you're right*, Charlotte thought, with a mingling rush of glee and dread. *He will love the additional humiliation factor.*

She allowed herself to be led, shuffling, trying to keep the knickers from falling further, across the cell and back out to the corridor. Making a bolt for it was not going to be an option, especially when the knickers finally slipped to ankle level on the way down a flight of stone stairs. She was tempted to just kick them off and leave them there, but the guard seemed patient enough with her slow gait, bringing her to an echoing chamber where her muffled slipshod steps were amplified alongside the guard's heavy tread.

Eventually, they stopped. The air around Charlotte's head seemed dense and full of dire forewarning. There was somebody else in here with them. Somebody was looking at her. And she couldn't see him.

He must have made some gesture to the guard, perhaps a nod or an upheld hand, because suddenly the blindfold was removed from Charlotte's eyes. She was still blinking, finding even the gloom of this subterranean chamber too bright for her long-sealed eyes, when the guard whipped off the tape gag, causing her mouth to sting and a gasp to fly out of its newly open lips.

'Thank you, Saunders,' said Collins. 'Return to your post now.'

Slowly Charlotte's eyes refocused, and the lean shadow behind the blocky shadow revealed itself to be Collins sitting at a desk, fingers steepled in the way she remembered so well, spectacles on, face absolutely impassive.

'Miss Steele,' he enunciated. She felt she needed to fill the subsequent silence, but she could not decide how. She breathed in a giant lungful of air, grateful to have that ability once more, feeling that she might have need of it sometime soon.

'I gagged you. I didn't cut your tongue out. Do you have nothing to say to me?'

'I ... thought I needed your permission to speak?'

At that, he smiled and a fleeting fondness crossed his

face.

'Yes,' he said softly. 'You are so good at this. It is why I can't let you go. But, regardless of your ability to give me the perfect answer, there is a reckoning to be made. Explain why you left without saying a word to me, Charlotte.'

'I didn't say a word to Bryant either, sir.'

'Master.'

'Sorry, Master.'

'That doesn't even begin to answer my question. Well?'

'I couldn't make a choice. You were asking me to make a choice.'

'Yes, I was. And I'm going to ask you again. A different choice this time. Stay here with me, or walk away. Make the choice, Charlotte. What do you decide?'

Collins rarely, indeed never, showed emotion, but Charlotte could see that his steepled fingers were just that bit more tensed. A knuckle cracked, shocking her into reply.

'I want to stay with you,' she blurted. Yes. Colliton was wrong for her, but Collins was right, so right. Never mind Bryant. Bryant had not gone to the lengths of finding and organising her perfect fantasy kidnap. Forget about him. Right here, right now, she could start a whole new chapter of submission, love and pleasure, with this man she had come to adore.

The fingers quivered and he broke their position, pushing the spectacles back up the bridge of his nose in the few seconds it took for him to collect himself.

'Good,' he said, calm restored. 'I think you have chosen well. On this occasion.' His brow furrowed again, and Charlotte remembered that she should be feeling a little anxious. She bit her lip and looked down at the floor. 'But we still have outstanding matters to address, don't we? Your reluctance to make a choice – when you have proven yourself more than capable of such a task – is an inadequate excuse. And I have yet to hear a word of apology from you for the pain you have caused me.'

Pain, she thought in surprise. *He feels pain. He is not impervious, nor superhuman. He has vulnerabilities too.*

'I'm sorry. I really am. I never meant to … hurt you.' How odd the words sounded, spoken by her, to him who so often meant to hurt her! But his hurting was at her unspoken behest, always, while she had caused a true and less easily-assuaged pain. 'Please forgive me.'

'I will forgive you,' he said, rising from his chair and walking over to an old metal cupboard in one corner of the room. 'But first you have to pay the price of that forgiveness. I'm sure you're expecting that, anyway. And I hate to disappoint.'

He opened the cupboard, took a length of rope, a cane and a box from it.

'Let's not deviate from your script too far, though, shall we? I think we should maintain the illusion of this forced kidnapping I took such pains to set up, just for a while. Don't you think?'

'If you wish, Master,' said Charlotte, trying not to smile. Oh, the cane. Oh, how she hated that thing. And yet she had been hoping for it … dreaming of it, back in her bed in Colliton.

'Saunders!' he said sharply, and she remembered the guard, turning around and seeing that he had been standing by the door all along. 'Bring in the punishment equipment.'

What? Was that not it, that stuff in his hands? Rope, cane, box full of dubious toys … seems like punishment

230

equipment to me.

Saunders wheeled in a strange item of furniture, something like a stepstool, padded all over in black leather.

'I think we need to send a few photographs with the ransom note,' Collins said to his henchman. 'Make sure they realise that we are in earnest. When they see what we've done to her, they'll be sure to start finding the money.'

Saunders came up behind Charlotte and untied her wrists, which she was allowed to stretch and rotate briefly before she was marched over to the stepstool affair and made to kneel on its ledge, arranging her upper body so that it lay along the slope on the other side, her face almost at floor level. The padded top of the device ensured that her bottom jutted out, presented in full curvaceous display mode, while a spreader bar fixed between her knees meant that she had to keep her thighs wide too.

'Take off her top,' Collins ordered, and Saunders darted over, pulling the garment over her head, then, without prompting, unclipped her bra as well. The smooth leather was cold on her nipples and she was conscious of the guard's eye, sizing up her breasts even though they were squashed to the slope of the punishment stool.

'As for that skirt ...' said Collins laconically, and then his hands were on her, tugging it down while she gripped the sides of the slope. The knickers were long gone now, and they were swiftly joined by her shoes until she lay, entirely naked and exposed, ready for the two men to dispose of her as they saw fit.

'You're very compliant,' noted Collins, his tone sharp, and Charlotte had to rouse herself from the luxury of her submission to play the role of agitated victim about to undergo cruel and unusual treatment.

'You can't do this!' she exclaimed. 'You … when the police get hold of you … you bastards!'

Collins laughed, deep and long. 'We are the police,' he said chillingly. 'Aren't we, Saunders?'

'That's right, guv.' Saunders was tying her ankles to the stool now, then looping the rope up and around her torso, lashing her to the fetish furniture until she was almost a part of it.

'You're here until we get our money, young lady, and until then, we will do what we want with you. Do you understand?'

Collins forced her head up, taking her chin and wrenching her neck to meet his iron gaze.

'I understand. But you can't make me accept it. I will never accept it.'

For a fleeting second, Charlotte thought about spitting in his face. But no. Collins would absolutely *hate* that. He did set such store by elegant behaviour in all situations.

'You will accept what we give you. All of it. Starting now.' He straightened back up to his full height and watched Saunders complete his expert bondage work. 'Good. Trussed up like a little chicken, Charlotte. Tied up and ready for your whipping. Because you are going to be whipped. Long and soundly, until your bottom is red and hot enough to glow in the photograph we will take of it. What do you think of that?'

'You evil pervert!' she cried, finding the line laughably hokey even as she said it. Ah well. She wasn't best placed to hone her improvisational skills, bent double over a leather punishment stool, naked and in knots. 'You won't get away with this.' She tried to struggle in her bonds, but Saunders had an impressive way with rope, and the best she could do was squirm.

'No? Well, if you're going to call us perverts, I suppose we ought to live up to our billing.' Collins brought the box down beneath her nose and opened it, selecting a large black silicone butt plug and wafting it in the air before her. 'I think you've earned this, young lady.'

'Oh my God! No!' she squealed, recognising the plug as Collins's favourite Instrument of Sanction. He had used it on her in the past, at times of extreme displeasure with her, and it commanded serious respect.

'Did you hear that, Saunders? I think she's starting to get the message. We mean business. Lubricate her.'

Charlotte was unable to prevent anything they wanted to do to any part of her, and all she could do was lie there in her tethers while Saunders greased a finger and began to circle her tensing anus with it, massaging it into the sensitive skin of her cleft until she could feel her muscles begin to pulse and twitch, helplessly betraying her arousal.

'I think she wants it!' Saunders was amused.

'Is she wet?'

Charlotte's breath hitched at the touch of another finger at her lower hole, dipping in and then slicking out.

'Is she ever! Fuck me, she's dripping.'

'Hmm, wait till after the caning, then. I bet she'll be even wetter.' His hand descended briefly on the back of Charlotte's neck, ruffling the hair at her nape affectionately. *He knows I will.*

Saunders re-lubed the finger and sent it, in one clean swift stab, up inside her puckered ring, wiggling it about a bit to get a feel for her size and stretch. Charlotte wanted to roll her hips so very badly, but she could not so much as jiggle them. She gritted her teeth and lay flat, resigned, while Saunders introduced the large fat plug slowly into her captive backside.

'How does that feel, Charlotte?' asked Collins, interested, though her faint squeaks and moans were providing quite a detailed answer.

'Uncomfortable,' she gasped. 'Please ...' The widest part of the plug was now stretching her ring, making tears blur her eyes. 'I can't.'

I could safeword. But the thought was gone before she could even have articulated it, and the plug was past the barrier now, firmly seated and unignorable, showing her her place in this scenario.

'Let me see.' Collins came around to the back and rotated the plug a few times, then he pulled it partway out, making her babble and plead for mercy, before popping it back in and then, for good sadistic measure, repeating the process. 'I love this one,' he said. 'It really is my favourite. The inflatable one is good as well. Perhaps another time.'

When he came back into Charlotte's line of vision, a quick strain of her neck muscles informed her that Collins was no longer carrying anything. So where was the ...?

'You may begin when I give the word, Saunders.'

Charlotte meeped in dismay – so she was to be caned by a stranger, not by the expert Mr Collins? His shiny shoes, so close to her nose, splayed outwards a little, and then he was crouching before her, so close that the expensive cloth of his trouser hem brushed her face. He held her by the chin, keeping her pale face upraised towards his.

'You are going to look at me, Charlotte,' he murmured. 'Hold my eye. If you look away, it will be the worse for you.'

'Oh ...' Charlotte was beyond words. She had never had to do this before. In the past, she had always been able to shut her eyes and become the pain, weightless in subspace. This thing Collins was asking her to do was almost unimaginably difficult – and yet she wanted to do it. She wanted to go the extra submissive mile, because he was doing this for her, and she loved him for it. Would it be easier if he relaxed his expression just a fraction, was ever so slightly less convincing a cruel, authoritarian kidnapper? No. He was Collins. He was what he was. He played every scene to the hilt, and that was how she wanted him. Relaxation could come later.

So she breathed in, set her jaw and opened her eyelids as wide as they would stretch.

'She's ready. Give her ten, Saunders. Hard.'

She looked at him, steadfast, through every burning stroke. Her broken cries, her hisses, her contortions of expression, never interrupted the line of contact between Charlotte and her master. Each swish of the rod was a pulse of energy setting her on a journey through pain and love, a journey that set her on fire, that tested her limits, that took her deep inside herself, but that eventually would see her home safe.

'No more,' she begged on the eighth stroke, but she didn't mean it. She didn't use her safeword. The plug send shockwaves through her every time the cane landed, and then the ferocious fizz of pain streaked across her skin. Two more. Just two more. Her eyes were swimmy now, but she could still see Collins's face, looking so cold, because it had to, because that was the rule – her rule as much as his.

The ninth stroke made her body convulse, straining against the bonds, sweat beading on her brow. 'Thank you, sir,' she whispered, and she saw he was struggling against an impulse to smile. She had won. She had done it. She had not given in.

'Make the last stroke a good one, Saunders,' said Collins, his voice very low now, dark smoke in the echoing room. Charlotte let the rod whistle, let it lay its stripe across the hot, stretched skin of her bottom, let the sting grow and grow and grow while she whimpered, then she blinked, hard and looked back at Collins.

'I love you,' she said.

He cupped her cheeks in big, warm palms. 'I know. I love you too,' he said. 'Saunders, take a photograph, would you? Then you may go.' He dropped one kiss on her damp forehead, waited for the camera to flash, then moved back around behind Charlotte, trailing one fingertip along her spine, down into the small of her back, up again and into the crevice of her buttocks. Charlotte began to gasp, feeling the sting and the sensation together, especially when he stopped at the butt plug and gave it a little tap before proceeding onward, to the water valley beneath.

'Oh, wet, as ever, oh, you are ready. I'm going to take you.'

There was nothing Charlotte could have done about it anyway, but she uttered a silent prayer of thanks, trying to thrust her bottom further towards him, but finding it impossible. He was there, quick and sharp, wide and long, inside her again. She sighed and purred, drenched in lust and emotion, sure that she would come without permission, she was so close already.

'Please, Master, may I come?' she asked, before he was even fully sheathed, causing him to chuckle as he placed his hands on her burning backside.

'So eager, Charlotte. I should refuse you, but tonight I

find that I can't do that. You may come as many times as you wish.'

She took him at his word, feeling her tremors build as soon as he began his initial thrusts. He rode her through two more, pacing himself so perfectly that she was weeping by the time he relented and finished emptying inside her, the tip of his cock nudging against the butt plug with each foray forward.

'I love your tears,' he said, wiping himself off and grabbing her hair at the nape of her neck, pulling it gently but firmly. 'But you must stop crying, Charlotte. I'm going to untie you now, and we are going home.'

'Home?'

He began to loosen the cords, leaving her to gather herself until only periodic sniffs betrayed her emotional overflow. His fingers traced the patterned lines the rope had left, stroking the woven indents. Charlotte might have been untied, but she was no more mobile than before, her limbs heavy and stiff.

'I should take out the plug,' mused Collins. 'I know you hate this bit … brace yourself …'

But she was too tired and she let him pull it out without her customary mild fuss and resistance, though she still yelped with the momentary pain.

'You're bad at that usually, but that was better. Was that obedience or sheer exhaustion?'

'The latter,' she murmured, happily bent over the stool, enjoying the residual throb of her caning – always a moment to treasure.

'Charlotte … can you stand?'

'Uh uh,' was all she could manage. Collins tutted fondly, then picked up her naked, welted body and carried it out of the chamber.

She must have fallen asleep in the back of his car,

because her next memory was of cold leather against her very sore, nude bottom, and a seatbelt crossing between her breasts and … Collins sitting beside her, one hand on a thigh while he frowned at a mobile phone screen.

'Where we going?' she mumbled. 'Where's this?'

'You've never been to my home before, have you? We're going there.'

'You're not …'

'Not what?'

'I asked Bryant once if you were married … he never did answer me … I just thought …'

'The things Bryant leaves unsaid are usually the ones that reveal the most about him,' frowned Collins. 'I'm not married. Unattached. Never found a submissive who wasn't needy or wildly attention-seeking or irritating in some other way. Until now.'

'Until me?'

'Until you, Charlotte. You know what you are, and you get on with being it. You make it all so simple and so pleasurable.'

'I am more than a submissive, you know.'

'I do know that. Of course I do. But you don't bang on and on about it, unlike some. I know you have other ambitions and interests. I will respect that. Outside the bedroom … or should I say, the dungeon … you will be treated as my equal always.'

'So we're … establishing a partnership … are we?'

'If you like.'

'Will I get to know you? I don't know you at all.'

'I don't let my guard down until I know I can, Charlotte. I think I might be able to … just slightly … perhaps, now. I used to be a punk, you know.'

Charlotte gasped then choked out a laugh. 'What? What? You?'

238

'Hmm. Tartan trousers with safety pins. Down the 100 Club every Friday and Saturday. Can you imagine it?'

'No! Not at all!'

'Well, if you're a good girl, I'll show you the photographs some time. Not the ones with the unfortunate lime spray-paint job on my hair though. They may be lost for all time.'

'Were you in a band?'

'No. I managed one though. Bryant was in it. He played bass. Or so he claimed. I don't think he knew more than one chord.'

'You met … through *punk rock*?'

'Is it so strange? Lots of kinky sex in the punk iconography, you know.'

'Well, yeah, I suppose that's true. But wow all the same.'

'Wow indeed.'

'So you and Bryant go right back to the Seventies.'

'Further than that. We were at school together. Hated each other, though. It was music that brought us together – I don't think anything else would have worked.'

'It seems a shame …'

'A shame? What seems a shame?'

'The agency. All your work. Your … you had such a dynamic together. You were like psychic twins. You always understood what the other was going to do. Is it really all over?'

Collins did not reply, because the car had descended into an underground car park, indicating that the destination had been reached.

'Is this a public car park?' asked Charlotte nervously, once the door had been opened by Saunders, the chauffeur.

'Yes.' Collins smiled charmingly. 'Out you get then.'

Charlotte was allowed one consternated expression before having to step gingerly out of the car, wincing as her cane stripes peeled reluctantly from the leather. Collins came out behind her, pressing her bottom to his trousered thighs and urging her on, barefoot across the concrete, to the elevator shaft.

'It's cold,' she muttered, teeth chattering, but Collins was busy thanking Saunders for his work tonight and promising that the cheque would be in the post tomorrow. The elevator, like the car park, was mercifully empty, though when it stopped at the lobby to let Saunders out, there were a couple of people standing across by the main door who could have caught a flash of Charlotte's nude front view. The lift doors shut before anybody's decency was outraged, though, and they continued up to the top floor and out into the landing of the penthouse suite.

Collins's apartment had floor-to-ceiling windows on every side, and from them all of London could be seen. A galaxy of lights surrounded them, from the yellowish glow of the neighbouring apartment blocks to the circular fluorescence of the London Eye. The eternal wink of the Canary Wharf tower could be seen from the bathroom, while the bedroom looked out towards Heathrow, the undercarriages of aircraft flashing red and green as they took their diagonal upward path to the skies.

'You live in the sky,' said Charlotte wonderingly.

'It's the only way to escape the constant crowds in London,' he replied, coming up behind her, pressing her to the window, which was as yet uncurtained. 'They would love to see this.' He dipped a hand down across her belly, placing his palm flat on her navel, and kissed her neck.

'Perhaps they can,' she said nervously. Some of those other apartment blocks were only a few yards away. Most of them were lower, but not all. It was conceivable that somebody could be looking out of their window, up to Collins's eyrie.

'I don't care,' said Collins darkly. 'I don't care what they see. I'll display you any time I see fit. What do you think of that?'

'Oh,' was all Charlotte could say, the sound coming out as a moan. Collins's fingers were sliding lower, positioning themselves at the juncture of thigh and crotch.

'I am your master,' he said into her ear. 'Say it.'

'You are my master.' She let her feet slip further apart, let him push his fingers up inside.

'Good. So let's have you kneeling on the rug now, shall we?'

Charlotte, perfectly obedient, waited for him to withdraw his fingers before placing herself as ordered on the thick cream rug. She tucked her arms into the small of her back, the stance Collins always favoured for the way it made her spine arch and breasts jut.

'Shut your eyes, Charlotte.' Collins's voice was seductive smoke, wafting over her sensitive skin. 'Don't open them unless you are told. Just allow yourself to be touched, felt, used.'

Charlotte shut her eyes, listening to the soft footfalls around her, then feeling a hand on her shoulder, then a cupping of a breast. Her nipples swelled, and a circling thumb sent messages lower down, resulting in an answering bloom in her clitoris. She waited patiently while the hands took their sweet time, examining every inch of her breasts before inspecting her marked bottom, cruelly pinching at the welts so that she jerked and cried out, but did not open her eyes. The hand smacked at her sore bottom until she was gasping and whimpering, but she never broke position and she kept the eyes tight. Then, ah yes, then it was where she wanted it, in the wanton wetness between her legs, giving her pleasure after the pain, giving her what she needed. She kept as still as she could, trusting her master's hand to know how best to bring her to her crisis, letting it flick and rub and press. While one set of fingers kept up this work, another set speared her hot, tight cunt, penetrating it with wicked efficiency. Charlotte was going to come soon, she knew it, and she did not have to ask permission today, so she simply let her breathing pattern give Collins the clue he needed, coming closer and closer, panting for air, feeling the tiny ticklish curl of her incipient orgasm, building, building, building ... There were hands on her breasts now, two hands, and yet there were still hands ... on ... everywhere ... oh, oh, ohhhhhhhh.

She let the tornado blow through, and then she dared to open her eyes.

Bryant was smiling at her, while Collins lurked at her hind.

'Hello, Charlotte. That looked nice. Would you like some more?'

Lucky Stars

LONDON LEGEND HAD IT that the building had been, at various times, a church; a music hall; the headquarters of an occult secret society; a prison; an illegal drinking club. Now its upper floors functioned as a cutting edge arts space while the crypt – in which the ceremony was to take place – hosted a variety of events, including the monthly meetings of the city's most exclusive sex club.

It was a beautiful, if rather chilly, almost intimidating place, Charlotte had thought when they had gone to inspect its suitability as a venue for the scene they had in mind. But then, given what was going to happen there, perhaps these were all good qualities.

Charlotte was so nervous her hands were shaking, so she was grateful for the help with her preparations.

'You look stunning,' Lady Markham assured her, retracting the mascara wand after the final waterproof layer. 'You know they will think so too. Now, stand up, dear, and I'll see to the finishing touches.'

The finishing touches involved rouge on the nipples and the labia, so it was a good thing Charlotte and the peeress had built up such a cordial relationship over the course of the last few months at the agency.

'Why are you so nervous?' scolded Lady Markham, smoothing gold-sheened oil all over Charlotte's belly and breasts.

'How many people are out there?' she wondered.

'Oh, scores, darling. I had the invitations printed by my stationer. I'm sure we ordered a hundred.'

'*A hundred?*'

'Those boys have never done things by halves. This will be no exception. Goodness, dear, you've been their partner in crime all this time. Surely you know that!'

Charlotte wanted desperately to peek through the keyhole of this small anteroom off the main crypt and see if she could identify any of the guests, but that would probably ruin her eye make-up, and Lady Markham might reprove her poor etiquette.

'How long have you known them?' she asked, raising her arms obediently to facilitate Lady Markham's full access to her body.

'Most of my life, dear. Jeremy was my first lover.'

'Bryant! No! Really?'

'Yes! We do have rather a lot in common, Charlotte. At least one element of which must be obvious to you.'

'Well. Yes. Did you … was it love? At the time?'

'It was infatuation. More on my side than his.' She sighed, and her hand slowed a little in its oiling. 'Twenty years ago, darling. You were still at prep school.'

'I didn't go to prep school.'

'You didn't miss much. Anyway.' She put her hands in a basin of water, ostensibly washing them, but also appearing to wash away the intrusive memory. 'Jeremy and I have both moved on, as it were. I have a wonderful new mistress, and he … well, he has you. Could you spread your legs a little wider, dear? I can't leave your thighs untouched, now, can I?'

'I'm so glad it's all worked out between you and Krysztyna,' said Charlotte, smiling, a little ruefully. 'It sounds like the perfect arrangement.'

'Oh, it is, my dear. I think I might prevail upon her to move in permanently soon.' Her long fingers with their oval polished nails massaged the oil into every crevice and cranny of Charlotte's legs and thighs, until she shone golden from the noblewoman's attentions. 'I think you'll do now. Hand me the corset.'

The corset was an underbust model, constructed of whaleboned satin with ribbon laces. Charlotte loved it and had chosen it herself, but she still could not help thinking that such a restrictive, ferocious item had no business being so delicately beautiful. She held her breath and kept her shoulders well back while Lady Markham pulled at the laces with such force it seemed for a moment like revenge. *You've taken Bryant, you've taken Collins, now you can take this!* But that was just paranoia, of course. 'You'll have to hang on to the door knob for all you're worth,' said Lady Markham through gritted teeth, and she pulled and tugged as if trying to rein in a runaway horse, finally succeeding in getting Charlotte's waist to little more than the span of a large man's hands.

'I must admit,' Lady Markham continued, picking up the gossamer silk stockings, 'I've been to a few of these collaring ceremonies in my time, but never one like this. Never one submissive and two Dominants. It will be quite unusual. Lift up your right leg, dear, and I'll put this stocking on you.'

Charlotte let her roll the tissue-thin silk up her calf toward her thigh, clipping it to the snaps that hung down from the corset.

'Jago obviously loves you to death.'

Charlotte fought the urge to giggle, as she always did whenever she heard someone use Collins's given name. She would never be able to call him it, she realised.

Never. Ever. Disloyal and cruel though it made her feel, she found the name too absurd. He would be Collins, forever and always, to her.

'Do you think so?' she asked, trying to mute the sudden uprising of hysteria. She couldn't laugh. It was just too uncomfortable in this corset.

'I know so. To want someone so much he would actually *share* her ... well. Even if it is with Jeremy, who is like his blood brother.'

'Were you a punk too?'

'Me? God, no. I did get into the New Romantic thing a bit though. There.'

The stockings were on, the hair sleeked back and held in a tight plait, both sets of lips crimson and hairless. 'Sit down. I'll do the shoes.'

Charlotte held out her feet, watching Lady Markham wrap the slender ankle straps round and round before buckling them firmly, imprisoning her feet in the criss-cross leather.

'He really does love me? They both do?' Charlotte's words came out in an anxious tumble, a plea for reassurance.

'Charlotte, who could not love you? Yes.' She sat back on her heels and smiled, genuinely. 'You're a lucky girl. They will treat you like a goddess. A goddess who likes to be whipped, that is.'

Charlotte rose to four-inch-heeled feet, holding her arms out to the sides for a moment until she had found her centre of equilibrium and was able to remain still atop her towering footwear.

'And you look like one too,' said Lady Markham, stepping back with her hands clasped in appraisal. 'A goddess.'

She was not looking so undeific herself, swathed in a

white silk toga with gold adornments, including a wide band around her waist and a torque at her throat. Her sand-blonde hair was piled up and pinned in place by a plain gold tiara. She looked rather like a Roman version of Wonderwoman, Charlotte thought, and her legs, emerging from the abbreviated hem of the toga, were every bit as good.

'Just the cloak then, and we're set.'

Charlotte felt a dry fear grip her, and she cast about for something to delay the inevitable moment – an extra spritz of hairspray, a slick of lip-gloss, more oil for her calves. It was strange that she should feel this stage fright when she had been on display many times before, often in front of a crowd. This was different though. This meant something and, though there was no legal basis to it and it could be taken back any time, the weight of commitment hung about the ceremony.

A cloak of heavy satin, clasped at the collarbone, was placed about Charlotte's shoulders. The fabric was cold and slick against her naked areas, pressing down on her shoulders. It slid deliciously over her uncovered buttocks and breasts, prompting the first prickly heat of arousal just as Lady Markham unlocked the chamber door and stood one step outside, indicating to the crowd that Charlotte was ready and the service could begin.

Hundreds of candles cast flickering shadows on the flagstone walls of the crypt, and the crowds of people who stood in knots around the vaulted room looked golden and glamorous, like dream representations of their real selves. Charlotte remembered to cross her arms across her chest and approach the far wall of the building with her eyes downcast. She was not meant to see her 'grooms' until their hands were upon her, so Lady Markham acted as her eyes, leading her along the aisle created by the dividing crowds.

Charlotte's ears tried to pick out phrases from the murmuring that accompanied her slow path forward, but it all merged into a buzz, adding itself to the jangling of her nerves and the heady tingling of erotic anticipation that underlaid everything.

When Lady Markham drew to a halt in front of her, she felt a hand on each shoulder, urging her down, to kneel. Charlotte was heartened to find a velvet hassock placed on the cold flags, sparing her delicately-stockinged knees, and she risked a sneaky glance upward, where Collins and Bryant stood, seeming endlessly tall and dark-suited, their heads somewhere far above her.

Lady Markham, now established at the front of the hall, held up a hand for silence. It seemed that she was to conduct whatever proceedings were to follow, and indeed, London's most famous submissive certainly seemed to command respect, for not a sound could be heard. Charlotte glanced sideways, and caught sight of a cushion, piled up with all kinds of remarkable things. She swallowed, clenched her thighs together, and found them wet. This was going to be a night to remember.

'Ladies and gentlemen, masters, mistresses and slaves, tonight is a momentous night,' intoned Lady Markham. 'It has been my privilege to know Mr Collins and Mr Bryant for a number of years, and nobody could be more delighted than me to know that they have reached the end of their search for the perfect submissive. I hope you will join me in celebrating the Collaring of Charlotte. Today she enters into a covenant with her two masters, signalling the beginning of a wonderful journey into committed submission and all that it brings. She will be loved, cherished and mastered by two absolutely superior men, and they in turn will enjoy the devoted obedience of their bond servant. Charlotte, you may kiss the feet of each of your new owners.'

Charlotte turned instinctively to the right, placing her lips first on Collins's highly polished brogue, then she repeated the process with Bryant.

'Now I would like to hear Mr Collins and Mr Bryant repeat after me the vows they have personally created to best reflect their hopes and plans for Charlotte.'

Collins and Bryant spoke in perfect unison, echoing the words Lady Markham spoke next. They promised that they would give Charlotte everything she needed. They would demand her submission without ever hindering her growth. They would love and cherish her. They would devise strict rules and would strictly enforce discipline for any breach of them. They would be consistent, firm and fair. Well, not always fair. But consistent and firm. They would endeavour to provide an atmosphere of stability, harmony and peace where Charlotte could continue to flourish and enjoy her life. If they ever failed her, they would not prevent her from ending the contract.

And now it was Charlotte's turn to speak. She lifted her face to Lady Markham's and repeated the phrases in a clear, distinct voice. She owed it to her audience that they should be able to hear the terms of her surrender.

'I, Charlotte Steele, promise my full and complete submission to Mr Collins and Mr Bryant. I will be honest about my needs, desires and ambitions. I will respect my masters, in thought, word and deed. I will be obedient in the bedroom, and tolerant outside of it. I will not refuse an order without a valid reason. I will give to them every part of myself, whenever and wherever it is required of me. If these vows ever become untenable, I will give fair warning of my intention to leave. I will wear my collar with pride and will work tirelessly at being the best submissive I can be.'

Of course, these were just the broad brush strokes of the contract. There were details, and devils in those details – many, many clauses and sub-clauses lurked on the parchment, in the copperplate hands of Mr Collins and Mr Bryant. Charlotte would be fenced in with duties and requirements, just as she had always dreamed of being. Her mode of dress, her daily timetable, even her personal grooming, would all be strictly controlled and subject to regular examination. They had sat up, night after night, thrashing out the new world order – sometimes literally thrashing it out – until the perfect compromise of submission and humanity had been established.

The vows exchanged, the ceremony moved on to what Lady Markham called 'The Demonstration of Commitment'.

'Mr Collins, would you place the collar on Charlotte.'

She had not known what the collar would look like, or be made of, so she was mildly surprised to feel the familiar rough underside of a common leather dog collar placed around her neck. A metal tag flapped its chill rim against the hollow of her throat; Charlotte could not see it, but she guessed there must be an inscription of some kind. She held her chin up while Mr Collins, behind her, fastened the buckle with care, making sure it was tight enough without being too tight. The leather was stiff and Charlotte was sorely tempted to put a hand up to it, to try and soften its hard edges. She had been half-expecting something fashioned from a precious metal, or something so subtle as to almost not be recognisable as a collar, but she realised that it was important to her masters that her position of subjection be blatant and clear to the world at large. She would not be allowed to conceal her submission, even on the bus or in the supermarket. It was a fact of her life. There was no lock, no key, just a buckle that she could undo at will, and this also struck her as symbolic. She had the freedom to uncollar herself. She was not a slave; the buckle was the mark of a woman who gave herself willingly, and could take herself away as soon as that will deviated from its current course. Collins and Bryant had no interest in being seen as throwbacks to the recent age of patriarchy – that would have offended them. She congratulated herself on having found such a pair of enlightened, intelligent sadists.

But now it was Bryant's turn to place the ring on her finger and all pondering ceased under the weight of the heavy metal circle.

'Remove her cloak, gentlemen, and commence the Endurance Ceremony.'

The satin poured off Charlotte's shoulders, leaving them bare. Now the congregation would be able to see her pale flanks and bottom, her breasts spilling over the cage of the corset, nipples erect in the stone-walled cold.

Bryant took her chin and angled it up – at last, she was permitted to look at her newly-minted masters. She essayed a tentative smile, and then gasped with shock as Collins took a firm grip of one breast and applied a silver clover clamp to the nipple. Charlotte had never quite understood the appeal of these devices; her breasts were sensitive and the spring-loaded jaws of the clamps caused her to suck in her breath and use all her powers of mental displacement to pretend they weren't there. Both Collins and Bryant loved the fierce, eye-rolling cast of concentration this gave to her face, and used them all the more for it, naturally. The first one fixed, its twin was pincered into place, causing Charlotte to vent an involuntary whimper of pain. She disappeared to the place inside her head that denied the sharp pressure and embraced the submission, letting her swimming eyes fixate on Bryant and his eternal indulgent smile.

He kept his finger beneath her chin when Collins placed a hand beneath her armpit and hauled her to her feet.

'Let's show you off,' he said under his breath, spinning her round to face the crowd. 'Ladies and gentlemen, may I present Miss Charlotte Steele, the possession and plaything of Mr Jeremy Bryant and Mr Collins.' Charlotte, despite the burning heat that was now seeping into every fibre of her being, suppressed a grin at Collins's avoidance of pronouncing his full name.

Bryant left her briefly, only to return with the velvet hassock under one arm and a solid wooden block under the other. He placed the block in front of Charlotte, and then set the hassock to its right hand side, indicating that she was to kneel and rest her stomach on the block, presenting a profile view of her upthrust bottom and dangling breasts to the appreciative crowd.

Charlotte did not need her wealth of experience to tell her what was coming next. The only thing she could not predict now was the duration and intensity of the whipping – and which of her masters would be first to flex his whip hand.

Collins opened the batting with a strap; a good, supple, well-oiled specimen that laid thick red stripes across the broadest section of her bottom, one after the other, sometimes overlaying each other, engendering a slow and inescapable burn that had her twitching rather more than she wanted to be, given the unpleasant consequences sudden movement had for her nipples.

As always when experiencing public chastisement, Charlotte gave herself up to it, gorging her psyche on the spectacle she must be making, opening herself up to the shame and humiliation, wishing that everybody in the whole world could be here to witness her reddening bottom and the telltale glisten between her thighs. She sometimes thought she would not be satisfied until her spread legs and roasted rump were advertised on billboards across the world, until she could not walk down the street without sly glances and pointed remarks about how much she needed everything she got. Charlotte let herself sink deeper and deeper into fantasy, imagining queues of people called upon to spank her and penetrate her with sex toys, imagining satellite broadcasts of her having her well-whipped bottom fucked by anyone who cared to pass by, while Collins plied the strap over and over again, its satisfying slap cracking out through the ancient crypt.

She was given a minute to catch her breath before Bryant stepped up with a French martinet. The effect was of a different type and magnitude; where the strap had been a relentless juggernaut of fire, the knotted ends of the flogger sent a multiplicity of stinging sparks across her skin in a way she found strikingly pleasant. She sighed and relaxed her muscles, pushing her bottom out, inviting a stronger swing, a faster swish, more and more of the little firework pops that lit her up.

The lashes stopped earlier than Charlotte had expected them to, and she felt Bryant's hand swiping itself up between her legs, finding the sweet swell of her clit amongst the heat and wetness that surrounded it and giving it a shocking little pinch.

'She's so wet!' he proclaimed to the crowd. 'She's loving it! Just as well – we aren't done yet. But before we continue … an interlude.' Bryant's hand was replaced with a length of something cold and rubbery that stroked the inner side of her thighs, gathering up the dew from her skin. When it reached her ripe snatch, it began to vibrate with a low purr, sending its radiations through her, shockwaves and aftershocks, flowing from skin to nerve until her epicentre was pulsing in time with it.

She was moaning and gyrating on the instrument, the pain in her nipples and the fire on her backside forgotten now in the face of this deeper craving.

'Oh, she wants it,' chuckled Bryant, and he drew lazy circles around the opening of her cunt, watching it contract and spasm, trying to suck the rounded end of the vibrator inside. 'She wants it badly. Should I let her have it? What do you think?'

To Charlotte, the echoing laughter and chatter of the crowd came from afar, like waves crashing on a beach, indistinct and fragmented outside the enormity of her lust.

The audience must have been on her side, for the next thing Charlotte was aware of was the thick round-ended baton travelling tantalisingly up inside her, sometimes stopping for a slow revolution, sometimes teasingly pulled out a fraction, until it was inside her, vrooming away, causing her walls to quake prior to the grand tumbling-down that would come soon, and then again, and again. 'Hold it in, Charlotte,' Bryant instructed, and she clamped her muscles down on the shaft, knowing that there would be a penalty if it slipped out of her. The vibrator ensconced, Bryant then fitted a moulded buzzer to her clit. Within seconds of its activation, she was begging to be allowed release.

'No, permission is not granted,' said Bryant and a sound of animal frustration howled from her mouth. Pain would be welcome now, and she tried to concentrate on her nipples, although they were almost numb from the ferocious grip of the clamps. Perhaps her bottom, but the heat soon subsided when she wasn't being actively dealt with. No, she had nothing to think about but the maddening invasion of her cunt and clit, driving her to certain disobedience unless she could ... unless she could ...

Ah. Oh. Yes. Mercy. Collins had had mercy on her. An unusual definition of mercy, perhaps, for the form it took was a cane stroke. Its swift lightning strike almost caused her to lose the vibrator from within her, but she managed to keep suitably clenched even as she hissed out her surprise, tensing in preparation for that intense afterglow that made caning so memorable, and such a favourite recreation of hers. The little clit stimulator buzzed away merrily, but it was no match for the searing majesty of the rattan, and it was with warped gratitude that Charlotte breathed out the first count.

'One, sir. Thank you, sir.'

The mob was closing in now, curious eyes feasting on her ritual humiliation. She kept her eyes closed and thought about breathing, about the patterns of breathing, about the way it filled her lungs and made her chest rise and fall. She visualised it every way she could, every trick in the book to take her mind off her constant bubbling-under of orgasm. Even the cane strokes weren't taking the edge off now, but she was past the pain, flying towards the pleasure through the starry, foggy void of subspace. She belonged to Collins, belonged to Bryant, belonged to everybody, took this flogging and this exposure and this manipulation of her sex for everyone, for her own good, for the pleasure of anyone. She submitted.

'I submit,' she whispered under her breath before calling out, 'Six! Six, sir! Thank you, sir,' and then the permission was granted and she screamed, bucking and jingling, threatening to collapse on her side with the flogging block clutched to her middle while the climax continued to shred her body to ribbons.

Afterwards, she was so flaccid and drained she could have slept, but she knew there was more to come. She was glad of the respite afforded by her display: still bent over the flogging block with her thighs spread wide, she lay calm and still while every member of the audience paraded past her, allowed to lay a hand on her hotly striped rear and her still-drenched quim in tribute to her and her masters. This took a long time – Lady Markham had not exaggerated the guest numbers – so she had time to recover a little of her breath and a lot of her shame, sparking her arousal back into life as she contemplated her position, with the help of Collins and Bryant, who sat in her line of vision, sipping urbanely at glasses of champagne.

The finale of this section of the ceremony was provided by Charlotte, knees to the hassock once again, accepting Collins's favourite plug into her stretched arse and having her wrists tied behind her back. Thus incapacitated, she was to drain first Bryant and then Collins of the masterful essences contained within them by sucking their cocks dry. This was difficult, as she knew, without the use of her hands, and she used every ounce of the suction skills she had learned under their tutelage, lapping at their balls and taking their shafts deep down beyond her mouth until they spurted the hot jets of salty liquid into her hardworking mouth.

She was spent now, jaw aching, eyes wet, nipples sore, bottom throbbing, cunt slick and vibrated into numbness, and her masters showed her to the crowd, who applauded her heartily while Collins and Bryant propped her up beneath her armpits in case she slid to the floor. They laid her tenderly on a low leather mattress while Lady Markham addressed some words about food and wine to the still-hooting crowd. Charlotte felt her nipples blaze back into life as the clips were removed, then submitted to the ever-hateful removal of the butt plug before her clit and cunt were also freed of their impositions. She was taken. She was owned. And there were witnesses. Perhaps even more than those here tonight, she thought, watching Dimitri's camera zooming down for a close-up of her depleted body.

Collins cradled her head in his arm and kissed her, a long, slow smooch that only ended when Bryant rather querulously demanded his turn.

'I think you need to eat,' he observed once he too had sucked the nectar from her lips. 'You've had quite a test there.'

'Did I pass?' she asked sleepily.

'With flying colours,' Collins chimed in. 'Now, shall we?' Taking one of her arms by the elbow, he yanked her to her feet, leaving her other arm to Bryant. Thus sandwiched between her two dark knights, Charlotte was escorted through the well-wishing sea to the distant shores of the dining tables, where she was to be toasted all night long.

Happily Collared Life

THE MORNING RITUAL WAS almost always the same. The alarm woke Charlotte at 6 a.m., and her first task of the day was to check her bedfellow – which could be Collins or Bryant or, as it was today, both – for signs that attention was required.

On this morning, one month after the Collaring had been performed, Charlotte faced the eternal dilemma of *Who first?* Collins, at her right hand side, and Bryant, at her left, both exhibited the telltale stiffness and, as she yawned and rubbed sleep's residue from her eyes, she found herself straining to remember whose turn it was.

Collins helped her out by raising one eyelid, releasing a shaft of gimlet stare that made her mind up for her.

'About time too,' he muttered, once she had drained the glass of water by the bed and slid her soft wet lips along the rigid shaft, settling in on her knees for a long, slow suck.

Her first breakfast swallowed and digested, she watched Collins depart for the shower, then she turned her attention to Bryant, who had awoken by now and watched the final portion of the fellatio interlude with keen interest.

'Oh, you're the best, Charlotte, the best,' Bryant, always more vocally demonstrative than Collins, avowed, shooting jets of warm saline liquid into the depths of Charlotte's deep throat.

Collins emerged from the en suite bathroom to dress, while Bryant took his turn in the shower. Charlotte was permitted a ten minute respite during this period, which she made the most of, leaning back against the pillows, breathing in the man smell of the linen and watching Collins dress. Watching Collins dress was one of her favourite activities; in fact, she often pondered secretly filming him so she could watch it while he was away on his periodic work-related trips. He had so many interesting accessories for a start – clippy things to stop his socks falling down, cufflinks, often a waistcoat with a gold fob watch. She drank in the faultless crispness of his shirts – Charlotte was forbidden to iron them, as her technique did not meet his high standards – and admired the perfect crease of his trousers. She quivered when he slipped his flexible leather belt through the loops of his waistband, pulling it taut and buckling it. She wanted to touch herself, but she knew it was not permitted, so she swallowed hard and focused grimly on his long slim fingers working on the cufflinks, then the waistcoat, button, button, button, then the jacket, handkerchief placed at such a precise angle in the top pocket. Hair dealt with next, briskly and efficiently, then spectacles on, then the shiny, shiny shoes. Sometimes, if they weren't shiny enough, Charlotte was called over to kneel, naked, and give them a brief buff-up, but this time they passed muster, it seemed, and now the fully-formed, 100% suited, booted and deadly J. Collins Esq was ready to unleash himself on an unsuspecting world.

'I'll start breakfast,' he said, unnecessarily, because he always did. Collins was the best cook of the three, and was visibly tense when either of the others tried their hand in his kitchen.

As the delicious cooking scents began to fill the air, Bryant strolled out in a towel, leaving the shower free for Charlotte. She performed her ablutions unaccompanied – which was not always the case, especially when she was alone with one or other of her masters – and stepped into the shower. This was a difficult time for Charlotte – she so often wanted to pleasure herself beneath the warm spray, but she had to wait, had to obey, had to be trustworthy. So she would content herself with folding the fragrant gel into her intimate places and lathering it up, allowing the tingle to build and the juices to flow, but bidding herself wait. She would be seen too soon enough. Patience, Charlotte, patience.

But patience was a virtue, and she wasn't big on those, so she whizzed through the wash as quickly as she possibly could and dried her hair with vigorous urgency before making her way to the kitchen, clad only in the sheer babydoll nightdress and high-heeled marabou-trimmed mules that constituted her morning uniform.

'Good morning, Charlotte,' her masters formally greeted her, Bryant smiling over the top of his newspaper while Collins put the cafetière on the table and slid eggs out of the frying pan. Charlotte stood by the door, waiting for Collins to finish all the fussing with grilled tomatoes and sprigs of parsley and sit down, then she took the plates and served the breakfasts, bending over to pour coffee and offer cream or sugar. Neither of them ever had sugar in their coffee, yet the offer must always be made before Charlotte was allowed to sit down and eat.

'No thank you, you may sit now,' said Collins, pouncing on his own newspaper and reading as he ate, leaving Charlotte to watch the pair of them, absorbed in the stock market figures and details of grisly crimes as they masticated bacon and tiny triangles of toast. It was a peaceful time, but Charlotte could never see it as such, for she knew what was to come, and her thighs were tense and shiny-damp with the thought of it.

The last traces of egg yolk wiped up by bread, the dregs of the coffee consumed so the caffeine could start its diabolical work in all of their bodies, the papers laid flat on the table and the dishes transferred to the sink, there was nowhere else to look, nowhere to run.

'Well, Charlotte, I think it's time,' said Bryant lightly. 'And you have the pleasure of us both this morning. Goodness. Did you sleep well?'

'Yes, sir' she said meekly, beginning to make the arrangements, pulling the high kitchen stool out from underneath a counter top, climbing on to the low rung and resting her stomach across the padded seat.

'What do we think, Collins? What are you in the mood for this morning? Hands? Kitchen spatula? Belt? Hairbrush?'

The morning spanking was always a DIY affair; the masters did not like to bring out their dedicated implements unless there was a proper scene to be played, or punishment to be administered.

'I'm intrigued by that rubber spatula Charlotte picked out at John Lewis last weekend. We still haven't tried that, have we? And I'm told rubber has a uniquely painful characteristic.'

Charlotte winced in advance, cursing herself for buying the brightly-coloured set of baking spatulas, even though she had always known they would be used for this purpose. But they were so *pretty*. She had the feeling that the prettiness might conceal something vicious, though, like a toxic jellyfish or sea anemone.

'Ah,' Bryant said. 'I suspect the rubber spatula will challenge Charlotte's tolerance at this time of the morning. So I'm minded to be generous and use my hand for a little warm-up. Shall we?'

The men stepped closer to Charlotte. Collins placed his hand at the back of her neck, holding her in position in a way that always created a spasm of needy joy in her pussy. The gossamer-thin fabric of the nightdress was hoisted up over her bottom, which was snowy white and unmarked this morning, because Charlotte had been on her best behaviour since the collaring. This morning routine was designed to remind Charlotte of her place rather than to create any lasting effect – she was left with a sore, red bottom for the next hour or so, and then the evidence faded, to be replaced the next day or – more likely – later on.

Bryant applied his hand weightily but without real malice, watching and revelling in the slow colour change wrought on Charlotte's rear. She squirmed and squeaked, but she was a long way from her limits and she settled into the spanking, keeping her bottom pushed out, rolling her hips occasionally and clamping her thighs in an attempt to steal some naughty pleasure from her abasement. But Bryant saw what she was doing, and ordered her legs apart, feet at either end of their supporting rung.

'You're in a hurry, Charlotte,' he reproved. 'You know you have to wait. But my goodness, aren't you wet? I can see why you don't want to. Getting nice and red now … lovely …' He smacked on, slowly and harder now, while Charlotte was made to listen to a lecture on the evils of importunate haste and impatience. By the time he finished, she was glowing and panting, her thighs sticky-wet and her clit feeling as if it had ballooned to the edges of her lips. But nobody was going to put her out of her aroused misery yet.

Collins and Bryant switched places, Bryant's gentler hand on her neck now while Collins took the largest of the rubber spatulas – a shocking pink – off its hook and weighed it in his palm.

'How many strokes do you think, Bryant?' he pondered. 'I think this will be more painful than the wooden one we broke on her last week. So perhaps not so many ... perhaps ten.'

'Ten sounds good.'

The rubber splatted against the curve of her bottom and Charlotte howled. Collins was not wrong – the rubber was fiendishly painful, with a lasting burn, outdoing its wooden counterpart by a factor of about five.

'It really does hurt,' mused Collins, rubbing a hand over the patch of skin that had been inflamed. 'Ten light strokes, or five heavy? I'm going to ask you, Charlotte. Which would you prefer?'

Oh, the quandary! Five would get it over with, but heavy strokes with that thing would probably have her squirming at the desk all day long. And besides, she didn't entirely trust that Collins's definition of 'light' strokes would coincide with her own.

'I think five,' she said, and a sudden hot blaze fell directly over the first.

'Five, *sir*. That one is extra.'

Charlotte would have kicked herself, if she had been allowed to bring her legs together, for her elementary error, but she gritted her teeth and told herself it would soon be over.

'Five, sir. Please, sir.'

Collins laid each one of the four swats at the sit spot,

where bottom cheek and thigh overlap, ensuring that she was quite correct to think that her wooden desk chair was not going to be the most comfortable of billets that day. The heat seemed to permeate the pores of her skin, pouring inside to burn her very core.

'That's a serious implement,' said Collins with surprised respect. 'I shall certainly be using it more often.' Charlotte, from the corner of her eye, could see the deep crimson patch at the lower end of her generally red bum in the shining surface of the chrome and steel oven. It was almost purple.

'Will it leave a mark, sir?' she wondered, hoping that she hadn't bruised. They wouldn't spank her for a day or so if she was bruised.

'I don't think so,' Collins replied. 'I think rubber is my new favourite substance. Bryant, let us invest in a rubber plant. The Goodyear Brothers were on to something, I feel.'

Bryant chuckled, releasing his grip on Charlotte's neck.

'Who's going to do the honours?'

'Why don't you? I'm afraid I've an early meeting with a client and I'm going to have to leave soon. Tell me which vibrator you want to use and I'll find it for you.'

'The one with the clit stimulator. The black one,' Bryant added, recalling that there were so many variations in their collection that specificity was required.

Collins fetched the sex toy and placed it on the kitchen table before dropping down to his haunches to deposit a fierce goodbye kiss on Charlotte's lips.

'Be good,' he whispered, then he put a finger to her cheek. 'I love you.'

'I love you too,' she whispered back.

'I'll be back around eight. Behave yourself. Goodbye.'

As the door of the apartment clicked shut, Bryant fired up the vibrator, putting it on its maximum setting and pressing it to Charlotte's damp thighs as if in warning.

'Would you like this?' he murmured, teasing her, pressing it deep into the skin of her inner thigh, letting its tip touch her clit for a microsecond before whipping it back down.

'Oh, yes please, sir,' she moaned. 'Yes please.'

'Dirty girl, bad girl, getting wet during a spanking. You need it, don't you? Tell me.'

'Yes, sir. I need it, sir.'

'Badly. So badly.' The vibrator was pushing at the sides of her lips, circling the entrance.

'Really badly, sir.'

'If I let you have it, you must promise me your arse tonight.'

'Yes, sir, I promise.'

'Good.' The vibrator disappeared inside her, throbbing mightily, its clitoral attachment snug against the rich, fat nexus of nerve endings. Bryant barely needed to move the instrument before Charlotte was coming over the kitchen stool, thrashing so wildly that Bryant had to place a hand on her back to prevent the whole structure toppling over.

'That's all it takes, isn't it, Charlotte, to control you? You're not a slave to anything but your own rampant wantonness. That's what rules you. Your cunt. Am I right or am I right?'

'You're right, sir,' she sighed, defeated, red-faced, floppy, spent.

'I wouldn't have it any other way.' He kissed her ear, nipping the lobe. 'Go and wash and dress before the housekeeper arrives.'

Charlotte washed the proof of her orgasm out from between her legs, then she dressed, as yesterday's memo had instructed. No knickers, no bra, short but classy black silk shift dress that outlined her every curve, sheer seamed hold-ups, high-heeled strappy sandals – this was her typical working wardrobe on a day when she wouldn't be expected to leave the apartment unless it was to meet one or both of her masters for lunch. The thought that she might be called out to cross the city in this outfit that so blatantly advertised her underwear-free state made her toes curl and her treacherous pussy begin to dampen anew – she both dreaded and hoped for a summons later on.

By the time she was dressed, Bryant had left, and she thought she might as well make a start on some work. The new housekeeper, a Polish woman, was due at nine and would keep her company for the morning, in her unique way. Charlotte brewed herself some more coffee and drank it by the picture window, looking out over the vast spread of the city while she waited.

'Good morning, Krysztyna,' she sang, hearing the key in the lock.

'Good morning, Charlotte.' The housekeeper peeked in, smiling brightly. 'How are you today?'

'Fine, thanks. A bit sore, actually.'

'Oh, they were hard on you this morning. May I see?'

Charlotte flipped up the back of her skirt, displaying the remnants of the rubber's worst work, eliciting a low whistle from the new member of staff.

'What did that? A paddle of some kind?'

'A rubber kitchen spatula. I'm not going to be sitting

266

comfortably today, Krysztyna.'

'No. But you like that, no?' The woman smiled, her frost-blue eyes twinkling. 'Perhaps I shall get one for Drusilla's kitchen.'

'Mr Collins would definitely recommend it.'

'I'm sure. Well, I'll see to the dishes and then perhaps we can have tea.'

'OK. I'd better get to work myself.'

Charlotte watched Krysztyna turn tail for the kitchen, then she sat down at her computer, winced, shifted position, and booted up the machine.

She had eight e-mails. The subject header on the first one was: 'I WOULD LOVE TO TAKE ON A RUGBY TEAM'.

She smiled, opened the letter and began to read.

Please review me – thank you!

www.xcitebooks.com

To join our mailing list please scan the QR code